MEET NICK MEYER

He's heir to millions—the legacy of his father, the principal benefactor of the famous Harry Meyer Hospital. The foremost center of organ transplantation, the Harry Meyer is where the rich, the powerful and the celebrated of the world are treated. Here breakthrough experiments are conducted, vital data accumulated and donated parts stored to fill the needs of the future.

Will Nick Meyer continue his father's involvement and give to this humanitarian enterprise? The prime movers at the hospital expect him to give...to give until it hurts!

**ARE THERE WARNER BOOKS
YOU WANT BUT CANNOT FIND IN YOUR LOCAL STORES?**

You can get any Warner Books title in print. Simply
send title and retail price, plus 50¢ to cover mailing
and handling costs for each book desired. New York
State residents add applicable sales tax. Enclose check
or money order only, no cash please, to:

WARNER BOOKS
P.O. BOX 690
NEW YORK, N.Y. 10019

SPARE PARTS

by

David A. Kaufelt

WARNER BOOKS

A Warner Communications Company

WARNER BOOKS EDITION

COPYRIGHT © 1978 by David A. Kaufelt
All rights reserved

ISBN 0-446-81889-5

Cover design and photographs by Gene Light

Cover sculpture by Judith Jampel

Warner Books, Inc., 75 Rockefeller Plaza, New York, N.Y. 10019

Printed in the United States of America

Not associated with Warner Press, Inc., of Anderson, Indiana

First Printing: August, 1978

10 9 8 7 6 5 4 3 2 1

W A Warner Communications Company

For Dick Duane, Jeff Brown and, of course, Lynn, all of whom helped me to put *Spare Parts* together.

I wish to thank Lowell J. Deehl, M.D., for providing me with appropriate medical texts and advice, and for helping me to keep *Spare Parts* within the realm of future, if not current, feasibility.

—David A. Kaufelt

CHAPTER 1

*   *   *   *

From the *New York Times,* "Notes On People,"
April 17—Eugene Kirk, former Columbia
College quarterback (1947), former Assistant
Secretary of the Treasury (1967–1972), current
chairman of Kirk Industries, Inc. and one of the
President's closest advisors, is thought to have
suffered a heart attack yesterday when his car
went out of control, colliding with a parked
utility van in Arlington, Virginia. Mr. Kirk
suffered rib fractures, multiple cuts and bruises.
He is being treated here in Manhattan at the
Harry Meyer Hospital where a spokesman
declined to comment further on his condition.

*   *   *   *

COMPUTER READOUT - 34017-t-4/17

MatchCode: WGER-WILDFLECKEN-ALTMAN

```
-23-M-USARM-POT.DON(A=)
HEART(PRIMARY) - Liver
(2) NOKIDNEY

(CROSS REF: ZIP20020-
KIRKeu-52-M-GVRNMNT
RCPNT(A+))
```

*   *   *   *

As Frau Mueller walked down the eighth floor corridor of Munich's luxurious Bayerischer Hof hotel, she checked the keys at her waist. It was a ploy that enabled her to snub both the new maid (who would not last, she could see that already) and the noisy young couple coming out of 814.

She knocked on the door of 816 and waited. Frau Mueller always "did" 816 herself. Not because she had to. Because she wanted to.

Frau Mueller had a special affection for Herr Brown, who had occupied 816 for seven years. Herr Brown was a man who deserved to live in a palace like the Bayerischer Hof, not like the young trash who had just emerged from the neighboring room. She smiled with pleasure, thinking of Herr Brown's scrupulously polite manners, his gentlemanly way of greeting her. She knocked again. And entered.

The room was one of the Bayerischer Hof's larger ones, overlooking the rear gardens. The bathroom was on the far side, away from the entrance. Frau Mueller walked through the gold wallpapered vestibule and into the room.

It was only then that she realized her mistake. With horror, she saw the bathroom door opening. Had she not been so unnerved, she might have had time to retreat.

She saw Herr Brown, a towel wrapped around his thin waist (thank God), shutting off the shower with one hand and opening the bathroom door with the other to let the steam escape.

To her surprise, instead of immediately shutting the door, he came out into the room, placing himself between her and the bed.

"I beg your pardon, Herr Brown. I knocked but..."

"Do not trouble yourself, Frau Mueller. I was in the shower. I could not hear." He moved a step backward, closer to the bed, as if he was attempting to block her view of the open black leather bag on it, half filled with clothes and other objects she could not quite identify.

"Leaving us, I see," she said, wondering why he was so unlike himself. He had been almost brusque.

"For a few days, Frau Mueller."

"Visiting with your sister?" Several times a year, she knew, he went to spend long weekends with his sister.

"A small holiday."

"In Frankfurt-am-Main?"

"Yes." He pulled the thick towel tighter around him.

"Ah, I have never been."

He was looking at her impatiently. Almost angrily. In all the years he had lived at the

11

Bayerischer Hof, she had never seen this side of him. What on earth was the matter? Surely he wasn't so modest. The towel covered more of him than an ordinary pair of lederhosen would.

His eyes moved slightly, and she realized that his concern was for the open case on the bed.

She had a sudden fantasy that the case was stuffed with black lace lingerie and pink high-heeled mules. Every man, she knew, had a hidden life, and to date Herr Brown had shown evidence of none.

"Have a nice trip, Herr Brown," she said, smirking, attempting one last look around his surprisingly broad body.

"*Danke schön*, Frau Mueller."

"*Bitte schön*, Herr Brown."

He waited until the door had closed behind her before he finished toweling himself dry. He folded the towel and put it back in its place in the bathroom. He went to his closet and began to dress. He chose a dark-grey suit, a light blue shirt, a woolen tie that appeared to have no color at all. He looked in the mirror on the inside of the bathroom door and was satisfied.

In the bedroom, he crossed off, on the check list in his mind, each item in the open suitcase. It was a habit he had developed over the years. He disliked being in a strange city and suddenly finding himself shy of a handkerchief or the cough lozenges he was addicted to.

The lozenges were there. And the handkerchiefs. His Phillips electric razor. His toothbrush and toothpowder. An extra shirt.

Underclothing. A pair of dark socks. The grenade. Brush and comb.

He closed the overnight case, carefully buckling the finely tooled leather straps, and studied the train schedule one last time before putting it in his jacket pocket and leaving the room.

It was not a schedule for trains which stopped in Frankfurt-am-Main.

*   *   *   *

COMPUTER READOUT - 34100-t-4/19

Revised
MatchCode: WGER-WILDFLECKEN-ALTMAN-
              23-M-USARM-(=)HEART (=)
              Status 4/19: PRJCT XCTD

              (CROSS REF: ZIP20020-
              KIRKeu-52-M-GVRNMNT-(+))

*   *   *   *

From the New York *Daily News*: Wildflecken, West Germany, April 20 (UPI)—An American soldier was killed in his apartment yesterday in an accidental explosion of a United States Army grenade he was saving as a souvenir, the West German police said today.

The police spokesman said that the blast in this Bavarian town had been of such intensity, there was virtually nothing left of the soldier's body.

13

The grenade was traced to a nearby U.S. Army installation, the spokesman said.

American and German police searched the homes of U.S. military personnel in the area and found six other grenades, three of them German-made.

An Army spokesman identified the dead man as Sgt. Wayne Altman, 23 years old, of Bismark, N. Dakota. He was a nephew of Eugene Kirk, the politically influential industrialist.

*   *   *   *

From the *Washington Post:* New York, June 1 (AP)—Long past his originally scheduled time to leave an exclusive private hospital in Manhattan, Presidential advisor Eugene Kirk, 52, was described by a friend as being "in great spirits, having a lot of fun, and kidding with the nurses." Mr. Kirk was thrown from his car on April 16 on his way to the White House.

He appeared at first to have suffered a heart attack but a long-time associate said yesterday: "His heart is in A-one condition. What he hurt was his tailbone when he was thrown from the car. He didn't feel much pain at the time but when the shock wore off, it hurt a lot more than he anticipated. Gene won't leave the Harry Meyer Hospital until he can walk to his car and that may not be for several days."

CHAPTER 2

Nothing was happening. Journalistically or personally.

One wasn't the loneliest number in the world, he decided. Zero was.

He had just spent six weeks in D.C. where nothing was happening. No new Watergates. No new drunken senators. No sex (journalistically or personally), no graft, no spies, no nothing. And none of the various Mrs. Carters wanted to be interviewed. Not by Nick Miller of "OFF!" magazine, at any rate.

He had returned to Philadelphia, to his editor and best friend, Tony Lyle, with empty hands and empty pages. "OFF!" (named in the heyday of Watergate and not nearly as anarchistic as it sounded, being more of a consumer watchdog than a call to revolutionary action), would have to get its sensations from the wire services.

He sat around the office playing backgammon with Tony for a few days. In between games, they tossed around a lot of boring special feature ideas—segregation in the suburbs, filth in downtown restaurants, corruption in the school system. Finally a spaced-out stringer for an underground press service called him.

"I hear they're going to pick up 'The Child of Scorn' mañana."

"They've been picking him up for the last five months." Nick said. The Child of Scorn was the self-proclaimed name of a child murderer who had been operating for almost a year in Philadelphia suburbs.

The stringer gave him an address in downtown Philadelphia.

"It's a long shot," Tony Lyle said. "How the hell would that junkie get a hold of something like this? But let's check it out. I'll send along the new photographer."

"What's she like?"

"You'll see."

She was all wrong. That was his first thought when he met her early the next morning.

"You Nick Miller?"

"Yes."

"I'm going under the name of Carol Vasquez for professional purposes but you can call me Carla, okay?"

"Fine with me."

"I mean like my real name isn't Carol. It's Carla. But the Vasquez lets you know where I'm coming from and I've been having enough trouble breaking into the business without a heavy Puerto

16

Rican trip hanging over my head, right? Jesus, you ever see a building like this?"

They were standing in front of the south entrance to Philadelphia's city hall, a monumental birthday cake, William Penn standing where the central candle should be.

"I bet it's lousy with history," Carla went on. "You know, I been in Philly four weeks and already I know more history than I did living in New York twenty-four years."

She was wearing a burlesque of a tweed hunting jacket cut too high under the arms and too tight across her slim breasts. Her culottes were turquoise and her boots were red. Two cameras in beige leather cases were strapped across her like a couple of ambassadorial decorations.

Because of what he later came to think of as her "special effects," Nick almost missed the fact that she was long and lean with a pale, perfectly featured face—big, heavily lashed black eyes; Grace Kelly's nose; lips that belonged in a lipstick ad. And someone had gotten her to the right beauty salon: her jet black hair, all curls, was cut short and chic.

"You from Philly?" she asked as they walked south on Broad past the Battlement Club, the last bastion of all male, all white, all Protestant Philadelphia.

"No. Jersey."

"You sound fancier than Jersey."

"Does it make any difference where I'm from or how fancy I sound? All we have to do is get through the next hour or so together."

17

She stopped in front of the Academy of Music. "You don't dig me, do you? I can tell you right now, I can't work with a guy who doesn't dig me. I don't mean sex, man; forget that. I mean vibes. I mean the vibes you are shooting off in every direction will show up in every fucken shot I take. I mean, man, this is no way to do a job. No way. I mean, let's just call up Tony and tell him—"

"Are you out of your mind? All we have to do is go stand in front of 1743 Lombard Street. You snap pictures of anybody the cops drag out and I write down their names and addresses. And that's that. What are you carrying on about?"

She looked up at him for a minute through her long lashes. "Why don't you like me? I do anything to you?"

In the early morning light, in her outrageous clothes, she looked like an appealing fashion victim, someone the media had taken advantage of. He felt sorry for her. "Who said I didn't like you? I do like you. You are refreshing and unusual, happily different from the usual run of cameramen I have to work with. All right? Can we get going now?"

She didn't move when he took her arm. She kept looking up at him. "Go ahead. Tell me what you have against me. Who knows? Maybe I can change."

He almost resisted but in the end he couldn't. "You look like Mrs. Astor's pet horse in that get-up. You come on too strong. You talk too much. I'm with you two minutes and you're telling me I don't like you. We have an ordinary, probably useless job to do and you're having a confrontation all by yourself on Broad and Sansom Streets."

"I'm nervous," she shouted at him as several proper Philadelphians walked by, pretending not to hear. "Guys like you always make me nervous. Look, Nick, we got time for a cup of coffee?"

He looked at his watch, sighed, and said yes, they had time for a cup of coffee. He piloted her into a booth in the Harvey House.

He watched her put four teaspoons of sugar into the cup of half coffee, half cream. She took a sip and smiled at him over the rim of the cup.

"I haven't had a thing to eat this morning. I was on pins and needles because—"

"I know," Nick said, drinking his milk. "Guys like me make you nervous. Whatever that means."

"Well, it means that you're big and cute and I know I'm not supposed to think about big and cute when I'm on a job but still, you're big and cute and it so happens I like big and cute. Two, you're rich."

"I'm not rich."

"Bullshit. I could tell a mile away you're rich. You got that rich smell, you know what I mean? Besides that, only rich people can get away with wearing a shirt with a hole in it."

"Listen, Carla, maybe I do come from a privileged background. But believe me, I am not rich now."

"Doesn't matter. It's in your blood. And I don't know what to say to you. You and Tony and all your little friends playing reporter, driving around in fancy sports cars, puffing on fifty dollar an ounce grass. Shit, man. You know where I grew up? On the Lower East Side. Not in government housing, baby, but in your basic two-room tenement. My father spoke three words of English and my mother took off when I was ten. You know how many times my own father tried to get into my pants?"

"Listen, Carla, Carol: I don't want to know. I don't want to hear your life story. I want—"

"But I'm telling it," she shouted. "And you goddamn well better sit down and drink your fucken milk and have the courtesy to listen. I been in this town a month and not one of you on that goddamn magazine has said, 'Hello, Carla. How are you, Carla? Where you from, Carla? You feeling okay, huh, Carla?' Now I'm telling *you*: I'm fucken lonesome. I hate it here."

His first reaction was to get up and go and call Tony and tell him the brilliant new photographer, the "street smart" chick he had hired while Nick was in Washington, was having a nervous breakdown in the fifth booth on the right in the Harvey House and maybe he had better send Ira Levy and his trusty Nikon down.

But suddenly she stopped crying. She stood up, took her jacket off and sat down again, smiling.

"I knew this fucken jacket was a mistake. I thought it would make me look like Vassar." She drained the coffee cup and said, in her tough, sweet voice: "I'm sorry, man. I'm so uptight about being away from New York, about this job, I don't know what I'm doing. You got a nice face. What can I tell you? Today was the day I had to stop being scared and let Carla out of the closet. You happened to be standing in the way, man."

He put his hand over hers, trying not to look at the black nail polish. "Just be yourself, Carla. That's all it takes."

"I'm trying, baby. I'm trying."

"Very trying," he said gently.

She looked up at him as she applied bright red lipstick to her mouth. "You ever curse, man? I mean like I been with you an hour already and I never heard you . . ."

He looked at his watch and they ran the rest of the way to Lombard Street. They sat on the steps of the brick row house across the street from the address the stringer had given, pretending they lived there, watching the three empty, double-parked Philadelphia police patrol cars.

A front door across the street opened suddenly and a group of police came out, some in uniform, some not. Two not in uniform were holding onto a pale, moon-faced fat man in his early thirties.

"Child of Scorn?" Nick asked the nearest policeman.

"I'll eat my badge if he's not."

"Jesus," Carla said, shooting picture after picture. "Jesus. Do you see that bastard?"

The Child of Scorn smiled obligingly at her

while Nick got his name and address from one of the neighbors, all of whom were out in full force.

They took a taxi to the lab that did "OFF!"'s work, and while Carla waited for the photos to be developed, Nick called in the story to Tony who had a man on his way down to police headquarters and the wire services on his other phones before the call was a minute old.

"Congratulations, Nick," he said.

"Don't forget Carla."

"Who could forget Carla?" Tony said as he hung up.

Carla came out of the lab waving pictures of the Child of Scorn, a big smile on her face. "Tony's going to come in his pants."

The lab technician, a sixty-year-old man with ivory-white skin, coughed and went back into the darkroom.

"What's a matter with him?" she asked Nick. "My language not refined enough?"

"Do you think you could possibly close that mouth for a moment and decide about having dinner with me tonight?"

"You asking me to go out with you to dinner?"

"That's what I'm trying to convey."

"I thought you hated me."

"I don't hate you. I told you: I find you refreshing."

"Cute."

"That's me, Nick Miller, big and cute."

"Now you're being patronizing and cute."

"Do you want to have dinner or not?"

"Only if it's Dutch treat."

"We'll charge it to 'OFF!' Then we can both enjoy it."

They left the photographs with Tony, and that night he took her to Bookbinder's where she ordered a steak ("this is a lobster place"/"so why do they have steak on the menu, big shot?") and then he took her home to the studio apartment she was subletting on Locust and 16th Street.

"You coming up?" she asked.

"I don't think it would be a good idea."

"Don't shit where you eat, huh?"

"Another appetizing expression."

"You know it would be good."

"I hadn't thought about it."

"Bullshit. You been thinking about nothing else since we left the restaurant. You don't want to come, you don't want to come. I'm not exactly used to begging."

She went inside and walked up the narrow, badly carpeted stairs.

Ten minutes later, he was knocking on the door of her apartment.

"I changed my mind," he said.

"I thought you would."

"You took your culottes off."

"I put them in the garbage."

As he put his arms around her, he realized how good her body was. "You're beautiful," he said.

"So are you, Nicky. You want to take a shower first or you want to do it natural?"

"Natural."

He was aware that he had spent most of his life in the rigid confines of the upper middle class, where even the rebels had a certain predictability about them. His peers were constantly monitoring their responses, pausing to take their emotional temperatures. It was difficult, he felt, to react naturally to anything.

Over the next few months, he found that what most fascinated him about Carla was that she was able to do and say what she felt without thinking about it. She was spontaneous. He knew where he was with her. When, very often, he didn't know where he was with himself.

"Man, I am a proud Puerto Rican woman," she told him one night. "I am what you have been missing all your life. Those uptight WASP pussies you been playing around with didn't know what it was all about. When they go to bed with a man, man, they got one hundred million other thoughts in their head. 'Am I giving too much?' 'Am I giving too little?' 'Is this wrong?' 'Is this right?' They been thinking about sex for too many centuries to do it natural. And those big selfish Jewish princesses who keep circling around you, they just want to eat you up, man. They want to get back at you for the things their father did to them for being girls. Now me, I am different. I am here to give you what you want and need, no strings. You have always needed a lady with hot island blood to unblock your hang-ups, to set you free."

"*Muchas gracias.*"

"De nada."

She had been brought up by her older sister, Luisa, who forced her to go to school, who kept her off heavy drugs, who sent her to the neighborhood settlement house where the photography teacher, a woman with her own method of solving social problems, had encouraged her.

"I ripped off my first camera, a little Kodak Brownie, from a store on Delancey Street. Baby, the day I saw those photographs, I was so high, I didn't know what to do next. I never robbed another camera. Bess, my teacher, saw to that. She was a good lady, man. She got me jobs around the neighborhood, shooting weddings, bar mitzvahs, anniversaries, everything you could think of. I had my first one-woman show when I was only fifteen. At the settlement. Bess got the *Daily News* to come down and they printed one of my photos. Man, she was one beautiful woman."

"Was?"

"Big C. And she didn't have any bread, either. She died in a city nursing home. I was sitting there, reading a magazine, rapping away when she coughed and zip. Man, I am not going to die in a city nursing home. I'm not going to die in a city anything."

She had worked for a second-rate fashion photographer while putting together a sample book of her own work. She sold a shot of a fire to the *Post*, one of Mick Jagger's wife hugging someone who wasn't Mick to the *Voice*. A friend told her about the job at "OFF!". "Like I never

25

heard of the magazine until I heard of the job. And if you think it was easy just packing up and leaving everything I knew, I'm here to tell you it wasn't." She stopped talking long enough to roll a joint as big as a cigar. "Anyway, it was time to split."

"Boy friend trouble?"

"'Boy friend trouble'! You are funny, Nick. The way you put things. Man, in plain English, this *schlemiel* was a lover whose time had come and gone."

"I'd best get prepared."

"You got a long ways to go," she said, putting her lips against his, blowing marijuana smoke into his mouth.

"But," she went on, sitting back, laying her leg across his stomach, "I'm still poor. Okay, I'm not living in a tenement, but I'm not on Fifth Avenue either."

"You're not going to get rich working for 'OFF!', Scarlett," he said, running the tips of his fingers over the smooth muscles of her thigh.

"You don't know. Every goddamn publication in the world picked up that shot of the Child of Scorn, right? Tony's getting ready to send me out on some real assignments, right?"

"You may get famous. Not rich."

"What about your family? When we have a little half-Rican kid, think they'll come around, give us some bread so we can bring him up in the style his father's accustomed to?"

"I have no family. My parents are both dead."

26

He reached for the joint. "Let's talk about something else."

"Cool with me, baby."

She moved into his apartment two weeks after they met, carrying each of her few possessions in herself.

"What the heck is that?"

"'Heck'! Where were you brought up, man, Kansas? This happens to be an African violet. It goes wherever I go. It does whatever I do. I love it. My sister Luisa gave it to me."

"It's ugly."

"Yeah, but it's mine."

She watered it too often and gave it too much plant food. It never changed, its grey-green leaves never quite dying, never quite living. She put it in the center of the bamboo coffee table they had bought together in a thrift shop. "You don't have a home unless you have a coffee table," she had informed him.

"Now we have a home," he had said, looking at the oval table with its pink legs.

She kissed him. "We sure do, baby."

He wouldn't say it, not even to himself, but he was happier than he had ever been in his life.

"Seeing you two together is like watching the Duke of Windsor walk down the aisle with Charro," Tony said one afternoon while they were sitting in the office ("Off the 'OFF!' office" someone had written on the wall in blue Magic Marker), going through press releases, looking for filler for the next issue.

"You know Joan Crawford was seventy-five when she kicked the bucket?" Nick said, reading from a press release.

"Another item of lasting political significance."

"What about campaigning for new marijuana laws?"

"We do that in every issue."

Carla came in and sat down on the edge of Tony's desk. She had been trying to convince him to send her to California to do a photo essay on the Chicanos. "You know, man, you are missing the chance of a lifetime," she said, still trying. "I speak the fucken language."

"What language is that?"

"We could win a fucken Pulitzer."

Tony picked up another press release. "Hey, I see where the King of Hiharan has checked into your old man's hospital."

"What old man?" Carla asked, "I thought your folks were dead, Nicky."

"They are. He's not my old man. I was adopted. I haven't talked to him in years."

"He owns a hospital?"

"Not exactly."

"What's it called?"

"The Harry Meyer. As he is."

CHAPTER 3

From the New York *Daily News*: New York,
May 1 (AP)—King Abu Assein of Hiharan
checked into the Harry Meyer Hospital here
yesterday for what was described as a routine
two-week physical examination. Hiharan is one
of the smallest and richest of the Mideastern oil
producing countries.

*   *   *   *

COMPUTER READOUT - 38001-t-5/1

MatchCode: ISRAEL-JERUSALEM-ASSEIN-
              18-M-STU-POT.DON(A=)
              LIVER(PRIMARY) - Heart
              (2) - Kidney (2)

              (CROSS REF: HIHARAN-
              ASSEIN-48-M-GVRNMNT-
              RCPNT(A+))

* * * *

"With your talent for languages, doll," Donald A. Schwartz, president of American Family Pharmaceuticals, said, "you could make a lot of money."

"I'm not in Israel to make a lot of money, Mr. Schwartz," Sonia Brown told him without looking up from her Steno pad.

"There's no law you have to stay in Israel, doll," he said, putting his fat hand on her shoulder.

Sonia Brown looked up at him with cool grey eyes. Mr. Schwartz removed his hand. "Anything else, Mr. Schwartz?" she asked, standing up.

"Not today, doll."

She left the room.

When international businessmen and diplomats visit the King David Hotel in Jerusalem and find themselves in need of a multilingual stenographer, they often request the services of Sonia Brown.

Sonia, who is in her late thirties, is an excellent stenographer, fluent in a surprising number of languages. Nice looking, she could be more attractive if she tried; or so the businessmen think as she expertly and rapidly translates their thoughts into Hebrew, French, Greek, Turkish, German, English.

Sonia Brown is not a person who invites discussion. When she is not at work, she spends her time in her room. It is located in an annex of the hotel and furnished only with essentials. The one luxury is a telephone.

It is rarely used. She has no friends in Israel. She keeps her co-workers at a distance; but she is not so much disliked as she is ignored. With so many vivid personalities blooming in the hothouse Israeli atmosphere, she does not find it difficult to fade into the background.

It is generally understood that the telephone is not for Sonia Brown's convenience but for that of her relatives. She has a number of them, all elderly, all survivors of the Holocaust. She is the only member of her generation who escaped.

A few of these relatives—uncles, aunts, cousins—have settled in Israel, but others have ended up in Greece, in Turkey. "Leaves," Sonia Brown said once, in a rare confidence to a co-worker. "They fell where they were blown. I am a daughter to them all."

When there is sickness or death or unbearable loneliness, Sonia Brown receives a telephone call. She herself shows no emotion as she takes her small kit, leaves a note for Nate Mazaltov, assistant manager of the King David, and catches a bus for Haifa, a plane for Athens or Ankara. She is often back a day or two later.

At nine o'clock on Monday morning, May the second, Charles Fournier, the young vice-president of Fournier Aircraft International, whose base is in Paris, was awakened by a call from Nathan Mazaltov. Mr. Mazaltov regretted to inform him, in heavily accented French, that the stenographer he had engaged had had a family emergency. As a result, she would not be able to continue working with him this morning.

31

Mr. Mazaltov was certain that Miss Fiebach would prove as exemplary as Miss Brown.

Fournier wasn't. He had enjoyed Sonia Brown's reserve. But he told Mazaltov to send Miss Fiebach up.

* * * *

COMPUTER <u>READOUT</u> —3804—t—5/3

Revised
MatchCode: ISRAEL—JERUSALEM—ASSEIN—
18—M—STU—(=)LIVER (=)
Status 5/3: PRJCT XCTD

(CROSS REF: HIHARAN—
ASSEIN—48—M—GVRNMNT—(+))

* * * *

From the *London Times*, May 4—Two Arab youths were killed yesterday in a clash with Israeli occupation forces near the West Bank town of Jenin. One was Prince Dalal Hassan Halil Assein, a leading figure in recent PLO activity, and a brother of King Abu Assein of Hiharan. His association with the PLO is thought to have caused a rift in his relationship with the conservative King Assein.

An Israeli spokesman said that Prince Assein and an unidentified companion were riding in a jeep at Qabatiya, near the biblical Dothan Valley, when a PLO gasoline bomb, aimed at a lorry filled with Israeli soldiers, misfired and struck the prince's vehicle.

In a subsequent skirmish, three Israeli soldiers were wounded.

The body of Prince Assein, the Israeli spokesman said, "is not recoverable." King Assein, undergoing medical examinations in New York, could not be reached for comment.

*　　*　　*　　*

From the *Washington Post*, June 2—King Abu Assein of Hiharan met with President Carter today to discuss international oil policies. The King later attended a private dinner party where he spoke to American oil company executives about investment in his country. He will return to Hiharan next week after a lengthy stay in the United States.

CHAPTER 4

My dear Winslow,

I know that it's going to come as a shock that I'm here in New York at the the Harry Meyer, not two blocks from that gargantuan townhouse you call home, and I haven't so much as lifted the receiver. But you, of all people, will understand that I simply can't see anyone (even you) at this moment.

As you can probably guess (or already have), I'm here in a last ditch attempt to see if something, *anything*, can be done.

I suppose you know HRM met with his ministers last week and they offered him the much expected ultimatum. To wit: either he divorces yours truly and marries a "fertile" (disgusting phrase) woman who can bear him heirs (they've already picked her out; you should see the bovine creature, the Air Minister's daughter, no less), or he steps aside and gives the throne to some cousin they've unearthed. Not bloody likely.

At any rate, HRM resolved the problem in his

own inimitable way by asking them for an extension (granted, but not very graciously) while he went into the temple to pray. I was supposedly sent into purdah and told to follow suit.

To put it bluntly, if I don't become pregnant soon, "The American Society Girl Who Became An Empress" will be an ex-Empress, *sans* husband and empire, for what that's worth.

I can't say I relish the idea but that seems to be my kismet unless the doctors here can do something about my, not to put too fine a word on it, plumbing.

Oddly enough, they're holding out hope. Some sort of new enzyme or hormone has been developed. I'm to be their royal guinea pig.

Do I sound hysterical? I am, of course. I'm rambling and my style has become parenthetical and florid, always a sure sign of mental disturbance.

Actually, the real reason I'm writing to you, dear Winnie, is not to air my already too well ventilated problems but to ask a favor: use your influence with that foundation you head up to give the Harry Meyer Hospital money for their research.

I shan't go into the details of what they're hoping to achieve (you'll find it all in the attached magazine article and the proposal they'll send separately) but suffice it to say that they do manage to save a great many very important lives. They certainly could help you, personally, out of a dicey situation if one day something of yours should go on the blink.

Obviously, if you plunked down five million dollars *Americain*, you and yours would be first in line. Think of it as a kind of very pricey insurance policy.

I don't think I was supposed to write that. The fund raising woman (so earnest and terribly Radcliffe; she reminds me of poor Jackie though of course she's better looking and years younger) asked me to write a *few* lines, if I would be so terribly kind and here I am recreating *War and Peace*. (I wonder how they knew I know you; but I suppose they work on the very sound principle that everyone knows everyone else.)

Don't come popping round here, there's a dear. And *don't* write or call. And *do* swallow this letter (you can wrap caviar in it and pretend it's a blini). It would be utter disaster if the powers that be at "home" found out I was here, eating chocolates and reading cheap novels instead of on my knees in front of that hideous clay goddess with all the arms.

But do send the Harry Meyer people a check, Winslow: they do do good things.

Love, Alexandria.

*   *   *   *

NEW YORK MAGAZINE
—Reprint, Cover Story
THE NEW FOUNTAIN OF YOUTH: Only the Very Rich or the Very Powerful Need Apply!

Item—A white Cadillac limousine pulls up to what appears to be an ordinary millionaire's apartment house at Fifth Avenue and 70th Street, one of Manhattan's plushiest corners. Out steps a black man whom twenty-seven percent of the world's population regard as their spiritual leader. He is ushered into the building by a tall white man wearing gold-rimmed glasses. His most trusted aide follows them, looking upstaged. The bodyguards are sent around the corner to the garage, along with the chauffeur and the Caddy.

Item—A famous blond starlet, television's "biggest grosser," according to her agent (and some critics), announces that she's taking a four-month vacation from the filming of her latest and most expensive series. The work stoppage will cost her studio, Hollywood pundits guesstimate, somewhere in the neighborhood of five million dollars. She is last seen on the arm of a tall man wearing gold-rimmed glasses, walking into an apartment house on the corner of Fifth Avenue and 70th Street.

Item—In the middle of the night, one of the nation's most respected senior statesmen is rushed from his apartment at United Nations Plaza to an address between 70th and 71st Streets on Fifth Avenue. He exits from the same address three months later, "fit as a fiddle" and ready for the latest go-round in the Arab-Israeli confrontation.

What is it at 70th and Fifth Avenue that's attracting the big, the bad and the beautiful? What goes on behind those ordinary, if expensive, brass doors, guarded by doormen the size and personality of Texas Rangers?

No Big Secret

The Harry Meyer Hospital, founded and constructed in the mid-1960's, is the joint creation of an English surgeon (Cecil Paine) and a colorful American supermarketeer (Harry Meyer).

Like most private hospitals in New York, it will mend broken limbs, fix awkward noses, remove a painful appendix.

You've Got To Have Heart (miles and miles and miles of heart)

But unlike any other hospital in New York—or in the world, for that matter—the Harry Meyer specializes in the new science of transplantation.

According to staff doctors, who understandably wish to remain anonymous, the Harry Meyer completes over 500 heart transplants each year...

...Successful Heart Transplants...

even though the official score keeper—the Organ Transplant Registry in Chicago—reports only 350 since Christiaan Barnard performed the first in 1967.

What's more, the Transplant Registry records show that only 80 such patients have survived!

Thousands Cheer

According to *New York*'s informants, there are literally thousands of men and women walking (well, riding) around with new hearts. And not only new hearts—new livers, kidneys, lungs.

Each and every one transplanted at the Harry Meyer.

They've Got A Secret

Why doesn't the Harry Meyer want the world to know of its phenomenal success? Why keep it a secret?

Think about it.

The South American strong man who went back to his country last August with a new heart isn't anxious for his comrades (at home and abroad) to know he has a weak point—an Achilles' heart, so to speak.

If you were the governor of a New England state who had his eyes set on a *much* higher office, wouldn't you suppress the news? (Who'd vote for a Democrat with a transplanted heart?)

The president of one of this country's biggest automobile companies isn't looking for *that* kind of publicity.

Nor is that aforementioned blond TV starlet. (The producers might worry that she'd turn into a genuine angel in mid-season!)

And don't forget the famous Chinese fortune cookie message: weak hearts, failing kidneys, faltering lungs all presage loss of power. Which may explain why so many highly-placed but aging Chinese politicos have found it expedient to visit New York of late.

What Is Transplantation?

Although it has only recently come to popular attention, transplantation is, in fact, a very ancient form of medical practice.

Hindu doctors were recreating the noses of criminals (who had been punished by having that member cut off in a public ceremony) with skin transplants from other areas of their bodies one

39

thousand years before Christ was born.

Chinese documents from 300 B.C. describe organ transplants.

Two third-century physicians (later saints), Cosmas and Damian, reportedly transplanted the leg of a dead Moor onto a gentlewoman from whom they had amputated a cancerous limb.

Where Are We Today?

The first modern transplant was corneal. It was performed on a camel in 1835 by a British army surgeon, S. L. Bigger, while he was imprisoned in Egypt.

It was not until 1905, however, that the operation was successful with a human being: an Austrian opthamologist gave sight to a blind workman with a corneal transplant.

At the time, and indeed for many years, it was not understood why corneal transplants were successful when all other "donor" transplants failed.

Eventually, however, the cornea was understood to be what is now called a "privileged site." It has no circulation and no real connection with the body's immunological system (the complicated but extremely effective defense mechanism which protects your body from succumbing to every bacteria and virus that comes its way). When a cornea is transplanted, therefore, the newcomer is not recognized as a foreign invader, and the immune response is not triggered. (Another example of the privileged site is the womb, which does not resist the acceptance of a fertilized egg.)

The Operation Was A Complete Success. Unfortunately, However, The Patient...

Transplant operations are almost always successful; that is, the donated organ or tissue does begin to function in its new home. But then the immune response begins; the host body produces special protein molecules called antibodies, which seek out and attack the invading organ; the transplant is rejected.

Says Doctor Cecil Paine, Executive Director of the Harry Meyer, "We must educate the system's defenses to distinguish between good and bad invaders, since it cannot discriminate by itself."

Educating the System

Irradiation, drugs, corticosteroids, removal of the thymus gland—all have been used to break through the immunological system, none with any great success. The problem is that while the patient's resistance to the transplanted organ is substantially reduced, so is his resistance to infection of all sorts; unless he is maintained in an elaborate, germ-free atmosphere, he may be killed by common, garden-variety bacteria.

The need is for an ideal immunosuppressant drug, one which would leave unhindered the body's natural defenses against bacteria and viruses, while at the same time restraining the antibodies' effort to reject the transplanted organ. And nowhere has immunosuppressant research and experimentation been carried out with greater success than at the Harry Meyer, under the direction of the dedicated Cecil Paine.

Dr. Paine and his associates are reportedly

working on an entirely new concept: an immunosuppressant based on an antibody coating—formulated from the donor's tissue and injected into the transplant recipient—which would hoodwink the immunological system into accepting the alien organ, but otherwise leave the system itself intact.

If the Harry Meyer scientists succeed, a new age of miracles will have begun.

There will be new hope for victims of birth defects and deforming accidents. With all organs and limbs replaceable at will, a new longevity will be available to mankind.

But miracles do not come cheap.

Who Pays? Who Knows.

The Harry Meyer Hospital began with a grant by Harry Meyer of thirty million dollars. Its endowment is now believed to be in excess of *five hundred million dollars.*

The hospital has an annual operating budget of one hundred million dollars.

Where does it all come from?

Sixty percent of the hospital's budget comes in the form of grants from such diverse Federal goverment agencies as the Department of Health, Education, and Welfare, the Department of Defense, the United States Navy, the Office of Public Health (and Lord only knows what hush!-don't-say-anything secret organizations). Which means, of course, that this money is being supplied by you and me, the nation's taxpayers.

The other forty percent comes from the Harry Meyer's king-sized endowment, and from private contributions by corporations and individuals.

Who Benefits? Don't Ask.

As any reputable doctor or hospital will tell you, a patient's medical record is confidential. But how often do you run into a Jane or John Doe on whom the Harry Meyer has worked its transplant magic?

The discretion which cloaks the identity of those who have benefited from Harry Meyer's Fountain of Youth suggests that only the very powerful and/or rich need apply.

Cecil Paine spoke recently at a $500-a-plate fund-raising dinner for Ronald Reagan. "Someday the benefits will trickle down," the eminent doctor said. "Someday anyone who can afford ordinary hospital care will be able to replace a damaged heart, a malfunctioning kidney, a diseased lung."

For most of us, unfortunately, someday will be too late.

*   *   *   *

```
FROM THE JANE AND WINSLOW GOODMAN
FOUNDATION
1 Rockefeller Plaza
New York, N.Y. 10019
(212) 555-0602

CONTACT: John van der Veldt

------------------------------------

          FOR IMMEDIATE RELEASE

Winslow Goodman, executive dir-
```

ector of Jane and Carl Goodman
Foundation, announced today a grant
of five million dollars to the
Harry Meyer Hospital. The money,
Mr. Goodman said, will be used to
further research in the science
of organ transplantation.

############### JvdV/ik - 5/27

CHAPTER 5

From the *New York Post*: New York, July 1
(AP)—Only hours after arriving in St. Anthony,
Newfoundland, to confer with a conclave of
North American religious leaders, Pope Paul IX
was abruptly flown to the Harry Meyer Hospital
here. A hospital spokesman said the seventy-
eight-year-old Pontiff was suffering from severe
fatigue. The statement differed from on-the-spot
reports which indicated the Pope had had a
seizure or attack. A fast-growing group stood
outside the hospital last night, keeping vigil.

* * * *

COMPUTER READOUT -4000-t-7/1

MatchCode: ZIP70299-MASSOT-21-M-
             MCHNC-POT.DON(A=) KIDNEY
             (PRIMARY) -Heart (1)-
             Liver (2)

*   *   *   *

"Why the fuck can't Frank fucking Sinatra, Jr., have the fucking fifth floor?"

"Why the fifth floor, Anthony? Why not the tenth floor? Or the sixth floor?"

"Five is the kid's fucking lucky number."

"Look, we got a guy in 520 who pays for his room by the year. He's the one guy in the entire hotel who pays for his room by the year. Fifty two bucks a day! Do you think I'm going to—"

"Why the fuck don't you do me and yourself a favor and kick the fucker's ass into another fucking room on another fucking floor, Louis?"

"What do you want to start something for? Huh? Before you know it we'll have the press involved. You want to be on the 'Today' show discussing corruption in Vegas? Or you want to take the sixth floor?"

"Who the fuck is this guy?"

"Do I know? Some schmuck named Brown. Spends twenty-three out of twenty-four hours in his room. No TV, no radio, no booze, no dope, no nothing. Eats all his meals up there. When the maid goes in, he comes down and plays a little roulette. Nothing flashy. Then he goes back upstairs."

"You do a check on him?"

"What do you think?"

"And?"

"And no one ever heard of him. Leastways, that's what Carmen tells me. And what Carmen tells me, I believe."

"Yeah?"

"Yeah. And Carmen says to leave him alone."

"I'm not fucking touching him, am I?"

"Five, six times a year he gets a call, goes off for a day or two, chasing a piece of ass. Maybe she's an actress; she travels a lot. Sometimes she's in Frisco; sometimes in L.A.; last time she was in Tahoe."

"A fucking weirdo, huh?"

"Just your basic Vegas solid cit. So listen, Anthony, what do you want me to do about the kid?"

"Give him the fucking sixth floor, creep."

On July second, Louis was told that "the character" in 520 had had another one of those calls. He had left word he wouldn't be back until Friday.

"So Frank, Jr., could have had the fifth floor after all," Louis said. To himself.

* * * *

```
COMPUTER READOUT  -4009-t-7/3

Revised
MatchCode:  ZIP70299-MASSOT-21-M-
            MCHNC-(=)

            (CROSS REF:  ITALY-ROME-
            PAUL IX-78-M-CLRGY-(+))
```

*   *   *   *

From the *Los Angeles Times*, Los Angeles, Calif., July 10 (UPI) - The search for Neil Massoth, a twenty-one-year-old mechanic, was called off today after a week of scouring the Mojave Desert.

Police Lt. William Mercer said that the police and members of the sheriff's jeep posse had found nothing during their search of the southern and western parts of the desert with the exception of the clue which prompted the search, Mr. Massoth's abandoned sports car.

Mr. Massoth's deceased mother, Grace, was a niece of Pope Paul IX.

*   *   *   *

From the New York *Daily News*, Rome, Italy, August 10 (AP) - His long bout with illness apparently over, Pope Paul IX was able to hold his weekly general audience yesterday. He condemned "modern permissiveness."

CHAPTER 6

Harry Meyer finished his swim in the Harry Meyer Hospital pool on the ground level, took an elevator to the third floor of the hospital and entered the third floor of his triplex through a connecting door. He replaced the plastic MatchCode card in the pocket of his flame-red and ivory-white velour robe and wondered for the thousandth time about the sanity of the computer technician who had designed the security system for his hospital.

All those doors and elevators that could only be opened and operated by the MatchCode cards issued to anyone having long-term business in the Harry Meyer!

The time wasted over those goddamn little cards, he thought, as he crossed the wide, marbleized landing, passed through his pale, upholstered bedroom and entered the smaller room he called his study.

He stood at his desk, fingering the mail

Lawrence had placed there in neat piles, looking out the window at the block-long stretch of Fifth Avenue that was the western border of the Harry Meyer Hospital.

He was enormously proud of what he privately liked to think of as his empire, and even prouder of the skill it had taken to put the real estate parcel together, of the years of patient secrecy that had been required. They still talked about it as one of the great Manhattan land coups.

In 1958, the Mayfair Realty Company quietly took control of three white-brick apartment houses on Madison Avenue between 70th and 71st Streets. In 1961, the Sussex-Devon Company acquired all of the townhouses lining the south side of 71st Street between Madison and Fifth. *And* the houses on the north side of 70th Street. Two years later, he personally announced the purchase of the famous Winthrop House that had stood empty on the corner of Fifth and 70th for twenty years, awaiting old lady Winthrop's demise on her chicken farm in Saddle Brook, New Jersey.

What he hadn't announced was the fact that he had also purchased the two adjoining apartment houses on Fifth Avenue. Or that Mayfair Realty and the Sussex-Devon Company belonged to him.

It hadn't taken the papers or the block associations or the landmark nuts long to realize that Harry Meyer now owned the entire square block encompassed by 70th and 71st Streets between Madison and Fifth.

Jesus, how those bastards had bothered him!

The newspapers wanted to know what he was going to do with his block. The block associations wanted to make sure he wasn't going to open a string of cat houses in the middle of their fine neighborhood. And the landmark nuts wanted to make sure he wasn't going to tear anything down.

They were all reassured, more or less, when he and Cecil announced that they were going to build a hospital with a research unit specializing in immunology, and that the façades of the original buildings would be maintained.

It had taken until 1967 to get the goddamned thing built. But it had been worth it—real estate values had quadrupled. Harry usually thought of value in monetary terms.

He went into the pink-and-blue marble bathroom on the far side of the bedroom, removed his robe, and worked the mechanism on the wall which set the shower at exactly the degree of temperature and pressure he enjoyed. Before he stepped into the shower, he caught sight of the old stranger in the one wall that was a mirror. He massaged his round, hard stomach, pinching it, pulling it in and up, hoping it would go away. He'd have to do more laps in the hospital pool, he told himself.

Which reminded him of the swim he had just taken, of the two young doctors, mustached and side-burned, who had gotten into the pool while he was in it. They hadn't said *may I?* or *excuse me* or even *good morning, Mister Meyer*. He had a suspicion that they hadn't even known who he was.

He stepped into the shower quickly and

51

allowed the sharp needle points of water hitting his back to make him forget the incident. He knew if he let himself make an issue of it, it would eventually come to the attention of Cecil who would, in that solicitous, increasingly patronizing way of his, make him feel foolish. He wondered, as he reached for the lightly perfumed soap, why he didn't get the hell out, why he didn't move. Maybe take a place in Florida or in Los Angeles. Travel a little.

But he knew the answer. It wasn't because he was living rent free, or because the services offered him were better than those of any luxury hotel.

He lived in the Harry Meyer complex because he was afraid.

Afraid that one day his transplanted heart would stop ticking. Afraid that one day he'd have an attack on a street corner in some strange city hundreds of miles away from anyone who knew about transplanted hearts, who knew how to make them start working again. Living in the complex gave him security. It gave him Cecil.

He left the shower stall and rubbed himself dry with a large, plush towel. He avoided looking at the mirror. At sixty-eight, he looked older and he knew it. He was five feet ten inches tall, weighed one hundred and eighty-five pounds and felt, despite his height and weight, as if he had somehow shrunk.

He was a man who had done what he was going to do in life. He had peaked a long time ago. He knew that and it made him sad. There was something to say, he told himself, for late bloomers. At this point in his life, he wished he were one; he wished he were on the brink of some great success, some tremendous money-making coup that would put his name on the financial map all over again.

Still, life continued to offer some pleasures.

Not sex. He'd given that up long ago. But he still liked rich food and well-tailored clothes. And the fixed routine of his day: TV talk shows in the early morning, the newspapers later on, a swim in the hospital pool, a half hour with correspondence and then, at luncheon, the real business of the day.

At one o'clock, Pat Buckley, the fund-raising woman assigned to him, would come to the door on the third floor of his triplex and escort him to the hospital's executive dining room on the ninth floor for lunch with foundation executives and government grant givers. Sometimes she would take him to one of the patients' suites on the sixteenth or seventeenth floor, and he would lunch with the rich, influential patients who sat in their rooms, bored and scared and glad of the opportunity to talk to him. Some of them, the patients, saw him as a god; if he were propitiated, their transplants would take, they would leave the hospital with a new life ahead of them.

He understood the role he was to play: Andrew Carnegie with a Middle European accent. Naive but dedicated. An uneducated innocent who had amassed a fortune with ruthless single-mindedness—the American way—and was now justifying his tactics by helping mankind.

Pat Buckley played counterpoint, the prim Wellesley girl, teeth cemented together, skirt tightly drawn about her attractive knees. She spewed forth facts and figures as she played with the pearls around her neck, making the final pitch for the foundation and government grants.

Pat Buckley was the hard, modern reality: *We need sixteen million dollars for cancer research, Senator.* Harry softened them up, gave the transaction humanity and romance: *Wouldn't it be wonderful, Senator, if we found a cure?*

He enjoyed the game. Everyone at the table knew the Harry Meyer wasn't engaged in cancer research except on the most peripheral level. Everyone knew the Senator's wife had a weak heart. Everyone played. Especially the Senator, who had been told by his doctors that his own heart wasn't in the best shape.

Luncheon was the high point of Harry's day.

He folded the towel and replaced it on the heated rack in the bathroom. In the bedroom, he went to the larger of two walk-in closets and chose a grey silk suit, brown hand-made shoes, a white monogrammed shirt, gold cuff links, a dark blue tie. By the time he finished dressing, his silver desk clock read 12:50, too late to start on the mail. He tried to read the editorial in the *Wall Street Journal.* By 1:05 he was furious. Where the hell was the Buckley kid? Usually she was as punctual as he was, knocking on the third floor door at one sharp.

He grabbed the telephone and pressed the operator's button.

"Get me Pat Buckley."

"Do you know her extension, Mr. Meyer?"

"If I knew her extension, would I ask you to get her for me?" He heard his voice drop a level—not a good sign.

"I'll connect you immediately, Mr. Meyer." He didn't like the way she spoke to him. The way a lot of them did. As if he were a spoiled brat, making unreasonable demands.

A woman's voice, not one he knew, answered the telephone after it had rung four times. "Program Development."

"Pat Buckley."

"Not here at the moment. May I take a message?"

"Where is she?"

"Who is this?"

"Harry Meyer. Who the hell is this?"

Immediately the tone of the voice changed. "Pat's assistant, Mr. Meyer. Ann Honeycutt. Pat's out ill today."

"Why the hell didn't somebody tell me instead of letting me sit around like a goddamn fool waiting for her?"

He slammed down the receiver. Jesus Christ! They were treating him like some goddamned office boy. It was time to make an issue. It was time to have a talk with Cecil.

Without him, Harry Meyer, there wouldn't be a goddamn hospital.

He left the triplex by the third floor door that led to the hospital. He strode down the corridor, feeling his face grow red with anger and frustration, and slid the MatchCode card into the elevator call slot. When the car came, he used it again on an inside panel. The doors closed.

The twelfth floor was given over to examining rooms and doctors' offices. Cecil's office was the largest. He was just leaving it as Harry entered the anteroom.

A stethoscope hung from the pocket of Cecil's white surgeon's coat. Gold-rimmed glasses sat low on his hawk nose. He looks like what he wants to look like, Harry thought—a busy, not unkind doctor running an important hospital.

"How are you, Harry?" Smiling, Cecil removed the glasses and pinched the bridge of his nose with his thumb and forefinger. "Haven't seen you all week. Making tons of money for us, I trust?"

"You got a minute, Cecil? I want to talk to you."

"Wish I did, Harry. Wish I had a thousand minutes. But there's a crisis on fifteen, something in the operating theater and a meeting up on twenty..."

Cecil looked at his secretary, a plump woman in a flowered dress. She gave him a look of sympathy.

"Call upstairs, Sylvia," Cecil told her. "Tell him I'll be there in a few minutes."

She reached for her multi-buttoned telephone, not once having looked at Harry.

As he followed Cecil into the office, his reason for being there, for using up Cecil's time, evaporated. I'm hyper-sensitive, Harry told himself. A senile fool. He often felt that way when he was near Cecil, as if he were wasting Cecil's currency, spending it on the wrong things. Cecil could be on the fifteenth floor, performing some miracle of surgery. He could be up on eighteen, in Research, coming up with a new cure for some terrible disease.

The office was paneled in pale blond wood. A blue and white Chinese rug decorated the grey carpeted floor. The desk was Scandinavian and blond, as was the chair Harry chose for himself. There were old-fashioned wooden venetian blinds on the windows, slatted to offer an impressionistic view of Central Park.

It was a quiet room.

"Talk to me, old boy." Cecil sat down behind his desk, which was neatly piled with papers, books, magazines, and computer printouts. "Talk to me, Harry."

Harry talked. He aired his grievances. There were more than he had thought, a long laundry list of black insults, dirty little snubs. As he came to the end of the list, he looked up to see Cecil's huge hands working the keyboard of a computer console attached to an adjunct of his desk.

"You have to play with that thing while I'm trying to talk to you?"

"Sorry, Harry." Cecil studied a readout on the small screen above the console and looked up. "Go ahead. You have my undivided attention."

"There's nothing else. I just want everyone around here to stop treating me as if I were dead." For a moment, a bad moment, Harry thought he might cry.

57

"I'll talk to Patricia. I'll talk to the staff. They're very wrong, Harry. They're only here because you made it possible. But you must realize, Harry, that you're what they call 'a legend in your own time.' What do they know about legends? They're in awe of you, and they don't quite know how to act toward you. Most of them are afraid of you." Cecil stood up and came around the desk. He put his big hand on Harry's shoulder. "I will speak to them."

For a moment, the tears did come. Two tears. He turned his head and wiped them away. He wasn't feeling himself, he thought.

Cecil returned to his desk and said, as if echoing his thoughts, "Harry, you're obviously not yourself. I want you to have a checkup. Head to toe."

"Maybe I should."

"I'll get your MatchCode and you bring it over to Dick Carlson any time you feel like it. But make it soon." He turned to the computer console. "We have a new feature on the terminals. I get printouts as well as readouts. No need now to have poor Sylvia race up to nineteen every time I need something on paper."

"More gadgets," Harry said.

Cecil typed a few lines on the keyboard, studied the screen above the computer for a moment, and pressed a lever. Almost immediately a thin sheet of paper appeared in a tray at the side of the console.

"Now, old boy," he said, handing the printout to Harry, "give this to Carlson and he'll do you up." He took off the thin, gold-framed glasses and rubbed the red spot on the bridge of his nose while Harry looked at the printout.

```
MatchCode:   ZIP10021-MEYERh-68-M-
             EXCTV-(+)

             (CROSS REF:  ZIP10002-
             MEYERr-45-F-UN-(=)HEART
             (=) Status 11/21/55:
             PRJCT XCTD))
```

Years had passed since the computer's language had been explained to him, but Harry remembered it well enough. First came the subject's zip code, then the first six letters of his last name (if the name had less than six letters, the first letters of the given name were added), then age, sex and occupation. UN was the code for unemployed. (+) meant donation received; (=) meant donation given.

Harry studied the slip of paper hard, as if he had to memorize it, as if his life depended on it. But none of it was new to him.

"You bastard," he said, looking up. "You promised me no one would know—"

"And who does know? Or care? Harry, it doesn't matter to anyone anymore," Cecil said gently.

"Except to me."

"You know we can't discriminate against the information we feed the computer. That would defeat its usefulness. Harry, listen to me—"

A small square black box on the desk made a low, penetrating siren sound.

"I'm sorry, Harry. I have to go."

Sssst . . . ssst.
The acrylic, resin-steeled finger, one of seven, comes away from the switch on the instrument panel. The call buzzer glows now, a red pin-point, and then is dark.
Sss . . . sssst . . . shhhhhh.
He makes a slow turn toward the television screen which reveals the activity in Operating Room A on the fifteenth floor, then glances at the digital clock above the screen. Cecil is late.
Hssst . . . sss . . . ssssst.
Moving now, moving soundlessly across the specially coated floor, away from the instrument panel, away from the computer that takes up most of the north wall. Where is Cecil?
Pfffft . . . sssssssst.
He turns, moves back to the instrument panel.
Hsss . . . pfft . . . ssssst.
The arm extends, lifts, wavers, and reaches for the panel.
Sssst . . . ssst.
The acrylic finger moves forward. The call buzzer glows red again.

The sound coming from the black box made Harry put down the printout.

When the sound stopped, Cecil stood up, replacing his glasses. "I should have been up there ten minutes ago. You know how he is about time."

He touched Harry's arm as he crossed the room. "Go see Carlson. Get yourself a good checkup. And for God's sake, forget about that printout."

Harry heard the door close behind him. He looked down at the printout Cecil wanted him to forget. He crushed the flimsy sheet of paper in his strong, wide hand.

But he couldn't crush the memory. He sat back in the blond wood chair, and he remembered.

He hadn't needed the printout to remind him of the day: November 21, 1955. It was a day that was always with him, floating somewhere between his conscious and unconscious minds.

The events that led up to November 21, 1955, were a series of painful memories, memories of conversations in elegant doctors' offices and of infinitely slow, agonizingly embarrassing physical examinations in white tiled rooms.

He hadn't accepted Cecil's verdict that his heart was about to give out on him, that there was only one way in which he could go on living. He had consulted six doctors on three continents and each of them had confirmed Cecil's judgment. And when, at last convinced, he had gone to Bonn and talked to Gotlieb—then the most celebrated of the world's heart specialists—of transplants, that sober man had looked at him, not without pity, and said, "Perhaps in fifteen years, Mr. Meyer. Maybe ten. But not now. I am sorry."

He had flown back to New York terrified. Cecil was waiting at the airport with his, Harry's, car and driver. He remembered the car, an enormous midnight-blue Cadillac with a gold plated grille and a telephone.

Sitting in the back of that car, his hands nervously rubbing the plush of the seat, he had told Cecil yes.

But when Cecil said that he, Harry, would have to go and get her—"She won't come with anyone else, you know that"—he had balked, talked of his heart giving out under the strain. And when Cecil had discounted that, he had simply begged not to be made to go.

"They only know you, old boy. *You* have to get her, Harry."

They drove straight to East Broadway, that odd lower East Side street which seemed, at that time, the last outpost for immigrant Jews. Small, orthodox synagogues, kosher bakeries and butchers, the Educational Alliance and the Jewish *Forward* building lined the south side of the street. The north side was taken up by a park, a library, union housing and the yellow brick building where she was kept.

The Cadillac stopped in front of the yellow building, behind a white ambulance with no name on its doors.

The matron was waiting for him inside the windowless, tiled lobby. She had small, dark eyes set close together and a long, badly shaped nose. She knew why he was there. There was nothing to explain. Everything, she said, was in readiness.

"It's a mistake, of course," she said in her hollow voice.

She led him into an elevator big enough to carry wheelchairs and took him to the fourth floor. The carbolic odor made him want to throw up, to run from the place.

"Your sister is absolutely incapable of caring for any of her personal functions, even the most basic," the matron said, as if she were repeating the text of a pamphlet. "I cannot imagine how you're going to manage."

"I've hired nurses," he said, to keep her quiet and because he wished it were so. "Round-the-clock nurses."

"What I cannot comprehend," she went on, unlocking a gate that led to a long, dismal corridor, "is why this sudden decision. She is not especially unhappy here. She has not complained, has she?"

A door at the end of the linoleumed hall was open and he could see her peering out. "Harry?" she called, trying to whisper. "Harry, is that you? Harry?"

"Yes," he called. "It's me, Ruthie. Harry."

She opened the door a little more and he could see that she would have liked to have come running down the hall to meet him. But she was afraid of the matron. As was he.

When he reached her, she put her thick arms around him, and he kissed her cheek. The smell was worse now, disinfectant and urine.

He could not look directly at her. But of course he knew what she looked like. They were twins. One-egg twins. ("Your tissue," Cecil had told him, "is exactly the same on twenty-three counts.

63

That's why it's going to work. The skin graft healed perfectly. No hint of a scar. In China, Harry, they were doing it thousands of years ago. On twins. Only on twins." "She'll die," he had said, and Cecil had replied, "What does she have to live for? She was born with half a brain. It's not going to get any bigger, Harry.")

He looked at her now as the matron and a young nurse helped Ruthie to get dressed.

In her greyish-pink slip, she looked incongruous, as if she weren't made for such a garment. She had his same strong peasant build, the same thick nose and pale eyes. Even her hair was greying the way his was.

They put a shapeless dress around her, fitted heavy orthopedic shoes onto her feet. "You're taking me home, Harry?" she asked.

"Yes, Ruthie. Home."

"I'll be good, Harry. I promise. I can't do so many things, but I could cook maybe. A chicken. Remember the chicken Mama used to make on that stove in the apartment on Rivington Street? Like butter. It tasted just like butter, didn't it, Harry?"

She moved toward him, butcher's shoulders swaying slightly, broad feet turned out. Watching her was like watching a burlesqued version of himself.

"The wheelchair, Roberta," the matron said.

"I can walk. I can walk by myself. Can't I, Harry? Can't I walk?"

He looked out of the small window down onto

64

the tiny garden that was fenced in like a bird's cage. "Let her walk," he said to the matron, who shook her narrow head in disapproval.

Ruthie held his hand, looking at his face every few steps; it was like walking with a distortion mirror. She continued to hold his hand as they walked along the uncompromising hall, as they came out into the light, where the white ambulance was waiting with its rear doors open. Two male nurses stood by the doors, their hands folded behind them.

Ruthie said, "It's cold, Harry. Ain't it cold?"

The matron looked at him and attempted a smile. "If things do not work out well—and more often than not they don't in cases like this—you can be sure that your sister will be welcomed back."

He ignored her as he helped Ruthie, his sister, into the back of the ambulance and followed her inside. The sound of the heavy metal doors closing behind him made him feel, for a moment, as if they had been locked in an underground vault.

Then the lights were switched on, and he saw that the ambulance was outfitted like a miniature operating room. Glass fronted cabinets revealed gleaming chromed equipment, and there was an operating table in the center.

The ambulance began to move as the male nurses helped his sister take off the ugly dress and the worn slip. Before he looked away, he saw that there were grey hairs on her chest, as there were on his. When he looked again, they had gotten her into a disposable paper robe, the kind that opens in the back.

"What are they doing to do to me, Harry?" she asked, reaching for his hand, still confident because she was with her brother.

"They're making you comfortable, Ruthie."

"I feel like a little girl, Harry. Remember when I was a little girl, Harry? I had nice long hair. I'm not such a pretty girl anymore. But I would look nice with my hair all up in braids, wouldn't I, Harry?"

"Very nice," he said, holding her sweaty hand.

"You're not feeling so good, Harry?"

"No. I'm fine, Ruthie. Fine."

They had her lie down on the operating table with her knees up to her stomach.

"I'm scared, Harry," she said.

"There's nothing to be scared of," he said. But he felt the same fear.

"Is Cecil here?" she asked suddenly, sitting up.

"No. Of course not. Now lie back down like the nurse showed you."

"That's right, Miss Meyer," one of the nurses said, his voice deep and low, like a radio announcer's. "We're going to give you something to help you sleep, Miss Meyer."

"Oh, I don't want to sleep."

"But we have a long way to go," the nurse said.

The other nurse checked to make sure the spinal anesthesia tray contained all that he needed, while the first one, the announcer, prepared Ruthie's skin with alcohol and tincture of Zephiran.

"Is it going to hurt, Harry?"

"Maybe for a second, Ruthie."

"I hate it when it hurts."

She had to lift her back for a moment so that they could place a sterile towel on the table beneath her.

"Nothing's happening, Harry."

"Close your eyes and try to sleep. It won't take long."

She closed her eyes and reached for his hand again. Harry gave it to her. The silent nurse put his middle finger on her iliac spine and attempted to locate, with his thumb, the interspace between her fourth and fifth lumbar vertebrae. Having found it, he inserted the needle.

She cried out, "Harry!"

"It will be over in a minute, Ruthie." He thought, irrelevantly, that the ambulance must be on a smooth highway; there were so few jolts, so little noise.

The nurse raised a skin weal over the interspace with the short twenty-five-gauge needle attached to the syringe containing the ephedrine-procaine solution. He changed the direction of the needle to an angle of forty-five degrees, injecting her interspinous ligament. She let out a little cry, and held on to Harry's right hand with both of hers.

"Soon over," Harry told her as the nurse removed the needle and inserted, full length, the introducer, a large bore, short needle to develop a

67

tract through her tough interspinous ligament. She cried out again as he then reinserted the spinal needle. He withdrew the stylet from the spinal needle, allowing the fluid free passage. After a few seconds, he withdrew the spinal needle quickly.

Ruth opened her eyes, looking up at her twin brother. The two nurses turned her over on her back and began to set up an intravenous drip, checking the level of algesia, going about their business like remarkably well-tuned robots.

She let go of his hand. "I'm going to sleep now, Harry. Kiss me goodnight the way Mama used to."

The memory that was clearest, the one that caused him the most pain, was of leaning over his twin sister and kissing her on her lips, his tears mixing with her sweat. She had always been afraid of needles.

Harry Meyer looked at the blank, moon-colored screen on Cecil's computer console, and realized that in his rush to get upstairs, Cecil had neglected to shut it off.

He moved around the desk and sat in Cecil's chair. He studied the hated piece of machinery as if it were the face of an enemy, for it had come to him that if the computer knew he had received his transplanted heart from his sister, it might also have other knowledge it shouldn't have.

After a moment, he began to feed it information, clumsily tapping out words on the keyboard: a zip code; a name, an age; an occupation.

For a few seconds, the screen remained reassuringly blank, and he thought he had been wrong.

And then there was a hum, like that of an air conditioner, and words began to appear on the screen.

```
MatchCode:   ZIP19106-MILLER*-28-
             RPRTR-POT.DON(A==) ALL
             ORGANS - LIMBS (PRI-
             MARY) Status: PRJCT
             IMMINENT *name at birth:
             MEYERn

             (CROSS REF: NOT AVAIL-
             ABLE)
```

CHAPTER 7

She came into the bedroom, threw a beautifully gift-wrapped package on his stomach and ran out again, screaming, "I did it! I did it!"

He got up, put on a silk robe he had bought at Sulka when he was in prep school, and, holding the package by one of its many bright red satin bows, went into the living room where she was watering her African violet.

"I did it, Baby Love," she was saying to the plant. "I did it."

"What did you do, drown the plant?"

"Very funny. You get back into bed, Mister Miller. And without the overcoat. I'll be joining you shortly." She picked up the plant, kissed its grey-green leaves, put it back on the coffee table, kissed Nick on the cheek, and ran around him and down the long hall to the kitchen.

Nick went back into the bedroom, put the package in the center of the bed, took off his robe and lay down. He could hear her singing in the kitchen, banging cabinet doors. "I did it."

"I beg you," he shouted. "Tell me what you did."

"You should be too proud to beg," she said, coming into the bedroom with a tray on which sat a bottle of pink champagne and two plastic cocktail glasses. She wore her Kelly green high heels. She had taken the rest of her clothes off in the kitchen.

He reached for her, but she backed away. "First a toast, man. Then we can get into serious fooling around." She poured the champagne, handed him a glass, took her own and sat down on the bed next to him.

"California, here I come," she said, sipping the champagne. She stood up and walked around the small bedroom in her high heeled shoes. "Tony finally gave in," she said.

"You're beautiful." He reached for her.

"Hold it, Fauntleroy, and listen to me: I'm going to do the grape pickers. I got a letter from Chavez inviting me. Tony, even Tony Lyle couldn't ignore that. Not after the Child of Scorn, he couldn't. Now drink that champagne."

"Do I have to?"

"I paid a fortune for it, man. Six bucks."

He swallowed the contents of the glass. "Congratulations, Carla."

"You look about as happy as a hearse."

"I'm happy for you, sad for me. What am I going to do without you?"

"Beat off. Now cut that out and open your present."

71

He started to pick the satin bows off the package. "Why a present for me?"

"Because I care about you. Because I can't stand the fact you walk around with shirts with holes in them."

She pulled the package away from him and ripped it open. There were two shirts inside, both with soft collars. "Rugby shirts," she said. "I thought they'd be fancy enough for you."

"They're gorgeous."

"You don't like them."

"I love them. I'll wear them both while we're making love."

"You might mess them up." She took them from him and put them on the maple bureau. "You sorry I'm leaving?"

"I told you: I'm happy for you. I'll miss you but I don't suppose you'll be gone forever."

"A week. You want me to get you a glass of milk?"

"No. I'll have more champagne."

"You're just saying that."

"No. I like it." He held out his glass. She put it on the floor, and lay down next to him on the bed.

"How the hell did I ever get mixed up with a guy who drinks milk, doesn't curse and puts on a fucken bathrobe to go from one room to the next?"

He put his nose in her neck. He loved her smell. It was a combination of the perfume she wore and something better, something more real, more natural. It was always there, under the perfume. Just as she was always there, under the terrible clothes and the funny-serious manner.

"When do you go?" he asked, sliding his hand down her back.

"Day after tomorrow. You can live without me."

"No, I can't."

She pulled him over on top of her. He put a pillow under her head and, straddling her, went into her mouth. She looked up at him as she took him, her black eyes as innocent as if she were a child sucking on a stolen lollipop.

She wasn't like any other woman he had known when it came to lovemaking. She was as interested, as ready to start something, as he was. They made love three, sometimes four times a day. Once they made love in the office, on the floor. Once they excused themselves from a cocktail party in Tony Lyle's Rittenhouse Square apartment and went into the bathroom and made love.

He lay down next to her. "You like your new shirts?" she asked.

"I told you: I love them."

"You going to wear them when I'm in California."

"Every day."

"You're not going to screw around, are you?"

"I can make it through the week," he said, kissing her.

"Do me one favor before I go," she said.

"No." He shifted the pillow so that it was under her.

"It wouldn't kill you, man. Just say it, once, for Carla."

"I'd rather die young."

73

"You're going to die old, man, without ever saying 'fuck'? You'll be in Ripley's Believe It Or Not."

He pushed her legs apart. "Late at night, when you're sleeping, I tiptoe into the bathroom and say it."

"But I want to hear you say it, Nicky."

"It should be enough that we do it."

He put the tip of his penis into her.

"Anyone ever tell you, Nicky, that you got a big, fat cock?"

"Everybody," he said, thrusting it into her.

She arched her body to meet him, her arms around his neck, her legs on his shoulders.

He looked at her as he moved in and out of her. This time her eyes were closed. Instead of a mischievous child, she looked devout now, a fifteenth century virgin in a ruined Spanish church.

He pulled all the way out and then pushed himself back into her, trying to open her eyes. They opened when she came. He pushed harder and faster and she came again, this time with him.

"I love you," he said, kissing her. She snuggled up against his chest, putting her lips next to his ear.

"I love you, too, Nicky."

"Marry me."

"That marriage would last a hot thirty minutes, Nicky. I can see my sister Luisa now, coming down the aisle in her blond Dynel wig while you and Tony in your white tie and tails chat with my father if they let him out of jail."

"I'm serious, Carla."

"Marriage isn't for us, Nicky. We dig each other, sure. But you and me, we're different animals. You know what I'm saying? Someday you'll marry a tight-assed lady who went to a fancy school, and you can sit around swapping funny stories about your shrinks. Then you'll buy a nice house in upper Long Island, a brown Mercedes with a sun roof, and a big insurance policy. You'll go to the art museum on Wednesday nights, and she'll make you throw out all your worn clothes and buy you a Brooks Brothers—"

He put his hand over her mouth and they made love again.

Only later, after they had had dinner at the Red and Blue Diner on Chestnut Street and had come back to the apartment, did he tell her about the telephone call he had received that afternoon.

"No wonder you've been down," she said. "I mean, everytime I hear from one of my relatives, not counting Luisa, I want to pick up an ax. But maybe the old man wants to make it up with you. Maybe he wants to lay a little bread on you. Maybe he—"

"Have you ever considered taking a course in basic conversational English?"

"Fuck you, Nick. I'm serious."

"He sounded scared."

"So do you."

"I haven't seen him in seven years." He took a toke of the joint she was smoking. "He's coming over here. Tonight."

"What?" She grabbed the joint away from him,

put it out, and opened the window. "That's all he has to do is smell grass in here."

"Quit acting like the Queen's coming to tea. I don't care what he smells in here. I—"

"Why don't you be nice to the guy? What's it going to cost you?"

"My self-respect."

"You can take that self-respect and shove it up your ass, Nicky. That fucker is old. He may be getting ready to say good-bye. Say he wants to apologize." She kissed his forehead. "Now you be nice to that old guy, you hear me?"

"I hear you." He liked the way she sentimentalized age. Everyone, in Carla's book of facts, became good and kind on their sixtieth birthday.

Harry was due at nine. A few minutes before, she came into the front room where he was lying on the shabby green sofa, trying to read the John Dean version of Watergate. She had wrapped herself in a dress whose design was based on the American flag.

She kissed her plant—"little sweet Baby Love"—and sat down in a faded red wing chair, crossed her legs, placed her purse at her side, and stared at the door.

Nick laughed.

"I want to make a good impression," she said. "Now you be quiet, *mahedero*, and read your lousy book, huh?"

He watched her cross and recross her legs, reaching over every few moments to touch Baby Love.

"You nervous?" he asked.

"No. Yes. I don't know. I mean, it's not like I meet too many millionaires." She looked at him. "Why don't you just this once put on some clothes that don't look as if they went through World War II? What're you saving your new shirts for?"

"I'm aging them, gracefully."

"What's he going to think of me letting you run around in a patched shirt? And, man, those fucken sneakers..."

He went and sat on the arm of her chair, and kissed her. "Take it easy," he said. "Be cool."

There was a weak ring from the doorbell. He felt his stomach muscles tighten as Carla went to the door and opened it.

"Hello, Nick," Harry Meyer said.

"Hi, Harry," Nick said.

The man in the doorway looked familiar but that was all, like someone he had once seen but had not been introduced to. "This is Carla Vasquez, Harry," he said. God, he looked so old!

"Pleased to meet you, Mr. Meyer," Carla said, leading him into the room. "Won't you sit down?"

She played hostess ineptly, asking him if he wanted something to drink (he didn't; he never drank), asking him what he thought of Philadelphia, whether he had had his dinner (he had; he always had his dinner at seven), how long he planned to stay, if this was his first trip.

Nick watched him as he responded to Carla. He was so much smaller than Nick remembered him. The man he remembered, the big, vital, colorful

77

man, never able to sit still for more than a moment, had nothing to do with this man. This was some other Harry Meyer. Nick wanted to touch his arms to see if the muscles that had once impressed him were still there, under the expensive fabric of his suit. He wanted to stretch the skin on the face, smooth away the wrinkles, eliminate the double chin, the sagging stomach. Harry Meyer looked like a man about to be ill one last time.

"You drive down, Mr. Meyer?" Carla was asking.

"Nope. Took the train. The Metroliner. I don't know what they're all talking about. It's not so special."

He sat on the green sofa, dead center, his legs planted firmly on the worn carpet, his hands on his knees. He looked around the room as he talked to Carla.

He's evaluating the premises, Nick thought. And Carla. It was an old trick of Harry's. "I wouldn't give you two cents for the whole shooting match," he could hear Harry saying in his former, stronger voice.

"You staying in downtown Philly, Mister Meyer?"

"The Warwick. I got a nice suite there."

"I've always liked the Warwick."

Nick wanted to tell her to stop, but it wasn't necessary. She stood up, smoothed her dress, and shook Harry Meyer's hand. "You two probably have a lot to talk about," she said. She kissed Nick on his cheek and was gone, leaving them alone together, leaving an atmosphere suddenly unhealthy, polluted with the old ghosts of unresolved arguments.

CHAPTER 8

They looked at each other across the comfortable, seedy room filled with thrift shop furniture.

"Nice girl," Harry Meyer said.

"In today's climate, Harry, she's a woman."

"You going to marry her?"

"She won't have me."

"Probably knows what she's doing."

"What are you doing, Harry?" He was afraid to let himself be angry, afraid his fury would kill the inexplicably old man sitting across from him.

"I came to see you, Nick," Harry Meyer said, folding his hands in his lap, like a cautious child on his first day of school.

"Seven years ago, when I called you and asked you to send me fifty bucks so I could get out of jail, you hung up on me. I kind of thought, after that, that I'd never see you again."

"You were illegally undermining this country. America gave me everything. Was I supposed to help you ruin it?"

The words had been spoken without passion, as if he were repeating lines from an old, often-quoted poem. His mind, Nick thought, was on something else.

"You'll be happy to know, Harry," he said, "that they ended the war and got rid of Nixon without me."

"There were too many like you. Snot-nosed kids who thought they knew everything." Anger crept into Harry's voice. "You name me one goddamn President who didn't do what Nixon did. Name me..." He stood and walked to the mantel over the fake fireplace. "I didn't come here to rehash that, Nick. Seven years is a long time."

"What did you come for, Harry?"

"I'm not getting any younger, right? You see what I look like?"

"You don't look so bad."

"Don't bullshit me. How many years you think I got left? Tell me. How many years?"

Nick couldn't look at him. "Plenty. You have plenty of years left."

"More bullshit. Look, Nick, we both made mistakes, right?" His voice faltered, recovered. "I don't want to die with us not being friends."

Harry Meyer walked to the chair Nick was sitting in and held out his hand. It was still big and beefy. His hand hadn't changed.

His first memory of that hand was of its slapping him when he was five. He had been sitting in the back of the grey Cadillac, Harry driving, and Isobel, Harry's wife, sitting next to

Harry, wearing a dark mink coat. They were driving through the Holland Tunnel, on their way from New Jersey to Sunday dinner in New York with Isobel's rich, noisy parents.

Bored in the back seat, a little frightened by the tunnel, Nick put his hands over Harry's eyes, a game his kindergarten teacher had played with him.

Harry pushed the hands away quickly; there was no accident. Not even the possibility of one. But when they left the tunnel, Harry pulled over, got out of the car, opened the rear door, and reached in and slapped him.

Isobel, in the front seat, pulled the collar of her coat closer to her sallow face and said distinctly, "Bad blood."

She was referring to the fact, one that had been clear to him early on, that he had been adopted by Harry much against her advice or desire.

"Just tell me who your parents are," she'd say to him when she was angry (and she was often angry), when Harry was off on a trip (and he was often off on a trip). "Show me an orphan and nine times out of ten I'll show you bad blood." She liked to speak like that, like the ladies' novels she read. "Scum. How much would you like to wager they weren't married? Your mother left you in the emergency room of a hospital. And Harry Meyer, with the big heart for everyone but his lawful wedded spouse, took you up. You honestly believe you're going to get an inheritance from him when he dies? Over my dead body, Mr. Miller. Over my dead body."

When Isobel was not angry, she ignored him. As did Harry. When Harry spoke to Nick, it was usually to give him money.

On Nick's thirteenth birthday, Harry took him to dinner in New York City. (Harry had wanted him to be bar mitzvahed, but Isobel had put her foot down. "Who in the world knows who his parents are? Do you think they were Jewish? I seriously doubt it. Italians, maybe. Or worse.")

The dinner had been at Toots Shor's, a big raucous restaurant. Nick ate prime ribs of beef while his father talked to Shor, to the men in their broad-shouldered, narrow-lapeled suits.

Afterwards, on the way home, Harry stopped the Cadillac—a green convertible at that point— and opened the glove compartment. He took a thick gold-papered box from it and handed it to Nick. Nick opened it. The gift was a watch. A gold and chrome Rolex with three dials. He put it on his wrist. It was too big, but that was all right.

"No 'thank you'?" Harry said. "You know how much that watch cost?"

"Thanks, Harry."

They stared at each other, neither knowing what to say. "I wanted to give you a bar mitzvah," Harry finally got out. "You know that, don't you?"

"It's okay. I didn't want one, Harry."

"But *I* wanted you to have one. It was that bitch, that *schlong*." He looked at his son again. "Still, bar mitzvah or no bar mitzvah, today you are a man, Nick. You understand that?"

"Sure."

"No more kid stuff. No more kissing or anything like that between us. From now on, we shake." He held out a big, thick slab of a hand and Nick took it. Solemnly, they shook.

"But you know something, Harry," Nick said. "You never kissed me."

"Yes, I did," said Harry Meyer. "You don't remember. But from now on, we shake, right?" He switched on the ignition and they went back to the big mock Tudor house in Elizabeth, New Jersey, while Nick wondered who his real parents were. Whether or not Harry knew. And why not asking questions about his parents was one of Harry's strictest rules, never to be broken.

Nick stood up and shook Harry Meyer's hand.

"By-gones by-gones?" Harry asked.

"Sure. By-gones are by-gones." He waited until Harry had gone back to the green sofa before he said, "But Harry, I have a question."

"Save it. I got a little proposition for you."

"I was waiting."

"Cut that out and listen to me. You always wanted to be a writer, right?"

"I am a writer, Harry."

"Not that kind of writer. Not magazines. Real writing."

"I am a real writer, Harry."

"I'm talking about books. Big books. Books they make movies from. Books you win prizes for. You need money to write those kind of books. So you can go somewhere quiet, someplace else, and write, right? So I'm offering both the money and the place, as a good-will gesture. I have a friend who has a house hidden away on an island off the coast of Florida. Nobody even knows about the island, much less that there's a house there. You go down—"

Nick put his hands up, to stop him. "Are you crazy, Harry? I don't want your money. I have enough—"

"Living in a joint like this, you got enough money? Living—"

"And I don't want to get lost on some island no one ever heard of. I like what I'm doing. I like where I'm doing it."

"Think it over."

"I've thought it over."

"You always were a goddamned independent bastard."

"Bastard's the operative word, Harry." They stared at each other, the old enmity coming back. "Am I a bastard, Harry?" There was silence for a moment. "Who were they, Harry? I have a right to know."

"And I told you a million times: I don't know. They—"

"I'm not buying it, Harry. I know you. You get your dollar's worth. You wouldn't adopt a kid with unknown parentage. You'd want a perfect kid, Harry. You were paying for him."

Harry stood up so fast, Nick thought he was going to throw a punch. "You know, you're a dummy? Here I am, offering you the chance—"

"Harry, it's time. Tell me. Or get out."

"I'll tell you. On one condition."

"Jesus."

"That you consider my offer."

"What's it to you whether or not I write a book or—"

"All I want is for you to consider, for Christ's sake!"

"Tell me. Then I'll consider."

"Okay. Okay."

"Who were they, Harry?"

"Your mother, she was Italian," Harry said. "Twenty-one years old. Her name was Andrea Tonato, but she called herself Andrea Miller. She thought Miller was American. She was a secretary, working for a slaughterhouse on 14th Street, in New York. There was a man."

"I hope so."

"Cut out the shit, Nick. Or don't you want to hear this?"

"Keep talking, Harry."

"He was married. She had a baby by him. You. She died having you. Her parents were immigrants. Dumb immigrants. They went back to Italy after she died. They didn't want anything to do with you. They thought Andrea was a goddess or something, a big success, a secretary bringing home fifty bucks a week. They couldn't believe she was having a baby and wasn't married. They pretended she, you, never lived. They turned their backs on their own daughter, on their own grandson."

Harry sat down again. Nick looked at his

flushed face and felt his own stomach muscles tighten again.

"Go on," he said. "Tell me about the married man. Tell me about my father."

"Jesus Christ, Nick..."

"Tell me, Harry."

"I have to say it in words?"

"You have to say it in words, Harry."

"It's me, goddamn it. I'm your father. Harry Meyer. Me."

Carla came in at midnight.

"Where you been?"

"Getting sandwich fucked by two sailors. What're you lying in the dark for?" She switched on the overhead light, looked at his face, switched it off. "Pretty bad, huh?" She went to him and wrapped her thin, cool, comforting arms around him.

And he told her what Harry had told him, how he had asked why he had been allowed to suffer all those years, how Harry had tried to lay it all on Isobel. And sure, there was some justification for that. It must have been tough enough to persuade her to let him adopt a child. If she had known Nick was his, she would've been gone. And with her, her money. "That's what it all came down to. It always does with Harry. Money. He needed the money to make the supermarket empire possible. So he let me grow up thinking my parents had dumped me, and that way he got everything—me, Isobel's money, and the supermarkets."

And then he told her how he had lost his

temper, how he shouted at Harry to get out of the apartment, out of his life. And how, when he had heard Harry walking down the hall with his slow, sad old man's pace, he had cried.

Remembering, he cried again while Carla held him.

Later, she asked, "You going to see him now or in the morning?"

"What makes you think I'm ever going to see him again?"

"Man, I know you. You try to hide it, but you got a heart in there. Under all that wise-ass jive. You know that old cocker only came here to make peace. You're not going to let him suffer."

"Yes, I'm just a sensitive flower," he said.

"Why don't you go now?"

"In the morning. Let him sleep."

"Ten to one, he's not sleeping."

"You don't know Harry Meyer." Nick kissed her. And then he said, "You don't know my father."

CHAPTER 9

He woke at eight, thought about calling Harry, and then decided it would probably be better simply to show up at the hotel. They would have a brief and honest talk, shake hands, and then they could both go about their business.

At least, that was the way he hoped it would go. One never knew with Harry.

By the time he left the apartment, Carla had already fed the plant and gone off to talk to Tony about her California assignment. He took the bus to Rittenhouse Square, trying not to think about how nervous he was. Everything's so hard, he thought, as he walked across the square. September sunshine made it look like an illustration in an old magazine.

He entered the Warwick through a side door and decided to skip the desk and the house phones.

The elevator man, who looked as if he had been born for the job, his bland features and indeterminate age blending with the beige walls of his cage, didn't give him any trouble. "Only two of them special suites up there," he said. "I wouldn't want to tell you how much they'd set you back, per day."

"I wouldn't want to know," Nick said.

He knocked on the door the elevator man had indicated. It swung open. He stuck his head around it and looked in. "Harry?" He turned back to the elevator man, who shrugged.

"I didn't take him down this morning and I don't expect he walked. Must be in there," the elevator man said.

Nick pushed the door fully open and stepped into the suite. The small living room was filled with stock hotel-French furniture. His father's wallet and key chain lay on a gilt writing table. Harry had been a heavy sleeper, he remembered; perhaps he still was.

He knocked at the paneled bedroom door, then pressed down on the brass handle and went in.

The bedroom was cold and dark. And very quiet. Only the hum of the air conditioner disturbed the silence. He crossed the carpeted floor to the radiator cover that housed the air conditioner, flicked it off, and switched on the light. The room was another French reproduction—shirred blue satin walls, white and gold furniture. The bed, majestic in a calculated, music-hall way, had a blue satin canopy that touched the ceiling.

Harry Meyer lay on his side in the exact center

of the bed, his knees curled up, his hands folded beneath his cheek. The blankets and sheets were tucked in neatly all around him. He looked like a painting entitled "Blessed Sleep."

Nick went to the bed, looked down, and touched him, but he already knew. Harry's forehead was too cold, even given the chill from the air conditioner.

He sat down in an uncomfortable chair across the room and wondered, irrelevantly, if all hotel furniture was manufactured by one company. He felt stoned. A little drunk. He forced himself to look at Harry Meyer's face. They had the same bone structure, he decided. Little else.

He wondered if he was going to cry, found he wasn't, then wondered if he should. He decided that he was probably in some kind of detached state of shock. Detached was the word. He felt very detached. Unattached.

He should do something. He had to wait, though, until the knot of discomfort in his guts had settled itself into the dull, steady ache he was used to when events happened that made him nervous.

The knot didn't seem to be going to settle. He wondered how long he had been sitting in the chair. Too long. Trying to snap out of it, he reached for the color-coordinated telephone on the night table next to his father's body. He heard a noise and, startled, looked up.

"Something the matter?" An old man with jowls, wearing a vested suit, a thick gold watch chain crossing his paunch like a miniature suspension bridge, stood in the doorway. He looked strong and mean and rich.

"Something the matter, young fellow?"

"Yes," Nick said. "My father's dead, I think. Who are you?"

"Ralston-Brown, with the hyphen. Theodore Ralston-Brown. I live in the opposite suite. Who are you?"

"Nick Miller."

Incredibly, they were shaking hands. "Pleased to meet you," Mr. Brown said in a gravelly voice. "You sit down. Not there. Outside. I'll call the manager and put a match under his ass." He led Nick into the living room, sat him down on a pink sofa no one had ever sat on before, and went to the telephone.

Waiting for the operator to locate the manager, Ralston-Brown cupped his hand over the mouthpiece and said, "I saw your father come in last night. He looked like the dickens. Had to help him up to bed."

Nick didn't want to think about the implications of what Ralston-Brown had said. He tried to turn his mind off. He tried not to feel responsible for Harry's death.

The next few hours were both numbing and painful. The suite filled with officious members of the hotel's executive staff, various physicians (both state and private) and a constantly changing guard of policemen, beginning with a patrolman in uniform and ending with a captain in a double-knit polyester suit.

Sometime during the morning, Harry's body was carried away on a stretcher with a sheet thrown over it. Nick fought back a need to tear the sheet away, to shout that he was sorry.

He sat through it all on the absurd pink sofa, taking no action at all except to call the office so that Carla and Tony Lyle would know. They arrived minutes after he called.

"Go back to the office, Tony," Nick said.

"I got some time. Who's that fellow with all the charm?"

"Ralston-Brown, with a hyphen. He lives in the next suite. He helped my father to bed last night."

"Man," Carla said to Tony, "you ever in a place where you don't ask questions?" She sat with Nick on the pink sofa, holding his hand, unnaturally subdued.

The police captain sat down with Nick and Carla. A big, soft man, he looked uncomfortable as he ground out his cigarette in a tiny glass ashtray. "There's an ambulance downstairs, Mr. Miller," he said. "It's going to take the body to New York." He spoke as if he were talking to a child, slowly and with concentration. "And there's a lady in the lobby from the Harry Meyer Hospital who'd like a word with you." He pointed to the phone.

"I thought there were all sorts of procedures you had to go through before a body was released," Nick said. "The death certificate and a—"

"Not in this case, Mr. Miller. Not with someone like your step-father. Don't you worry;

I'm taking care of it all."

The captain got up and brought the phone over to him.

"He was my real father," Nick said.

"I must've got the wrong poop, Mr. Miller. Here's the phone."

"Hello? Mr. Miller? This is Pat Buckley," said a bright voice. "I worked closely with your father at the hospital. Dr. Paine—Dr. Cecil Paine, Executive Director of the hospital—sent me down to facilitate the funeral arrangements. I'm going back to New York now, and I wondered if you'd like to come along. The funeral will be at 11 a.m. tomorrow—in accordance, I believe, with your father's religious beliefs. If you'd like to pack a bag, I could certainly wait—"

"I'll come to New York tomorrow," he said.

"Oh."

There was a long pause. He could almost hear Pat Buckley thinking. "Dr. Paine specifically requested that he see you today," she said. "There's so much to discuss . . ."

"Tomorrow," he said.

Another pause.

"I see. You know, Mr. Miller, I could leave the car and driver here with you, and hitch a ride with the ambulance. The driver could pick you up at eight. Would that be convenient, Mr. Miller?"

"Very. Would you like my address?"

"No, we already have that. Well, then, I imagine I'll be meeting you quite soon. I am sorry about your father, Mr. Miller. And I know Dr.

94

Paine and the other members of the staff are as distraught as I am."

Pat Buckley hung up, and he turned to Carla, who squeezed his hand. He returned the pressure. "You all right?"

"Sure," she said. "Fine."

Eventually, except for her, they all left. Tony, the doctors, the hotel people, the medical examiner, the police captain. Nick went to take a last look at the room in which his father had died. The bed had been stripped and the windows opened.

"Harry always liked hotel suites," he said, as he closed the door.

That night Carla cried and Nick soothed her. "Talk to me," he said. "What're you feeling?"

"I'm scared."

"About what, Carla?"

"I don't want to die."

"You just started living."

"I know, Nicky. I know." She held on to him as if he were her life line.

In the morning, she seemed to have recovered her spirits.

She was going to New York with him, she announced. "I'll change my ticket and leave from JFK. I want to see my sister and I wouldn't mind eating a little real food for a change. Something with a little spice in it. Jesus, I can just taste some cuchifritos, plántanos..."

Brushing her hair, she looked out the window

at the limousine waiting for them. "Besides, I never been in a limo before. How come that woman left the car for you, Nick?"

"R.H.I.P."

"What?"

"Rank Has Its Privileges. I'm Harry Meyer's son. They're going to be very nice to me until they find out I don't get his money."

"You don't?"

"He cut me out of his will so many times, all that's left is confetti. Say you love me anyway."

"I love you anyway," she said, kissing him as the phone rang. It was Tony Lyle.

"I was wondering if you had left," Tony said.

"Twenty minutes ago."

"How you feeling, Nick?"

"Okay. A little sad."

There was a pause. "Listen, Tony, there's a car waiting for us..."

"I've been thinking, Nick."

"Always a bad sign."

"No. Listen to me for a minute. Yesterday, before you called from the Warwick, Carla told me why your father came down to Philly, what he offered you."

"So?"

"So the next morning he's dead."

"Tony, that's not the oddest coincidence I ever heard of."

"It bothered me. I went back to the hotel. And I asked some questions. The answers bothered me even more. That Ralston-Brown cat who had to help your father to bed?"

96

"Yes?"

"Nick, he has a reputation for never, ever, talking to anyone. Suddenly he's having drinks with your father and putting him to bed."

"Drinks? Tony, my father never had a drink with anyone in his life. He hated booze."

"I'm telling you, Nick, it gets funnier and funnier. I'm going to look into it a little."

Carla held her watch in front of Nick's eyes. "You want to miss your old man's funeral?" she stage-whispered.

"I've got to go," he told Tony. "I'll call you in a day or two."

"Good luck, Nick."

Carla went down the stairs carrying Baby Love in a plastic bag with holes poked in it so that the plant could breathe. He followed, carrying his old pigskin suitcase and her new red canvas one.

"Good morning, Mister Meyer," the chauffeur said. Nick didn't correct him.

CHAPTER 10

The limousine stopped in front of the James R. Pinder Nondenominational Funeral Establishment on East 82nd Street and First Avenue. The building was ugly—yellow brick with fake wooden columns pressed into its façade to suggest the manor house of a southern plantation.

"You call me at three o'clock," Carla said, one hand grasping his, the other holding onto Baby Love.

"Why don't you let him drop you off?" Nick said, nodding toward the chauffeur.

"Yeah, I can see it now: little Carla Vasquez pulling up at the front entrance of the Seward Co-operative Public Housing Project in a chauffeur-driven Caddy. Then Luisa would *know* that I'm dealing the hard stuff." She kissed him and got out of the car, her plant cuddled next to her breast, and ran across First Avenue, shouting at a taxi.

A woman opened the other door of the car for

him from the curb side. She was in her mid-twenties and looked as if she had been outfitted in the better-dress department at Bonwit Teller's. Her blond hair was thick, cut short. She wore tinted aviator glasses, the blue lenses making it difficult to see her eyes. Her clothes, Nick thought, were more for protection than attraction.

"Mr. Miller?" she asked with a bright, nervous smile she knew wasn't good enough. "I'm Pat Buckley. We spoke yesterday, on the phone."

"I remember. Thanks for arranging for the car."

"That's my job," she said. "Dr. Paine is waiting for you inside."

He followed her through the door and down a long, polished hall. A tall, big man stood at the end of it. He held a pair of gold-framed glasses in one hand while he massaged the bridge of his nose with the other. As they walked toward him, he put the glasses on and smiled.

"I'm Cecil Paine," he said, his big hand shooting out to grasp Nick's. "You must know how grieved I am. Your father and I were very close." He released Nick's hand. "We have a great deal to discuss, but I'm afraid it shall have to wait until after the service. We've been holding things up till you arrived." He had a deep, solicitous voice, tinged with a British accent. Nick felt, in a curious way, comforted by it.

Paine put his big hand on Nick's shoulder and piloted him through a side door into a chapel filled with men and women with neat haircuts and adult, serious faces. They stopped talking until Paine and Nick had taken their seats in the first row.

"We quite purposely kept it small, limited to staff," Cecil whispered. "There was the time element, and I know Harry would have preferred it this way."

Nick tried to get comfortable on the hard, wooden bench. "I wonder," he said. "My guess is he would have liked it held in Madison Square Garden on New Year's Eve with klieg lights, full media coverage and Barry Goldwater delivering the eulogy."

Cecil smiled. "Your father had become a great deal more conservative in the last few years."

"You knew he was my real father, Dr. Paine?"

"There's not much I don't know about Harry Meyer," Cecil said. "And please call me Cecil, Nick."

A small, dark man in black robes entered the chapel and the congregation became silent. He stepped behind a podium placed off to the left, his head bowed, his hands folded. He looked down at the podium and then up at the audience.

"We are gathered here today," he said, "to pay our last respects to a great humanitarian, a wonderful human being, Harry Meyer. Rising from the humblest of beginnings, this man, who was born in..."

Nick looked away, his attention focusing on the ostentatiously plain pine coffin that rested on a platform to the right of the podium. He shivered. It was hard to believe that his father, flamboyant Harry Meyer, lay inside it. It was even harder to believe that that complicated, infuriating, not altogether unlovable, man would never bother him again. At least in the flesh.

Trying to visualize Harry inside the long box, he understood the reason for open coffins, the need of the living to be assured that the dead were really dead.

For a moment he felt like jumping up and ripping the cover off the coffin to make sure that some hoax was not being played, that Harry was really inside.

He made himself look up at the high ceiling, at the stained-glass Star of David that hung discreetly from a chain. It came from a prop room, he supposed, where it was kept on a shelf beside a wooden cross. The man at the podium droned on about Harry Meyer's kindness and goodness; Cecil Paine polished his glasses with a large white handkerchief.

At last the eulogy was over, the light above the coffin dimmed, and Cecil indicated that Nick and he were to walk out together, down the center aisle. The other mourners looked up at them as they passed, offering small, disinterested smiles.

"Where's he being buried?" Nick asked as they came out of the funeral parlor and moved down the steps to where the car was waiting.

Cecil held the car door open for him while Pat Buckley got into the front seat next to the chauffeur.

"Buried?" Cecil said. "He's not being buried, my dear fellow."

"Why, are his ashes being strewn over Wall Street?" Nick said.

Cecil smiled. "All members of the hospital board pledge their bodies to medical science, Nick. It would be odd if we didn't. After all, the very reason for the hospital's existence..."

"What did he die of, Dr. Paine?"

"Cecil. You must call me Cecil, Nick." He waited until the car was moving out into the First Avenue traffic before he went on. "You must be aware that your father was the recipient of one of the earliest heart transplants. Did you know that I performed that operation?"

"I was just a kid, but I remember being told about it," Nick said. "I didn't know about you."

"But you probably do know," Cecil went on, "that the survival rate for heart transplant recipients is alarmingly low. Most die within a year or two from heart attacks resulting from something called ventricular fibrillation. Which means, in plain English, that the main pumping chamber of the heart suddenly beats irregularly and then stops. We don't know exactly why. Nor do we know why your father took some twenty years to develop the same affliction that does in most patients a few weeks or months or a year after the transplant. That is why the minute Harry's body arrived in New York I performed an autopsy."

"And what did you find?"

102

"Nothing, Nick. Nothing other than the usual degeneration of aging."

Cecil sighed, and put a hand on Nick's shoulder. "Harry thought about you a great deal during these last years. Were you and he able to make up? I know he planned to try."

"Harry certainly seems to have told you everything."

"Nick, we were two old bachelors living in close proximity. We had absolutely no secrets from each other. I might say that my relationship with your father was one of the most satisfying of my life."

Nick returned his smile of sympathy. It was hard to imagine Harry Meyer talking out his troubles and his secrets to anyone. Yet he could imagine confiding in Cecil. He seemed everything a doctor should be: interested, secure, wise. A big daddy who would make one well.

The limousine turned into a Harry Meyer Hospital driveway on East 70th Street, half a block from Fifth Avenue. An electronic garage door opened and the car drove down a ramp into a large garage. A dozen cars were neatly parked in marked spaces. There was room for five dozen more. The driver stopped in front of an elevator bank.

They got out of the car and Pat Buckley inserted a plastic square into a slot next to the elevator door, which then opened.

"It's like '2001'," Nick said when they were all in the elevator and she had used the card again by

103

the raised number three on the panel.

"We're very careful about security," Cecil said. "We treat a great many people who, for one reason or another, might be the subject of an attack." He laughed. "A friend of mine, a senator, recently told me he wasn't sure which was the greater risk—the surgeon's scalpel or the assassin's knife."

The elevator doors opened and they stepped into an expensively carpeted corridor.

Pat Buckley looked at the Cartier watch on her wrist. "You're due on twenty in a few minutes, Dr. Paine."

"Yes. Thank you, Patricia."

"Goodbye, Mr. Miller," she said, and walked in the other direction as Cecil led Nick along the corridor, which had a great many wood-paneled doors on either side. The walls were hung with English sporting prints.

"This doesn't look much like a hospital," Nick said.

"This floor doesn't, certainly," Cecil said. "It's called Executive Services—there arc meeting rooms, a doctors' library and canteen, even shower rooms and napping cubicles for the staff. I often think it is a great waste of space, but I'm something of a Spartan perhaps."

He stopped before a pair of teak-paneled doors and took his MatchCode card from his jacket pocket.

"You have to use that to get into every room?" Nick asked.

"Almost all of them," Cecil answered. "The security system used to make Harry frantic." He inserted his card into a slot. "This is the library and the gentleman waiting to meet you is Harry's lawyer, Elliot Sarno. He is, I might add, the hospital's principal legal advisor as well."

The library looked as if it belonged in a men's club. Wooden shelves filled with books ran the length of the room. Leather chairs were grouped about a large, low table near the heavily curtained windows. In one corner was a detailed model of the Harry Meyer complex, encased in a plastic bubble. In another corner, a hooded computer console sat on a small table. Both the model and the console looked like invaders from another, more advanced century.

Elliot Sarno was in one of the leather chairs. He was a thin, tobacco-colored man with a lined, sour face. His wrinkled blue suit was a size too big, as was his shirt. The dollar cigar in his hand seemed like a natural extension of his person.

"Elliot, this is Harry's son, Nick. Nick, this is Elliot Sarno. I leave you to him. When you're finished, just pick up that telephone, and tell the operator to notify me."

Cecil gave them both his smile and left, shutting the teak-paneled doors behind him.

Elliot Sarno shook Nick's hand without getting up from his seat. He crossed his knife-thin legs and lit his cigar with an old Zippo.

"Sit down, kid." He puffed on the cigar as Nick sat down in one of the leather chairs. "So you're

Harry Meyer's son. You don't look like him. You're better looking." He exhaled a perfect smoke ring. "You know how long I knew your father, kid?"

"How long?" Nick asked, liking the deadpan delivery.

"Too long, kid. Too long." He twirled the cigar in his fingers. "And maybe not long enough. Complicated man, Harry Meyer. Tough. Soon as take a poke at you as look at you. Yet he winds up in a set-up like this. Say, I remember..."

He talked about Harry Meyer for a half hour or so, remembering all-night crap games, lightning supermarket takeovers, junkets to Las Vegas, and one long-ago trip to Miami in a Lincoln Continental when they had run over a farmer's pig. "You should've seen the look on that sheriff's face when your father gave him the secret Masonic handshake. 'I didn't know Jews were Masons,' the sheriff said. 'Yeah,' your father said, 'and I didn't know sheriffs were pig farmers.' Cost us a hundred bucks to get out of that one, and that wasn't hay in those days."

Elliot Sarno relit his cigar. "Well, enough schmoozing. You come and see me some day after you're settled and I'll take you to a place your father and I used to go to, we'll talk some more. The best goddamned corned beef you ever ate in your life."

"Sounds good."

"Good? It's great." He looked at Nick as he ground the cigar out in an ashtray. "So let's talk about Harry's will."

"Sure."

"How much you think you're going to get?"

Nick laughed and stood up. He went to the windows, pulled the heavy curtains aside, and looked down at the cars on Fifth Avenue. "Let me put your mind at ease, Mr. Sarno. You're not about to break my heart. Harry made it clear a long time ago that he had given me all he was going to give me, that I was going to get nothing."

"Nothing?" Elliot Sarno said. "Seven million dollars is nothing?"

Nick turned. "What?"

"I'm sitting here wasting my time, talking to myself. Kid, you get—depending on the market, depending on when I can push the will through probate and a few other variables I'm not going into now—you get seven million dollars."

"Jesus." Nick felt his stomach knot. And, for an instant, he saw Harry's face, a benevolent, smiling hallucination.

"Jesus," he said. "Jesus H. Christ. What am I going to do with all that money?"

"A lot of people will try to answer that question for you."

"Jesus." Nick put his hand on his stomach. "Jesus."

"You got a remarkably small repertoire of exclamations, kid. You feeling all right? You don't look so hot suddenly."

"Yes. No. I mean, I'm fine."

Elliot Sarno stood and picked up his oversized briefcase. "Listen, kid, you take it easy. I have to get back to my office. I just wanted to drop the first bombshell today. We'll get together in a couple of days. There's more."

"Like what? I only get the money if I remain celibate for life?"

"You're a regular wisenheimer, kid," Elliot Sarno said amiably. At the door, he turned. "Fact of the matter is, he not only left you the seven million, he also made you, along with Cecil Paine, a trustee of the trust he set up for this hospital. And we are talking, kid, about a trust of more than one hundred million dollars. Your vote on how the income is spent will be just as important as Cecil's vote. That means you're a very important man, Mr. Meyer."

"Miller," Nick said automatically.

"Believe me, kid," Elliot Sarno said, "you're Mr. Meyer now."

He had the switchboard page Dr. Paine as soon as Elliot Sarno was gone. Five minutes later Cecil rejoined him in the library. But though he offered congratulations ("I'm aware of what Elliot has told you. How does it feel to be a millionaire, Nick?"), his mind was clearly on the hospital's work and needs. Nick tried to concentrate as Cecil talked on.

". . . the closer the tissue compatibility between donor and recipient, the more chance of a successful transplantion. The matching is all-important. A series of tests we've just completed proves conclusively that there's little chance of even the simplest transplant—say a skin graft—

taking between a German and a Japanese. But there's a ninety per cent chance of its taking between brother and sister, uncle and nephew, even between distant cousins, as long as the tissue is compatible. Thank the Lord for computers. You have no idea what headway we've made in tissue typing, Nick. We can . . ."

Cecil had removed his glasses and his eyes, usually so pale it was hard to distinguish their color, had become a luminescent blue. He seemed to Nick to have a kind of religious conviction about what he was saying.

". . . utmost importance. I have—" Cecil stopped talking in the middle of a sentence and replaced his glasses. "I am sorry, old boy. You must be tired and hungry, and if you're at all like me, in a state of semi-shock. News, important news, always throws my system completely out of whack. And here I am, dithering away about transplants. But the hospital and its work is my one abiding interest. When I go on too long about it, you must stop me. I must point out, however, that you now hold a very important role in the affairs of this institution. Not only because of your position on the Trust, but because you are Harry Meyer's son. I want you to consider taking your father's place here at the hospital."

"I'm not really all that sure what he did here," Nick said.

"A great many things, chief among them being a sort of good-will ambassador. Your name alone, assuming you take your father's, will help to provide both reassurance to our patients and continuity to our fund-raising efforts."

"I couldn't give you an answer now. It's—"

"No, of course not. But as Harry would have said, listen to my proposition. Stay here for a few weeks. Use your father's apartment. Let our Miss Buckley show you around. Get some idea of the width and breadth of what we are attempting to achieve. See with your own eyes what we are doing here, what our work will mean to mankind, what it is already doing for thousands of people, important people, who would be dead if it weren't for the Harry Meyer Hospital. And then think of our need for intelligent advisors like yourself." He stopped himself. "Dear me, there I go again, on the old soap box!"

Cecil smiled. "What you need now, Nick, is to get away from me, have a light dinner and a quiet night. Miss Buckley is waiting outside to show you Harry's apartment. We'll talk again soon." He patted Nick on the back and left.

Nick went to the telephone. Carla answered on the first ring. "You all right, Nicky?"

"I don't know."

"What do you mean, you don't know?"

"When I tell you what's happened . . ."

"So tell me."

"I'll tell you when I see you. I'm at the hospital now and all I want to do is get out of here. I feel like I'm being suffocated with money and good works."

"You stoned, Nicky?"

110

"Sort of. Listen, meet me at the Plaza in the front lobby in a half hour. I'll get us a room."

"The Plaza Hotel?"

"Cecil, Dr. Paine, offered me my father's apartment but this place is making me—"

"What's the apartment like?"

"I don't know." He took the receiver and walked over to the scale model. "I think it's a triplex. What difference does it make? I just want to get out of here, Carla."

"Is it on Fifth Avenue?"

"Yes."

"Does it face the Park?"

"Yes, it faces the Park."

"I hate hotels, Nicky. The bell boys making dirty noises at each other, the sad little rooms with the hard little beds..."

"Not the Plaza. Carla, I want to get away from here."

"But suppose it's fabulous, Nicky? Suppose it's the kind of apartment I've dreamed about all—"

"Then you stay there. I'm checking into the Plaza."

"Nicky! I never ask you for much, right? But please, just let's take a look at it. Jesus, how many people get to stay in an apartment on Fifth Avenue, facing the Park?"

"You have a wonderful set of values, Carla."

"Nick! Please..."

"Meet me on the corner of Fifth and 70th in half an hour, you materialistic, social climbing—"

"I'll be there in twenty minutes. I'll take a taxi."

"And we're just going to look at it. If I hate it, if I feel funny about it, I'm not staying. Right?"

He waited for an answer, but all he got was the dial tone.

CHAPTER 11

They stood in his father's bedroom, staring out the full-length one-way window across Central Park, at the lights of Central Park West.

"Man," Carla said, "this is most definitely where it's at. If I ever had any doubts, they are gone now." She began to unwrap the plastic bag in which she carried Baby Love.

He had agreed to stay in the apartment for "a while," and a giant doorman had brought in their suitcases and left them on Harry's circular bed.

Pat Buckley had given them a tour of the apartment, acting like a rental agent who didn't believe they were a couple who could afford something really nice. Carla didn't care. She just took it all in, her eyes Orphan Annie-round as they went through each floor of the triplex. Nick was amused, wondering what Harry had made of the decor, and who had talked him into it. There weren't many rooms, but all of them were large. The street floor, with a private entrance from

Fifth Avenue, had a marbleized foyer, a short hall, a kitchen, a butler's pantry, a bathroom. The second floor contained a circular living room and a small, square, formal dining room with a dumb-waiter, concealed by a Coromandel screen, connected to the kitchen below. The bedroom, the huge bathroom, and the small study were on the third floor. A door off the third floor landing led to the third floor of the hospital.

Most of the rooms were beige, white, and black. The furniture was modern, overstuffed, and overscaled. Enormous paintings—Stella, Pollock, Close—dominated the walls.

Only the study seemed like his father. It contained a large, ornate mahogany desk, a leather recliner that could be adjusted to eight different positions, a twenty-eight-inch color television set, and a small Chagall—a green bird on a white background.

Plastic MatchCode cards were not needed within the apartment, Pat Buckley explained; only the door on the third floor landing, leading to the hospital, required a card. She thanked Nick for his patience, said that she would arrange with various program directors for him to tour the hospital complex the following day, and left.

"That lady digs you," Carla said. "She'd like to get it on with you."

"Where do you get that stuff, Carla?"

"I'm telling you, man. To Carla she gave your straight yes–no answers. To you, she gave little pissy combacks, little cunty come-ons. You watch your step with that blonde bitch, I'm telling you."

"Don't tell me. Show me." He pulled her to him, but she broke away.

"Before we get into all that, I want to hear everything. And I want to hear it like a lady. Down in the living room. Over martinis, Nicholas. We spend entirely too much time in the bedroom," she said in what she thought was a high-society voice.

In the living room, she mixed drinks from a bar hidden in a carved Korean chest.

"How'd you figure out that was the bar?" he asked, taking the martini.

"You kidding me? Sloane's, Bloomingdale's, even John Wanamaker's carry them. Twelve hundred bucks and it's yours."

"I didn't hang out in furniture departments when I was growing up."

"You would have, big shot, if you never had any bread." She threw him a thick joint. "Courtesy of my sister, Luisa. Man, you look like you need it." She sat down across from him, reaching over the molded plastic coffee table, on which Baby Love rested, to light the joint with a gold duPont table lighter. "Start talking."

"Let's go upstairs and make love first."

"Nicky..."

He told her.

"*Madre de Dios!* Seven million bucks! Jesus."

She got up and started pacing the room, the martini in one hand, the joint in the other. "You know what you can do with seven million bucks?"

"You want to marry me now?"

"Man, not now and not *never*! The richer the guy, the easier it is for him when it comes to split time. You'll get a couple of goons to work me over, drop a check for a thousand bucks on what's left of my body and go on to the next one. That Buckley blonde, for instance."

"Anyone ever tell you you paint beautiful word pictures?"

"I seen it happen, man. They get divorced in poor nabes, too, you know. The guy always wins. Always." She took a long toke on the joint and a sip of the martini. "Seven million bucks. Man, you never have to worry again!"

"I never worried before," he said, getting up, reaching for her.

"Not here, Nick. Not in the living room."

She ran up the circular steps to the bedroom. He followed and pulled her down on the bed.

He kissed her, but she pulled her face away. "Shut out the lights, Nick." She pointed to the one incongruity in the decoration scheme, an overhead glass light fixture.

"What's the matter with you, Carla?" He sat up, letting her go. "Suddenly you want the lights off, and suddenly you have to be in a bed. Where's the free spirit you're always talking about?"

"I'm uptight, man. I admit it. But you got to admit I have plenty of reasons. I mean, I am leaving mañana for California and the Big Chance. I bring it off, I come back with really good shots of those Chicanos, I can write my own ticket. And then there's all this incredible stuff here—my teenage masturbation fantasy come true. Here I am, little Carla Vasquez, barely out of the tenement, having martinis in the classiest Fifth Avenue apartment I could ever imagine, sitting next to a handsome guy with seven million bucks in the bank and everything it takes to take what I got. So I'm trying to act like a lady, Nicky, instead of the hired help. What can I tell you? Maybe you could try and understand, huh?"

"I understand."

She put her arms around him and kissed him, her tongue going into his mouth. "Do me one little favor, Nicky. Just tonight, shut out the light. That big one-way window over there. It's giving me trouble. I mean how do *I* know it's one way?"

He laughed, got up and switched off the light. They made love.

She made all the right moves and sounds. But still, he thought, just before he fell asleep, something wasn't right.

In the morning, cameras strapped around her, she got into a taxi. "You call me," he said, kissing her.

"You take care of Baby Love. Water. Every other day. And talk to her. Give her kisses. That plant can't live without affection."

"Neither can I. You sure you don't want me to come to the airport?"

"Positive. I'm being brave this week."

"Good luck," he said. They kissed again, and

the taxi took off down Fifth.

He felt predictably lonesome, deserted. The empty feeling that had taken the place of the knotted feeling in his stomach began to creep into other parts of his body. He wondered if he were going to be sick. He couldn't bring himself to go back into Harry's apartment, past the jolly green uniformed giant of a doorman.

"You a permanent fixture?" he asked the man, who looked as if he should have been playing professional killer football. There was a Sony two-way radio attached to his belt.

"Yes, Mr. Meyer. My name is Lawrence. I performed small services for your father—may I say how sorry I am about his untimely demise, sir?—and should be happy to do the same for you."

"Thanks."

"Thank you, sir."

Nick looked across the street at Central Park. It was alive with joggers and bike riders, a trail of nursery school kids following their earnest counselors. It was a nice, sunny, early September day. Rich men in grey suits, briefcases under their arms, smiled as they passed him on their way to midtown offices.

He wished he was on his way to a midtown office. Or maybe a midtown asylum. Someplace dark where he could lie down and erase everything. He started to walk uptown, away from Lawrence.

"Will you be away long, sir?"

"I don't know, Lawrence."

"It's only that if there are messages or if Dr. Paine or Miss Buckley want to reach you . . . Your father always left word where he would be."

"Yes? Well, I'm not my father, Lawrence."

"Yes, Mr. Meyer, sir."

All he needed in his life, he thought, was a seven-foot doorman who looked like a Copa bouncer.

"Anyone ever call you Larry?" he asked.

"Never, sir. Not to my knowledge, sir."

He walked toward 71st Street. All the Fifth Avenue entrances to the Harry Meyer looked like any other Fifth Avenue apartment house entrance: green and white canopies, wrought iron grilles on the doors, two doormen in each of the doorways. But these doormen, unlike their counterparts on neighboring blocks, were of epic proportions and young.

At the corner, two shoulder-heavy policemen said good morning to him as if they knew who he was. Like the doormen, they wore Sony radios on their belts. Half-way across 71st, he turned. The cops were watching him, one of them talking into his radio.

There were two more on the corner of Madison and 71st. "Good morning, Mr. Meyer."

He suppressed an urge to start running. He crossed the street and walked north on the west side of Madison, feeling safer once he crossed 72nd, turning every so often to see if he were being followed.

The hospital, he thought, was better protected than the White House.

He concentrated on the crowd, wondering if he could even tell if he were being followed. All he saw were prosperous mothers in modest, expensive clothes, walking hand-in-hand with perfect little kids. Men in tight pants, open shirts, blazers, strolled in and out of the galleries. Short, stout women walked rapidly in and out of the specialty food stores. Young, painfully thin men with short haircuts and jewelry around their wrists peered longingly out of beauty salon windows. Cops, less buttoned up than the ones posted on Harry Meyer corners, walked around with their toes pointed out, looking benign.

He wondered if he were being paranoid. And realized it was a mistake to wonder if one were being paranoid because if one started wondering, one would surely become.

He knew he had to talk to someone. Someone smart. He had to ask the questions out loud.

He called Tony Lyle at the "OFF!" office but didn't make contact, the office not being Tony's favorite place on Saturday morning. He called Tony's apartment.

"Hello, honey." It was the answering service.

"Tony in?"

"No, sweetie. He won't be in all day."

"Any idea when he'll be in?"

"He didn't say, love. Want to leave your name?"

120

"I'll call back."
"Bye, dear."
He tried Shepard Gordon's number.

CHAPTER 12

They had gone to the same country day school, Chilton Hall. They had both been leaders, but with remarkably different styles. Shepard was blond and broad and went out for soccer. Nick was dark and thin and the fastest long-distance runner Chilton Hall had ever had.

Shep was a WASP who loved his parents, his school, his country, right or wrong. In the yearbook, under his photographed good looks, appeared his nickname: Straight Arrow. Under Nick's picture it said: Renegade.

Their relationship was based on curiosity—a need to understand how the other could live, could work, could think so differently. They were like two scientists from China and Russia, forced to work on a project together, each constantly misunderstanding, misinterpreting the other's words and actions; but constantly interested—and, in a way, constantly trusting. Each came to know instinctively that the other would not harm him, even in the savage world of Chilton Hall.

They might have stopped knowing one another had they gone on to different institutes of higher learning, but both went to the University of Pennsylvania. Shep (who had his heart set on Princeton) because his father and grandfather and great grandfather had gone there, Nick because Harry wanted him to—"They got the best goddamn business school in the country." He had envisioned Nick, even at that late date, taking over the supermarket empire.

Shep joined Sigma Chi, drove a TR6, switched from soccer to lacrosse, made Dean's list, bought his clothes at the Philadelphia branch of Brooks Brothers, and drank beer.

Nick flirted with the SDS, bought a Harley-Davidson vintage motorcycle, helped Tony Lyle start an underground newspaper, dropped out and back in during his sophomore year, owned one pair of blue jeans, smoked grass and took acid.

Yet they got together a couple of times a month, still attempting to dissect one another's motives, still trying to find out how they could think so differently about so many things. Still trusting one another.

Shep went on to Harvard Law, where he graduated fourth in his class and was promptly recruited into an organization called The United States Economic Recovery Program (TUSERP). Nick was never sure what TUSERP was, but he knew it wasn't what Shep said—a government agency dedicated to finding new ways to make old land and buildings profitable. Nick supposed it was some kind of federal surveillance group.

"How's the renegade?" Shep asked, when he came to the phone. "Sorry to hear about your father, Ace."

"Look, Shep, I have to talk to you. I'm in New York. Can I—"

"Come on over. All I had planned was watching football on the tube. Brendi would love to see you."

The taxi dropped him off at Park and 89th. He walked east to the narrow two-story brownstone Shep's father had given him for being a good Republican boy. Brendi answered the door.

"Hi, Nick."

"Hi."

She had been at Penn with them, the most sought after girl of her year. He had almost forgotten how good looking she was, how attractive he had once found her. She still wore her black hair parted in the middle; her polite patrician face was still made interesting by her dimples and by her alert, dark blue eyes.

They had slept together once, propelled into bed by the same curiosity that caused Nick and Shep to circle round one another. She had left Nick's not especially clean bed in the early morning and gone back to her neat room in the Women's Dormitory, confused, resolving not to see him again. He had thought, for a time, that he could love her.

"Sorry to hear about your dad, Nick," Brendi said now, kissing him on the cheek.

"Thanks." He kissed her back.

They looked at each other, remembering the night they had made love, still attracted to each other. He wondered if she had told Shep.

"Come in," she said, her smile discharging the electricity in the air. "You hungry?"

"I'm always hungry."

The three of them had lunch at a heavy mahogany table in a dark red dining room under a Tiffany chandelier, eating off Tiffany plates with Tiffany silverware.

A black woman in a white uniform served. Shep seemed as natural, as Shep-like, as he had always been. Brendi smiled her private smile and ate slowly, sitting between the two men.

"You like the shad roe?" Shep sipped his white wine and forked arugula into his mouth.

"Fish egg, isn't it?" Nick asked, avoiding the question.

"Shep likes it," Brendi said, "because he thinks it's low in calories."

"Got to watch the waist line," Shep said. "Now that I'm in an office most of the time."

"Recovering all those economies," Nick said, putting down his fork.

They had frozen yogurt on sticks for dessert. "I've got to lose five pounds," Shep said, as he and Nick carried their coffee cups into the den. "You should catch me trying to move around the track at the A.C. Little old arthritic men on crutches whizz past me."

Brendi put her head in the door. "I'll see you soon, Nick. I have to pick up the girls at dancing

125

school and take them to a party."

He stood up. "I forgot you were a mother."

"There are times I'd like to." She kissed Shep on the lips, Nick on the cheek. "Don't be a stranger."

She closed the door as she left.

"Still the prettiest girl in her class," Nick said, watching Shep fill his pipe.

"One thing we don't argue about. You want to smoke a joint or something, go ahead."

"Very loose of you, Shep, but this isn't the kind of occasion when one smokes a joint."

"What is the occasion?"

"I have some questions," Nick said carefully. "I need a mind like yours to help me answer them."

"What kind of mind is that?"

"Logical. Unemotional. Gentile."

Shep laughed. "I guess that's what I've got, all right." He puffed on his pipe. "Shoot."

"What do you know about the Harry Meyer Hospital?"

"Heap big powerful organization. Not to be touched. I'm fairly high up in the secret clearance department—I guess that's no secret—and even I don't have access to that particular file."

"Something smells funny there."

"You think something smells funny everywhere, Nick."

"Something usually does."

"What is it?"

"I don't know. Just listen to this sequence of events and tell me what you think."

He told Shep everything that happened, from

the moment Harry Meyer announced that Nick was his son to the moment when Elliot Sarno had told him he was inheriting seven million bucks and a place on a hundred-million-dollar trust.

"Jesus!" Shep took a deep breath and relighted his pipe. "Seven million bucks!"

"What I guess I'm getting at is that something strange is going on in that hospital, and there's something strange about my father's death. I don't know what it is, but I don't like it." He looked at Shep. "Go ahead. Tell me I'm having a paranoid fantasy brought on by the shock of Harry's paternal revelations, sudden death, and secret generosity."

"I don't have to tell you, Nick. You already know it. It's not as if this is the first time you ever thought someone was after you. At Chilton Hall it was that old fart, the Latin teacher. At Penn it was the head of the political science department. You ever consider talking to a shrink? I mean, if I were you, I would be ordering a Rolls Royce right now, not talking conspiracy with—"

"There's something wrong there, Shep."

Shep sucked on his pipe, realized it had gone out, and struck another match. "Look, even if there was something wrong with the way Harry Meyer met his maker, there would be zilch that you could do about it. Believe me, you cannot buck Cecil Paine and the Harry Meyer Hospital."

"Hot shit, huh?"

"Top of the pile. Nick, why don't you take your money and run? Go back to Philly and blow it on another underground magazine, or a hostel for unrepentant draft dodgers, or give it to the American Indians or—"

"I'm hanging around for a while. Remember, I'm a trustee. Besides, I want to see what I can pick up."

"You're not going to pick up anything, Ace."

"Suppose—just suppose—I do?"

"You won't."

"But suppose I do? Shep, I'm asking you to promise that if I find out something, you'll help."

"Listen, Ace—"

"If. I said, if."

"Okay. *If* you get some solid proof, not just more neurotic surmise, that all is not what it should be at the Harry Meyer Hospital, I will give you all the help I can. Which is, as I guess you know, a helluva lot. But don't go running around that place with a fire ax, breaking down every door you see. Try, for once in your life, Ace, to be a little subtle."

Shep gave up on the pipe and got to his feet. "Keep in touch. Let me know what you dig up, before you do anything crazy. At least promise me that."

Nick took his outstretched hand. "I promise you that, Shepard."

Shep walked with him to the front door and watched while Nick got into a taxi. Then he turned and went into the house. He stood in the vestibule for a few minutes, thinking, before he walked back to the kitchen.

"Maggie," he asked the woman washing the Tiffany plates. "We have any cake in this house?"

128

"You know we don't," the woman said. "On account of your diet."

"Maggie, I think it's time you went shopping for some cookies."

"Your special cookies, Mr. Gordon?" she asked, wiping her hands on a towel.

He smiled. "Right, Maggie. Emergency cookies."

He took a white card from his wallet, wrote a few words on it and gave it to her. "You give this right to the head baker, Maggie."

She laughed, found her purse, and headed for the back door. "Good thing these cookies don't have any calories, Mr. Gordon."

He went back into his den, lighted his pipe again, and waited for the phonc call.

CHAPTER 13

Nick walked back to the triplex, thinking that New York wasn't such an ugly city after all, at least not if you lived on the upper East Side and it was early September and doormen smiled at you.

He ignored his own doorman's "Good afternoon, Mr. Meyer, sir," and went into the kitchen and poured himself a glass of milk. They certainly knew enough about him, he thought, looking at the half-gallon bottle of milk someone—Lawrence?—must have put there that morning. Harry not only didn't drink alcohol, he never drank milk. He had been strictly a seltzer man.

Pat Buckley was waiting upstairs in the circular living room on one of the circular sofas.

"Mr. Meyer." She stood up, then leaned over to grind out her cigarette in an ashtray full of ground-out cigarettes. "We were scheduled for an early morning tour of the complex."

"You were," he said. "I wasn't."

"Well," she said, putting the strap of her purse

across her shoulder, "we can start now and continue tomorrow."

"You start now. I have some things to do."

"Mr. Meyer! Dr. Paine is most anxious that you become acquainted with the hospital as soon as possible, and—"

"I'll be available tomorrow morning," Nick said.

He could sense that she wanted to argue, but she didn't. She straightened her purse strap, put her clipboard under her arm and looked, for a moment, like a flight attendant without passengers. She turned to leave.

"Miss Buckley, I have some requests," Nick said. "Do I make them to you, or should I go directly to Cecil?" He sat down on the sofa she had vacated, facing a multi-colored, striped painting that took up most of the opposite wall.

"To me." She tried to smile. "I've been detailed to you, you might say."

"Then you should call me Nick. And if it's all right with you, I'll call you Pat."

"That would be fine, Nick."

"All right, to start with—and this is no reflection on you, but just a personal quirk—I don't want anyone waiting in my living room for me when I get home, or when I get up in the morning, or when I go to bed at night. I'm what you might call a very private person. Two, I want Lawrence transferred or sent on vacation or put out on loan to Ringling Brothers. He rubs me the wrong way. Three, when plans which call for my participation are made, I want to be let in on them

131

early, before anything is set in cement. You have all that?"

She had made notes on everything he said on a yellow pad attached to the clipboard. When she looked up, he was surprised to see little tears of frustration behind the aviator glasses. Oh, God, he thought. She comes from the school of "I-Can't-Do-Anything-Right!" and here I am, confirming it.

"Please don't take this personally," he said. "I just thought if we established ground rules, we—"

"I always used to wait here for your father."

He said softly, "My father and I are—were—very different people."

"And we certainly can't fire Lawrence," she said. "I'm not even sure we can transfer him. There's the union. Contracts have to be..."

She was about to light another cigarette, so he said, "If you don't mind, that's another thing. I used to smoke three packs a day. You know there's nothing like a reformed smoker..."

She put the cigarette back in its pack. "Well, then," she said, making an effort to be brave, "I'll see you tomorrow morning, Nick. At seven, if that's all right with you. We can meet at your third floor entrance to the hospital."

"Seven A.M.?"

"That's what we're scheduled for. Of course, if you would like to make it later..." Her voice rose and very nearly broke.

"No. Seven's terrific. I'll see you at seven."

He showed her out through the door on the

floor above that connected the apartment to the hospital, and went into Harry's study, the small, comfortable room that had been the interior decorator's one concession to Harry Meyer's taste. He took the telephone receiver off the cradle, held the button down with one finger, and unscrewed the mouthpiece with his other hand. There was nothing there, but that didn't mean much. Bugs could be in an infinite number of places; he could spend a month in that room and never find one. But something told him one was there.

At least it wasn't in the most obvious place. He put the receiver back together and called Philadelphia again.

Tony was home. "You okay?" he asked.

"No," Nick said.

"What's the matter?"

"I can't get into it."

There was a photograph on his father's desk, a picture of Harry taken in the late 1920's. He was wearing a thin tie and a double-breasted jacket; there was a cigar in his mouth, and he had one booted foot on the running board of an old touring car. He looked very pleased with himself.

"This is going to be one of your mysterious conversations, I take it," Tony said.

"Harry Meyer," Nick said, "left me seven million bucks. Plus one of the two places on a hundred-million-dollar trust, the beneficiary of which is the Harry Meyer Hospital."

"Great God in heaven!" Then there was silence.

"You still there?" Nick said.

"Barely," Tony said. "What're you going to do with all that filthy lucre?"

"I haven't thought about it."

"Start thinking. We could buy *Newsweek*."

"And what would we do with it?"

"Turn it into a revolutionary journal for the middle class." Tony whistled. "Seven million! I guess I won't be seeing much of you in the near future, Nick."

"Not for a while."

"You want to quit?"

"Horse manure. Consider me on leave of absence while I clear up some personal matters."

"Can you hold on for a minute, Nick?"

"Sure."

Waiting, he studied the picture of cocky Harry Meyer, trying to find a resemblance in it to cocky Nicky Miller.

Tony came back to the phone. "I thought I heard someone at the front door, but no one was there. And then I thought I heard someone by the kitchen door, and no one was there. You think maybe I'm a little nuts?"

"More than a little. Where were you this morning?"

"In Reading."

"Reading?"

"Yes, Reading. I was tracking down your Mister Ralston-Brown."

"The old guy in the hotel?"

"Supposedly he made his money manufacturing umbrellas in Reading. No one there ever heard of him."

"Maybe it was a long time ago."

"Even so."

"Why don't you leave him alone? Even if he made his money running a string of child brothels, so what?" He looked at the picture again. In the 1920's Harry looked as if he had a heart the size and texture of a football.

"I don't care." Tony said. "There's something strange about Ralston-Brown, and I'm going to check him out. Call you later." He hung up without getting Nick's telephone number.

Nick felt deserted, as if one more exit had been blocked up. He set the photograph on the edge of the desk and it fell off, its protective glass shattering. He picked it up and removed the pieces of glass, then took the photo from the frame. When he turned it over to see if there was any writing on the back, he found another photograph behind it.

This one was older, a family portrait, the family posed before a battered, thatched-roof farmhouse. It had an old-country look; probably it had been taken in Poland before Harry and his parents emigrated to America.

His father, clearly recognizable in a knicker suit and matching cap, stood in the center of the picture, striking his usual jaunty pose. He was holding the hand of a girl who looked exactly like him, as if the photographer had performed some trick with the lens. She was staring at Harry, not at the camera.

Harry's parents stood on either side of them, the mother holding Harry's other hand, the father with his arm around the girl. Harry's mother was short and stout, dressed in a long dark skirt with a shawl over a light blouse. She looked tough. The father was more elegant in a black suit that buttoned high up under a long, dark beard. He had sad eyes. Standing next to him, a little off to the side, was a tall young man, holding what appeared to be a large baby. His face was in shadow, but the baby looked out of his nest of wraps directly into the camera. He had the face of a doll, with round pale eyes.

Nick had heard of his father's twin sister, but who were those two? Cousins? Certainly Harry's parents were too old to have a baby.

He sat at Harry's desk for some time, staring at the photograph, trying to find some connection with it, some family line he could grab on to, something that would make him feel as if he belonged.

Later, he walked over to Third Avenue and fought his way through the Saturday afternoon crowd outside of Bloomingdale's. He went down to Clarke's, had a hamburger and two beers, rejected the advances of an amorous account executive and, depressed, tried to get Tony back on the phone. Tony was out.

He took a taxi back to the apartment where he said hello to the night doorman, Charlie, a dark-haired version of Lawrence. He wondered if all the hospital doormen were recruited from the Green Berets. He went to bed.

The telephone rang in the middle of the night and he had an unsatisfactory conversation with Carla. The connection was bad—her words seemed to arrive a few seconds after she said them—but she sounded up and happy. Her work was going well—"I got some dynamite shots, man"—and he resisted the temptation to tell her how miserable and alone he felt.

After that, for no reason he could think of, he went back into the study for another look at the family photograph. He wondered what Carla would make of it, as he slipped it back under the picture of his father and set the frame back in its original position on the desk.

He fell asleep wondering what Tony would find out about Ralston-Brown, wondering what Pat Buckley had arranged for him to see.

CHAPTER 14

They were in an anteroom of the main operating theater on the fifteenth floor.

"If we had begun the tour yesterday, as arranged, we would have started with the executive offices," Pat Buckley said as she strapped her feet into plastic conductive booties. "But since those offices are closed on Sundays, Dr. Paine suggested we observe an operation he's conducting this morning."

"The rest of the hospital doesn't observe the Sabbath?" Nick asked as the scrub nurse showed him how to slip the booties over his shoes.

"We're what you might call a twenty-four-hour, seven-days-a-week operation." Pat smiled. "No pun intended."

Nick tried to return the smile, but he couldn't take his eyes off the scrub nurse. Her face, with its enormous Italian eyes, belonged with the body of an Italian Renaissance madonna. Instead, it sat on top of Jayne Mansfield's torso. Enormous breasts pushed against the starched uniform, threatening to break through.

"You got a lot of inflammable gas in there," the scrub nurse explained, when he asked about the booties. "These are designed to prevent static electricity in the operating room. They keep you from igniting it." Her tough New York accent went more with her body than with her face, he thought as she positioned him on the conductometer to make sure he wasn't a hazard.

Her breasts brushed against his arm as he stepped off the conductometer, and he looked into her saint's face to see if it had been intentional. He couldn't decide.

She put a cap on his head which completely covered his hair, a mask over his nose, and helped him button the short-sleeved cotton suit he had been given.

"We have to be especially careful during an operation like this, when the patient has been shot full of immunosuppressants, not to bring bacteria or viruses in with us." Pat spoke in a determinedly cheerful voice that said that no matter how she felt about him personally, this was her job and she was going to carry it out to the best of her abilities like the good little soldier she was.

She led Nick into the operating theater, which was tiled in black. It does look like a real theater, he thought—an avant-garde one. There was a stage, its floor covered with a white rubbery material. The audience section of the theater, filled with cube-like armchairs, all of them empty, was carpeted in black.

They took seats a few tiers up from the stage. On the stage, under a huge kettledrum of lights, were two operating tables, some six feet apart. A surgical team stood by each table, flanked by draped Mayo stands holding surgical instruments. At the rear of the stage, behind thick Lucite screens, two anesthesiologists sat by their equipment. It looks like a set for a television game show, Nick thought.

Draped in surgical sheets, a man lay on one of the operating tables, surrounded like a horseshoe stake by a U of doctors in white coats and masks.

Television cameras suspended over the operating table relayed what was happening, in detailed and full color close-ups, to monitor screens placed in the backs of every other seat. Not two feet from him, Nick could see the lines under the patient's closed eyes, the beads of sweat on his forehead which a nurse was methodically wiping away.

Pat Buckley was still using her paid escort's voice. "The patient is a fifty-five-year-old man, a laborer, who has suffered for the last five years from heart disease."

"What's his name?" Nick asked.

"I'm not sure I know." Pat leafed through papers on her clipboard. "Does it make any difference? Wait a minute, here it is: Stanley Rosen." She glanced at him slyly. "You don't know him, do you?"

It was the first trace of humor she had shown, and he liked it.

"Only by reputation," he said.

"Should I go on?"

"Please."

"Mr. Rosen recently suffered a stroke that caused extensive damage to his brain, impairing his mental faculties to a point where, if he survives, he will have to be taken care of for the rest of his life."

"What's Mr. Rosen doing here if he's so far gone?" Nick asked.

"This is an experiment. It could only be performed on a patient who, not to put too fine a point on it, hasn't much of a future. There's a good chance Mr. Rosen won't survive the operation."

"And if he does?"

"He'll probably die fairly soon from something else."

"So what does he get out of it?"

"The knowledge that he has helped to benefit his fellow man."

"That's all?"

"Isn't that enough?" She looked at him calmly. "Shall I go on?"

"Sure."

"Mr. Rosen has been in and out of shock all morning."

"Ditto."

"His wife was asked for permission to go ahead with the operation, which she gave. The donor is being wheeled in now."

Nick looked down at the TV monitor in the back of the seat directly before him. The camera was moving in for an extreme close-up. The donor's face filled the screen. At first, Nick couldn't figure out what he was seeing. When he did understand, he stared at the monitor for almost a full minute before he turned to Pat.

"You've got to be kidding," he said.

"We couldn't be more serious. It's worked half a dozen times with kidney transplants. There's no reason, other than human prejudice, why it shouldn't work with a heart."

The face that filled the screen had large, outstanding ears. It was covered with abundant black hair, though the area around the mouth was white. The eyes were wide open, filled with silent terror.

The camera pulled back. The patient was a large chimpanzee. The camera pulled back again. It revealed a surgeon holding a scalpel in his gloved left hand, while his right hand smoothed the shaven skin of the chimp away from him. He poised the scalpel an inch above the center of the chimp's chest and looked up at one of the anesthesiologists. The anesthesiologist held his hand up, giving a "go ahead."

The surgeon put the tip of the scalpel deep into the animal, tilted it to a forty-five-degree angle, and slit the chest wall open. The monitor showed pulsating jets of arterial blood. Nick looked away and then back as the surgeon attached clamps to the large vessels that carried oxygen and blood to the heart.

"That's Dr. Paine operating," Pat said. "He has to be quick. The tissues of the heart die if they don't get their blood and oxygen."

An assistant put his gloved hands into the chimp's open chest and removed the heart. He held it for a moment in the palm of his hand. To Nick, it looked like an overripe tomato with its top cut off. The top had remained in the chimp's body. The rest of it, the two ventricles and the lower portion of the upper atrial chambers were dipped by the assistant in a jar filled with a salt solution.

Pat's voice was just above a whisper. "Now they'll attach the chimp's heart to a heart-lung machine. Mr. Rosen's own blood, taken yesterday, will be used to feed it until they can put the heart in his chest." She looked at him. "Are you all right?"

"A little nauseous."

She put her hand on his shoulder. "If you're going to throw up, Nick, you'd best leave now. You can't take your mask off in here."

"I won't throw up," he said.

"You're sure? The difficult part is coming now."

"I'm sure."

On the monitor, he watched Cecil make a long, slashing incision, opening Mr. Rosen's chest, and then use a bone saw to cut through the ribs. The saw gave off a chilling, dental sound.

Assistants set retractors in the cavity to separate the cut ends, to hold open the chest wall.

Cecil sliced through the pericardium, the membrane that enclosed the heart. An assistant folded it back as if it were a rare piece of tapestry, revealing Mr. Rosen's failing heart.

As easily as if he were filleting a piece of fish, Cecil's scalpel cut a perfect circle around the heart, freeing it. The assistant lifted the heart out of the cavity and dropped it into a jar held by a nurse. It made a light plopping noise, as if a heavy stone had been dropped into a lake.

Cecil turned to the leart-lung machine, took the chimp's heart carefully in his huge hands, and placed it in Mr. Rosen's body.

"Looks very small, doesn't it?" Pat stared at the close-up on the monitor, her voice still a kind of awed whisper. "But as long as it's still elastic and what Dr. Paine calls virgin, it will do the job."

Cecil had placed the chimp's heart so that its septum was lined up in the cavity with the remainder of the patient's septum. Another assistant came forward and, using an odd overhand motion, stitched the two edges together. Cecil then twisted the heart around, and the assistant began to sew again. He used a curved needle, plunging it down through the chimp's heart muscles and up through what was left of Mr. Rosen's heart.

The first assistant removed the clamps from the arteries and veins. He handed Cecil an instrument that resembled a conductor's baton.

"An electric defibrillator," Pat whispered. "The next moment will tell us whether the operation is a success."

Cecil touched the defibrillator to the chimp's heart in Mr. Rosen's body. Nothing happened. He did it again, and a jolt of current went from the instrument to the heart. The camera moved in for a close-up as the heart began to beat.

The assistants removed the retractors from Mr. Rosen's chest cavity and began the process of closing the chest wall.

Everyone on the stage stood very still, staring up at an electronic digital unit placed high in a tiled wall.

"They're watching the electrocardiogram," Pat said. "It's showing them that the new heart is beating at exactly the speed of an average human heart. You've just witnessed a miracle of modern science, Nick. A miracle."

There were tears behind the blue lenses of her glasses. Her hands were pressed together, the fingertips touching her lips as if she were praying.

He looked back to the monitor and saw the chimp's body, wrapped in a sheet, being wheeled from the operating room. A moment later Mr. Rosen was taken away.

The operating theater's lights dimmed and the monitor went blank. The surgeons on the stage began pulling off their masks, walking toward the doors, congratulating Cecil, who stood with his gold glasses in one hand, the other hand massaging his nose. He replaced the glasses, looked up at Nick and Pat, waved, and then allowed the surgeons to escort him out.

"Coffee?" Pat asked.

"Milk," he said. "And a little cocaine."

He looked at his watch. Three hours had passed.

"You'll get used to it, Nick. When I first came to work for Dr. Paine, these operations bothered me terribly. Now I find them fascinating. I mean, think about it! Someday there won't be any problems finding hearts or lungs to replace damaged ones. There'll be ranches of animals bred for the *sole* purpose of transplanting organs! Now, no one expects that patient to—"

"Mr. Rosen," he said.

"—to live very long. But the very fact that Dr. Paine has demonstrated that it can work, that an animal's heart actually is capable of pumping blood through a man's body, that's wonderful, don't you think?"

She stood up, taking off her mask. "I suppose my wide-eyed dedication seems ridiculous to you?"

"Not ridiculous," Nick said. "Maybe a little misplaced."

"After you've been here for a few days, I think you'll see that it's in the very best possible place. Now we just have time for your milk—and my coffee—before we're due in Program Development."

He followed her obediently out of the operating theater.

Pfffft ... Pfft ... Pffft ...
The arm reaches out, holds for a moment, then lowers itself to the table.
Pfffft ... Pfffft ...
The hand joints move, and two fingers grasp the cup, bringing it to mouth level.
Ssss ... Sssss ... Pffft ...
The lips sip from the straw. Watching the

146

transplant on the monitor screen has made the lips dry.

Pfffft ... Pfffft ...

The hand replaces the cup on the table; the arm returns to its resting place.

Vsst ... Vssssst ...

A turn toward the screen again. It shows two young people leaving an operating theater—a girl with a clipboard under her arm, a young man following

Pffft ... Vsssst ...

The monitor is switched off. The lips smile.

CHAPTER 15

Program Development was the Harry Meyer Hospital's euphemism for Fund Raising. It was located on the third floor of the complex, and reached through a waiting room filled with old-fashioned tufted sofas and potted palms. Wicker tables holding copies of *Foundation News* and other magazines aimed at the upper end of the demographic curve were scattered about the room.

Pat Buckley introduced him to the admitting receptionist, a plump woman with white hair and a pink rabbit's mouth, and then took him into the office area.

It was divided into a number of sections and sub-sections. "An operation this size," Pat said, "needs a large fund-raising staff. They're working on Sunday because this is a particularly busy time of the year."

Government contacts were handled by three young women of varying social backgrounds and accents. Someone to please everyone, Nick thought, as he shook their hands and listened to Pat explain who was in charge of federal grants, who headed up State, and who dealt with the City.

Foundation grants were applied for by a married couple, Martin and Isobel Barlowe, who looked as if they had sprung straight from the pages of the Social Register. He wore a fluffed up handkerchief in the breast pocket of his tweed jacket and was clearly a gentleman who had gone to school with all the gentleman who headed up the "really important family foundations." She was tougher, more deliberate, more intellectual. Her appeal, Nick guessed, was aimed at the experts who ran the serious, professionally administered foundations.

The international division, which dealt with foreign government grants, had the smallest and least impressive offices. A black man, who looked as if he had been pressed by a highly competent professional cleaner, sat smoking in one of them. His face was cicatrized and there were knife-edge creases in his royal blue trousers. Pat introduced him as "our Ugandan representative."

"Dr. Moshul is stationed in Kampala," she said. "He's in for a briefing with Dr. Paine." Dr. Moshul put down his cigarette and allowed his hand to be shaken by Nick.

"Do you mean to tell me we have a man in every little African country?" Nick asked as they walked up the corridor to the elevator bank.

"Of course not. Dr. Moshul used to handle almost all of Africa on a commission basis, but—"

"What's that mean?"

"He'd get a percentage of every grant brought in. Don't look shocked. It's common practice. Anyway, we had to segment the continent due to the political climate, and Dr. Moshul found it expedient to remain in Uganda."

"And Cecil gets directly involved in the fund raising?" Nick asked.

"Of course. Dr. Paine's directly involved with everything."

Pat put her MatchCode card into the elevator slot. "We're scheduled to do nineteen next. The computer."

On nineteen, they waited for several minutes in a narrow entry until Arthur Fox, Director of Electronic Data Processing, could come to open the door for them. Standing close to Pat, Nick found, was not unpleasant. He wondered what her body looked like under the tailored clothes.

The door opened.

"I knew your father only slightly, Mr. Meyer," Arthur Fox said, extending his hand. "But allow me to offer my heartfelt condolences."

Nick thanked him and followed Fox and Pat into what seemed like a square acre of computer hardware, all of it in action. A twenty-foot cube, looking like a contemporary artist's comment on the soul of modern man, stood in the center of the space, extending up through the ceiling into the floor above.

"Big Mama," Arthur Fox said. "That's what I call her. Officially, she's the Basehart CVR 100, modified to our own specifications."

He was a slender man with narrow shoulders, blond hair that had gone grey, and a slight Texas accent. He was very proud of Big Mama.

"Probably, for her size, she's the most advanced computer on the market," Fox went on. "Everything else you see is subsidiary. None of it could work without Big Mama here." He explained the MatchCode by having Pat type her own on the console keyboard. "Pat's been in on this since the beginning. She knows nearly as much about Big Mama as I do."

"She's a woman of many talents," Nick said, and enjoyed seeing her blush.

"She's just plain smart. Shoot, if I weren't already married, why I'd—"

"Arthur, we don't have much time," Pat said quickly.

"She's shy. That's her main problem," Fox said, smiling, and went on to explain how Big Mama controlled information output.

"Think of her as a big house filled with locked doors. You got the right code, Big Mama will let you in. But each door has a different code, and Big Mama will just let you go through the ones you got the code for, not the others."

"What information is secret?" Nick asked.

"I don't rightly know," Fox said. "When it gets right down to it, I'm just a programmer."

Seated at the computer's control console, he extolled its use as a search tool.

"Inside Big Mama's brain is a list of every American citizen who has ever had a physical examination, each name categorized by tissue and blood type. So say, the Lord forbid, that Miss

Buckley here needs a kidney. I feed into the computer twenty-two characteristics of her tissue, along with her blood type, and I get back in fifteen minutes a list of everyone who falls into her category, detailing what their current health status is, and whether or not they have signed the Uniform Donor Card giving their bodies to science after death. Usually—somehow, some-where—we find a person who is willing to part with an organ to help another human live."

"And when you don't?" Nick asked.

"If we fail on the twenty-two characteristic tissue level, we go to the twenty-one level and so on down the line."

"You seem very dedicated."

Pat said, "One of Arthur's sons had a kidney transplant two years ago here in the Harry Meyer."

"Saved the kid's life. I owe the Harry Meyer something for that," Arthur Fox said.

He went on to discuss some of the other components of the giant computer, winding up with an explanation of how Big Mama monitored other computers.

"We trade information on population characteristics, for example. And the Perge/Merge feature sure comes in handy then. Perge/Merge means that we never have duplicate names in Big Mama's brain. She's programmed to eliminate all redundancies. For instance, you must have had several physical examinations, even in your young lifetime, Mr. Meyer. Your name would be fed in each time, but Big Mama only records it once, thanks to Perge/Merge."

"He talks a lot," Nick said, when they had been released from the nineteenth floor.

"Big Mama's a silent mistress," Pat said.

He laughed. "Funny how you come out with things like that every once in a while."

"My mean streak. Well, it's almost six. Perhaps we could continue in the morning? At seven?"

"Fine."

She took him to the triplex entrance and let him in with her MatchCode card.

He went down to the kitchen, had a glass of milk, made himself a roast beef sandwich, watered Baby Love, tried Tony (the service said he had called in, honey, and she would give him the message), watched "Sixty Minutes" and a terrible movie on television, and went to sleep waiting for Carla's call.

CHAPTER 16

At seven o'clock the next morning, Pat escorted him to the eighteenth floor. The Research Division took up the entire floor—a series of windowless, sound-proofed rooms, some no larger than a cell, others running the length of the building. All of them had been painted a dull white and given rubberized industrial flooring. The researchers moved from room to room in white butcher's coats, clipboards under their arms, their faces serious, as if to prove they were engaged in important matters.

"They're very devoted here," Pat told him.

"To what?" Nick said. He had slept badly; Carla hadn't phoned. And Tony Lyle still wasn't home or in the office.

"To finding ways to overcome the immune response—and, of course, to Dr. Paine."

In Laboratory A-18, one of the researchers, a short, trim man with the unlikely name of Dr. Suet explained to Nick an experiment in the use of advanced radiation techniques to paralyze the immune reaction.

The subject was a brown and white cow that stood unprotesting in a stall in the middle of the room while the blood was pumped out of its body and run through a number of transparent tubes into an oblong nickel-plated machine. The machine, Dr. Suet explained, bombarded the blood with radiation in doses much greater than the cow would have been able to survive. The blood was then returned to the cow. Whether or not the immunity barrier had been overcome would be learned after another group in the department had transplanted various organs into the cow's body. This particular method of short-circuiting immunity, Nick was told, was called "extra-corporeal circulation."

"If it works, will you use it on humans?" he asked.

"Not necessarily."

"Why not?"

"My dear Mr. Meyer, you are naïve. What works with animals doesn't always work with man. It merely points the way."

Pat looked at Nick's face and immediately took him off to see the rest of the department. "You didn't like Dr. Suet, did you?"

"Not exactly an endearing personality."

"Researchers tend to live in their own little worlds."

"May I put that on my sampler?"

He was shown anesthetics being injected into

155

the ear veins of rabbits to prepare them for skin graft experiments.

He watched a dozen cats being irradiated in preparation for liver transplants.

He was shown a new method for detecting the imminent rejection of transplanted kidneys in dogs; the blood supply to the kidneys was measured so that the dosage of drugs could be controlled. "Dogs treated by this method," he was told by a researcher with terrible breath, "live twice as long as dogs treated by other methods."

"You know," he told Pat in the corridor, "I'm not an anti-vivisectionist but . . ."

"You have two buttons missing on your shirt. If you leave it out tomorrow, I'll have them replaced."

In Laboratory B-16, Nick was shown Spooky, a mongrel dog who had, for several months, been using the hind leg of another animal. "We seem to have overcome the immune response," a researcher told him, "by replacing in advance all of the patient's blood with blood from the donor animal."

Finally, he was shown Shakespeare, a very human-like chimpanzee who had had the head of a small white monkey grafted onto its back, so that it possessed two working heads.

"We've done it hundreds of times," a Chinese woman doctor said, amused by Nick's expression. "Shakespeare is remarkable because he's already lived for a month and a half, whereas all the others died within ten days to two weeks. Notice that though the extra head is living off its host, it can salivate and blink its own eyes. Wonderful, is it not?"

"Wonderful," Nick said, looking away. "But just tell me what that has to do with overcoming the immune response?"

"That would take much too long, Mr. Meyer," she said, giving the animal what looked like a bowl of corn flakes.

He had lunch with Pat in the executive canteen, a long dining room decorated to resemble an outdoor cafe. All he could get down was an English muffin and a glass of milk.

"That really upset you, didn't it?" Pat asked, taking a bite of her sandwich.

"When one day I see a chimpanzee's heart cut out, and the next I see a cow having its blood pumped out, I start to get all emotional about our dumb friends. They didn't ask to be here."

She put her hand on his arm. "They're never really in pain, you know, Nick. And think how they're helping us to—"

"Benefit mankind? Maybe those rabbits are more interested in benefiting rabbitkind."

"You're a funny man, Nick."

"You should see my imitations."

A young surgeon with bright red hair stopped by their table and told them that Mr. Rosen, the patient with the chimpanzee's heart, had died that morning. "The heart was too small to do the job. Next time we're going to try a baboon's," he said, heading for the cafeteria line.

"Well, here's to Mr. Rosen," Nick said. "I

wonder if he went to man heaven or chimpanzee heaven."

"You know," Pat said, puffing hard on a cigarette, "when I said you were funny, Nick, I didn't mean funny ha-ha. I meant funny-odd. I know my job is to show you around and be gracious and easy to get along with, but—my God!—of everyone I have taken through the Harry Meyer, you're the most sarcastic, the most off-putting! And you're Harry Meyer's son! Everything seems to call for some ironic remark. You think all this is being done for the fun of it? You think we like cutting up people and animals? We're trying to extend man's life! And if you could put down that phony, cynical shield you're always wielding and try to see that this is a great hospital, an honorable place with a humane mission, you'd have a better chance of learning something about your father. And about yourself!"

She stood up and went to the ladies' room.

When she came back, re-lipsticked, he took her hand. "I'd like to apologize," he said. "You're perfectly right. I *have* been wise-cracking my way through this place. It's a reaction I have, a kind of defense, when I see people or animals in pain. And you're right, too, about it not being fair to my father or the hospital or to you. Give me another chance."

She smiled an unsure smile and squeezed his hand. "I think *I* overreacted. I'm sorry. But I think you're good for me, Nick. I can't remember the last time I was angry at someone and let them know it."

"You certainly let me know it. Where do we go from here?"

"Storage."

Storage had its own elevator, from the street floor down two levels underground.

They came off the elevator into a small room in which a middle-aged man sat behind a desk.

"This is Mr. Rios," Pat said. "Mr. Rios's job is to check in the cadavers that are brought here."

"Yes," Mr. Rios said, smiling. "You know, sometimes when I get here in the morning, I got eight, maybe twelve cadavers waiting for me. The boys drop them off at night." He pointed to a conveyor belt that led, he explained, up into the courtyard. "Night deposits, we call them."

Nick shook Mr. Rios's hand, and Pat used her MatchCode card to get them through the steel doors that led into a narrow, low-ceilinged, refrigerated corridor.

"The dissecting rooms are along here," she said. "Would you care to—"

"At the risk of seeming callous and flip, I think I'll take a pass."

She led him past the dissecting rooms. A sickly odor came from them. He looked through a window cut into one of the doors and saw a grey, half-dissected body on a green-sheeted table. Its skin was partially peeled off; the top of its head was split open; its scalp was cut back. Its hair, once a coil of black braids, looked like a discarded wig. Where its stomach should have been was a wide black hole in which sat its organs, neatly laid out and labeled.

The smell of formaldehyde mixed with the vaporous, refrigerated air—he could hear the high-pitched sound of the refrigerator motors whirring somewhere above him—made him stop for a moment. He could feel the blood leaving his head.

"You all right?" Pat asked.

"I just need a minute."

His eyes went back to the window, and he caught a glimpse of a stainless steel sink filled with organs, floating in rose-colored water.

"Let's move on," he said.

They entered another corridor where thin neon tubes gave off a stale, dim light. The intense formaldehyde smell had given way to another odor, a less definable smell, like that of meat gone bad.

A stout, tall woman with blue-white hair stepped out of an office at the end of the corridor. Pat introduced her as Dr. Pollette.

"The temperature in these rooms," Dr. Pollette said, after telling Nick how much she had admired Harry, "is always kept at minus four degrees centigrade. You won't notice it too much because it is a very dry kind of cold." She had a very dry kind of voice, Nick thought, like a society woman in a Marx Brothers film.

Dr. Pollette pointed to a large steel dumbwaiter. "Now this is a contraption we couldn't possibly do without. It carries parts up into the operating theaters in a matter of seconds, so we can keep organs under optimum conditions until the very last moment."

She led them into a large room off the corridor where workers, ghost-like in the hazy light, sat at long tables, their gloved hands dipping hearts, livers, kidneys, lungs into glass jars.

"Bit like mass production, isn't it?" Dr. Pollette said. "You know, of course, that freezing organs is much more difficult than freezing blood. Ice crystals, which form under non-optimum conditions, can cause irreparable harm. What's more, a delicate balance is disturbed when organs are frozen, when the electrochemical equilibrium of the tissues is disturbed. But we've gone a long way in solving the problem. These workers are coating the organs with a mixture of dimethyl sulfoxide and a chemical solvent Dr. Paine has developed which extends their frozen life from a few weeks to up to two years."

She paused, as if waiting for applause.

"That's wonderful," Nick said, avoiding Pat's warning glance.

They moved back into the corridor and on into another room filled with silent people wearing the ubiquitous white coats. They were working on either side of a conveyor belt that traveled in a circle through a tower-like machine.

Dr. Pollette began again. "Here we sterilize cadaver bone using a technique developed at the Massachusetts Institute of Technology. It is very much like the one food corporations use to extend the shelf life of bacon and cereal. The machine is a Van de Graaff accelerator. It uses massive doses of irradiation to render the bone surgically sterile without the damage that sometimes occurs with chemical methods. Each piece of bone is frozen, and placed in a two-tiered envelope made of see-through plastic. Between the two tiers, we place a small glass bead which becomes brown after radiation. The conveyor belts take the envelopes through the radiation beam several times to ensure that all sides are radiated. Average exposure is eighteen seconds. The total radiation dose is one million roentgens."

She showed them a small room where frozen tissue—skin, cartilage, arteries, nerves—was stored. "One cadaver can yield up to one hundred and twenty-five pieces of tissue," she said, and added wistfully, "Arteries used to be in constant demand. Now, thanks to man-made substitutes, the demand is falling off."

"This may be a naïve question," Nick said, "but if you have all these organs and parts frozen and ready for use, why does the Harry Meyer need that elaborate computer system to locate new ones?"

"That is not a naïve question. That is a very good question." Dr. Pollette smiled at Nick as if he were her prize pupil. "We don't know why yet, but fresh transplants take better than frozen ones that have been brought back to normal temperature. The frozen organs you have seen here are used only for research and in experimental surgery. Very rarely in genuine transplants.

But Dr. Paine is convinced, as I am, that in the very near future, when immunology has resolved the immune barrier problems, all these parts will be put to good use. You might say, if you'll pardon the pun, that we're banking them against that day."

She paused for breath, beaming, and Nick realized that he would have to express some sort of appreciation.

"Fascinating," he said. It was the best he could do.

"Very few people realize," Dr. Pollette said proudly, "that what we do here is as challenging and complicated as open-heart surgery. You passed the dissecting rooms when you came in. Do you know that each of those rooms is equipped with a team of surgeons, nurses and hospital corpsman; that during each fourteen-hour procedure, every member of the team makes eight complete changes of clothing, drapes, gloves and masks; that the scrubdown is even more complicated than it is in live surgery?"

"Where do the bodies come from?" Nick asked.

"Accidents. Cadavers can't have any malignancy, infection or contagious disease. That leaves out the majority of corpses."

"What's stored in here?" Finding it difficult to keep looking at Dr. Pollette's shiny face, Nick pulled open one of the freezer cabinets.

Thin wisps of frozen air rose from the storage compartment, in which saline-saturated plastic bags containing arms and hands, legs and feet, were displayed like cuts of meat in supermarket cases. The skin was shaved and had turned blue-white, not unlike the color of Dr. Pollette's hair.

"I thought limbs were not transplantable," Nick said.

"Not at the moment," Dr. Pollette said, removing his hand from the cabinet door. She shut the cabinet and led the way out of the department. The touch of her hand had been unpleasantly warm.

At the entrance door, Dr. Pollette looked at her watch. "Dear me, I completely forgot about my appointment with Dr. Carlson. Dear Mr. Meyer, it has been a pleasure. Please, don't be a stranger. Any time." Smiling, she disappeared into an office.

They said good-bye to Mr. Rios. Nick was relieved to get away from the sound of the refrigerator fans, the smell of the formaldehyde, the cold, the low ceilings, and the fat, compulsively informative woman.

"Her only son lost both his legs in Viet Nam," Pat said in the elevator.

"Everyone seems to have a personal interest here."

"Dr. Paine has a gift for attracting committed people."

He wondered, as she walked with him down the third floor corridor toward the triplex, what her committment was based on.

"Dr. Paine would like you to accompany him on his morning rounds tomorrow," she said. "There are several patients he wants you to meet. I'll pick you up at ten o'clock."

"Don't you think it's time, Pat, that I got my own little white card—so you could go back to your job?"

"Oh, I don't mind, Nick."

"I'd still like to be able to come and go as I choose."

"I'll speak to Dr. Paine about it. And Nick—we do have a pick-up in Philadelphia. I wondered if you'd like me to have the man stop at your apartment and bring in some of your clothes?"

"Shirts with buttons? That would be nice, Pat. I'll give you the key." He took it off his key ring. "And perhaps they could bring Carla's things too."

"Yes, of course." She tried to smile, but it was worse than usual. "See you tomorrow, Nick." She waited for him to go into the apartment before she returned to the elevator.

CHAPTER 17

He took a shower in the huge marbled bathroom. The mirrored wall made him uncomfortable, distorting his reflection slightly, as if it were showing the image of someone else. He felt very much alone and spooked, the way he felt when he was a kid and Harry was off somewhere and Isobel was locked up in her room, the television blaring.

He tried to reject the images of the day, but couldn't: pulpy hearts, two-headed chimpanzees, cadavers, kidneys and frozen blood kept appearing on the screen in his mind. He made himself concentrate on mundane thoughts: it was nice for Pat to arrange to get his clothes; when was Carla coming back and would she phone tonight?; where was Tony—on some sort of a binge or digging into a story or just not answering his phone?

He toweled himself down with the largest, thickest bath towel he had ever seen outside of a

James Bond film and sat down for a moment on one of the two marble benches that faced each other across the circular, enclosed shower.

The thought of Tony, the need to talk to someone he trusted totally, someone away from the Harry Meyer Hospital, made him reach for the wall phone and dial the "OFF!" number, on the chance Tony had shown up. There was no answer. He tried Tony's apartment. After four rings, (the service was supposed to get it on the third), a woman with a whiskey voice answered.

"Is Tony Lyle there?" he asked, thinking he might have dialed the wrong number.

"May I ask who's calling?" She sounded as if she wasn't interested.

"Nick. Nick Miller."

There was a pause, and he thought he heard the woman catch her breath. Then she said, with perfect poise, "Nick, this is Tony's mother, Grace Lyle."

There was another pause.

He remembered having met Grace Lyle on three or four occasions—a good-looking woman with grey-blond hair and a way of moving that let you know she was very rich and very sure of herself. Nick had found her attractive.

"I have some bad news," Grace Lyle said. And again the pause, the caught breath. "Tony was killed last night."

"What?" He had heard what she said, but the words wouldn't register. "What?"

"Tony was killed last night," she said more easily, as if she was getting used to saying it.

"I don't understand. I don't—"

"Tony was killed last night in an accident on the Schuylkill Expressway. His car went out of control and hit a telephone pole."

"Mrs. Lyle, I just can't—"

"Last night, Nick. An accident on the Schuylkill Expressway. He was coming back from Reading."

Neither of them said anything for a very long time. He could hear her sipping some sort of drink.

"I'm sorry, Mrs. Lyle. So sorry," he said at last.

"I'm here in his apartment, sorting things out. My God, he kept the damnedest junk. There's a white dinner jacket in his closet we bought for him when he was fifteen years old. So unlike me. I never keep anything."

He heard her sob.

"We're going to have a quiet funeral, only the immediate family, but we're considering a memorial service next month . . ." She went on talking about services and arrangements and the stuff Tony kept in his closets and drawers. He let her go on, hoping that the simple recitation of facts, the unimportant details, would help her.

They didn't help him. His mind was racing like a motor out of control.

At last he got off the phone and, wrapping the towel around him, went through the bedroom into Harry's study. He was more frightened than he had ever been in his adult life. He wanted his motor, his brain, to stop adding and multiplying, to stop putting two and two together. He reached for his father's picture. Holding it as if it were an icon, he put his forehead down on the sturdy surface of the desk and began to cry.

Later, he called Shep.

"Tony Lyle was killed last night."

"What?"

"You heard me."

"Jesus, Ace, I'm sorry! What happened?"

"They made it look like a car accident."

"Who made it look like a car accident?"

"Whoever killed Tony and my father."

"Get off it, will you? You can't make every goddamn death in this country part of your conspiracy obsession. Ace, it's a tough break, Harry and Tony dying so close together. But Christ, Nick, you're as bad as the Kennedy-King nuts! Can't you let Tony die a natural death without getting your fucking ego all wrapped up in it, making it a part of a master plot to get Nick Miller?"

"They killed him because he was on to something, because he had found out something about Ralston-Brown, the last man to see Harry alive. Tony was checking—"

"Look, Nick, come over, have a drink. You need some company, some—"

"You know what you can do with that drink, Shep."

"What's that supposed to mean?"

"Don't patronize me. I'm not interested in what you think of my mental state. I just wanted to tell you what I know: they killed Harry and they killed Tony. I wasn't sure about Harry until today. But now—"

"All right. All right. Let's say I believe you. They killed your father; they killed your best friend. Why haven't they killed you?"

"I don't know."

"And what about your girl, Ace?"

"I'm keeping her out of this. I don't want her to know anything. She's—"

"Nick, listen to me—"

"I'm hanging up now, Shep. I'll talk to you in a couple of days. When I have more answers."

He got into Harry Meyer's circular bed and wished he had religion. He wished he had a rabbi or a priest or a psychiatrist he could go to for solace. He wondered if he was cracking up. He pulled the phone over, placing it next to him on the bed. He tried to make his mind a blank while he waited. The phone rang at midnight.

"Nicky, you okay?"

"No, I'm terrible. When are you coming back?"

"Friday," Carla said. "I miss you, Nicky. I miss you so much."

"Why Friday?"

"They're having a major demonstration against the Gallo boys Friday morning. I'll catch the first plane right after. Oh, Nicky, I'm getting great stuff! The real mother-fucken McCoy. Prize stuff!"

He knew he should tell her what had happened to Tony, but she was too up. He couldn't spoil it.

"I wish you were here with me," he said.

"*Yo tambien.* Nicky, you all right? You sound so fucken down. You want me to come back now, tonight?"

"No. I'm fine. You come back on Friday."

"You sure?"

"Sure I'm sure."

She said she would take a taxi from the airport. She asked again if everything was all right, and again he was tempted to tell her about Tony. But why ruin her trip? There was nothing she could do. He said yes, he was all right, but it was the middle of the night in New York, and he only had a pillow to hold on to and he was lonesome.

Later, as he held the pillow, trying to get to sleep, he wondered why, if she was getting such great pictures, she hadn't asked him to tell Tony.

171

CHAPTER 18

He woke too early, feeling as if he hadn't had any sleep. He kept his eyes closed, trying not to think of Tony, of this sudden new nightmare he was living.

He listened to the muted sounds of early morning Fifth Avenue, and then became conscious of a peculiar low hum that he realized he had heard throughout the complex. It was always there, background noise. He supposed it had something to do with the generator; somewhere he had picked up the idea that hospitals had their own generators to protect them against blackouts.

He got up and went down to the kitchen, thinking that the Harry Meyer not only had its own generator, it had its own police force, its own security system, its very own computer. It was a fortress. Pouring himself a glass of milk, he looked out the street-level window at Lawrence, still at his post. He wondered what Lawrence was thinking about as he stood in the September sunshine, his hands behind his back, his feet stuck firmly to the cement.

When he had finished his milk, he went into the windowless downstairs bathroom, a Spartan cell compared to the luxurious one upstairs. He shut the door, blocking out the kitchen light, not bothering to switch on the overhead bathroom light. Making a game, as he sometimes did at night, of trying to urinate on target in total darkness, he noticed that the low hum of the generator, or whatever it was, didn't penetrate into the bathroom. Hard to believe, he thought, that the little bathroom was sound-proofed. He remembered that the hum was also absent during the night, when the lights were off. He turned on the bathroom light. The hum began again.

He went upstairs to the marbled bathroom and noticed, as he brushed his teeth and shaved, that here too the hum could be heard only when the lights were on. He couldn't stop listening to it. He knew his mind was playing tricks on him, keeping itself occupied with small questions and small sounds so he wouldn't think of Tony. It didn't help. He was thinking of Tony all of the time.

He went to the closet where Harry's collection of silk and mohair suits still hung. Shelves had been built into the closet for shirts and underwear. Three of them had been cleared of his father's things, and his own undershorts and shirts were neatly in place. There was also an old suit of his and a sports jacket, two pairs of slacks and several

173

pairs of his shoes. He went to the other closet. All of Carla's clothes were there.

"How did all our clothes get into those closets?" he asked Pat when she met him at ten o'clock at the third-floor door to the complex.

"Lawrence brought them in. He didn't want to disturb you."

"I don't want anyone, especially Lawrence, coming in and out of this apartment—especially when I'm in it—unless I know. I thought I made that clear."

"He has to straighten up. Put food in the kitchen. I thought I was doing you a favor." The familiar mist was beginning to appear behind the blue tinted lenses.

"I appreciate your getting the things here so quickly. But I'm not used to—"

"Her things are in the other closet," she said.

"I know. Terrific."

"I do try," she said as she slid her card into the elevator slot. "But I'm forever sticking my foot in it." She tried a tentative smile.

"I'm sorry. I realize you do try. Never mind. Did you ask Cecil about my MatchCode card?"

"I almost forgot." She dipped into her Vuitton purse and came up with a small plasticene envelope. "*Voilà.* Your official card of entry."

"I feel as if I'd just become a Mouseketeer. Thank you, Pat."

She left him on the sixteenth floor, the patients' floor, where he was to meet Cecil Paine. "I'll pick you up for lunch, Nick."

"You're not coming?"

174

"No, I'm not especially good with important people unless I'm giving them facts and figures."

"You put yourself down too much."

"I'll try not to," she said as the elevator doors closed.

She had looked especially forlorn, Nick thought, in her Halston-inspired pants suit. He wondered, for the first time, what it would be like to make love to her.

The central corridor of the sixteenth floor was wide and expensive. The wallpaper was hand-screened with a jungle motif; the floor was inlaid with a pale green marble; light came from behind a translucent ceiling, simulating daylight. Bamboo benches with thick batik-covered pillows and little lacquered tables were placed every few feet along the walls.

A too-blond young man in a tapered green Eisenhower jacket with "Harry Meyer Hospital" stitched in white letters across the breast pocket stood at the exact center of the corridor, running his fingers along the crease in his military trousers. He looked like the major-domo of a Beverly Hills swim club.

"And may I help you, sir?" he asked Nick, smiling. His teeth were very white.

"I'm Nick Miller. Here to meet Dr. Paine."

"Miller? Miller?" He moved like a dancer to a chest-high desk and studied a chart.

"Meyer," Nick said, deciding to play. "Nick Meyer."

"Oh, Mr. Meyer. I am happy to meet you. My

175

name is Richard, and if there is anything I can do for you, please do not hesitate to call on me." The meaningless words were delivered as if Richard had overcome a speech impediment and was proud of his verbal dexterity.

Nick asked again for Cecil.

"Oh, Dr. Paine is in the atrium. Shall I take you to him?" The smile flashed again.

"Sure."

He followed Richard's trim body through wide double doors onto a glass-enclosed terrace that overlooked a small courtyard. The terrace was filled with plants, most of them exotic. Cecil stood at the end of it, talking to a woman Nick recognized as a senator from one of the midwestern states. He had heard her speak once at a press conference in Washington. She was smoking a cigarette, drinking from a demi-tasse cup, looking very much at home in the greenhouse.

Cecil glanced up, saw him, said something to the senator, and came forward. "Ah, there you are."

"What's she doing here?" Nick asked, nodding toward the senator.

"Her left lung has been giving her a certain amount of trouble."

"She should stop smoking."

"Of course, old man." Cecil led him back toward the central corridor. "You've been here a few days, Nick. What do you think of it?"

"I don't know, Cecil. I haven't assimilated it all yet."

"It will take you months to really get to know the place. What I'm trying to give you now is an overview. Once you begin to see recovered patients, lives saved, lives extended, I think you'll begin to understand the fervor that drives us all."

"Something very strong must drive you, Cecil. I can't imagine how you, personally, manage to find time for everything—surgery, research, computers, holding rich ladies' hands."

"I sometimes wonder myself. But I'm a very disciplined man, Nick."

"Who disciplines you, Cecil?"

"Not who, Nick. What. And the 'what' is the pleasure I take in my work."

They moved along the corridor, Cecil explaining the layout of the sixteenth floor to him.

"Each patient has his or her own suite. This is, of course, beneficial to the individual's state of mind. They are all, to a greater or lesser extent, undergoing the kind of stress that accompanies major change. It is not difficult to understand why so many of them are more than a little neurotic during their hospitalization."

"Where are the nurses?" Nick asked. "The starched dresses, the little trays with pills and paper cups full of watered orange juice?"

"Each patient is assigned his own attendant, and very often brings along one servant. You won't see starched white dresses, if that's what you're looking for. We're not that sort of hospital. Richard, for instance, is an expert paramedic. Those two comely young women at the end of the corridor are physician's aides. There's really not much for them to do until the post-op stage."

Dr. Moshul, the man from Uganda, appeared in a doorway and motioned to Cecil. The scars in the blue-black skin of his face were wet, as if he had sweated only in the cicatrized grooves.

"He wants a word with you," Dr. Moshul said.

"There's nothing I can tell the Marshal," Cecil said. "Except that—"

A huge black man in a filthy military uniform appeared in the doorway behind Dr. Moshul and pushed him aside. He looked like an angry blimp about to explode. He shouted something in what Nick assumed was Ugandan.

Dr. Moshul looked at Cecil for help.

"Tell the Marshal we have located the donor," Cecil said. "It will only be a matter of hours."

Sweat ran over the white collar of Dr. Moshul's shirt, making a black stain on the knot of his dark tie. He said something that appeared to mollify the Marshal, who turned and went back into his suite.

Through the open door, Nick saw a television set, a movie projector, a large new stereo tape recorder, and a very young girl so bleached she might have been an albino. She was wearing cut-off dungarees and a red handkerchief halter, half undone. Her breasts looked like small round loaves of white bread. The smell that came from the room was numbing, a mixture of sweat, sex and something Nick couldn't and didn't want to identify.

Dr. Moshul followed the Marshal into the suite as if he were on his way to his final session with the

178

Inquisitor, shutting the door quietly after him.

"Difficult man," Cecil said as he guided Nick around a corner into another handsomely papered corridor.

"That's the understatement of the decade."

Cecil stopped and put a big hand on Nick's shoulder. "I know you're a journalist by profession, and I wouldn't say this if it weren't vital. You must understand, old boy—and I'm sure you do—that everything you see here must be kept absolutely secret. We're responsible for these peoples' lives in more ways than one. If word got out that—"

"That you had one of the world's most infamous murderers and his fifteen-year-old mistress in a suite here, there might be trouble."

"I don't really care about politics, Nick. I'm here to save people's lives."

"One very sure way would be to let your Marshal die."

"I'm the doctor, Nick, not the judge," Cecil changed the subject, uncharacteristically smoothing down the back of his hair. "Now I'm going to introduce you to one of the world's most beautiful women."

He knocked on a door at the end of the corridor, and it was opened by a square, dark woman with a veil over the bottom half of her face.

"Please tell Miss Pace that Dr. Paine and Mr. Meyer are here to see her." Cecil said.

The woman just looked at them, her eyes hostile above the veil, and they went around her.

Nick thought he heard her praying as they walked through a small, arched foyer into a long room with fireplaces at either end.

The room belonged in a summer mansion. Doors with glass panes led onto a terrace that overlooked Fifth Avenue. The curtains and slipcovers were pastel chintz; the wood floor was painted a washed-out blue; there were large turquoise vases filled with yellow and pink flowers on the mantels.

Reclining—it was the only word for it—on a wicker chaise lounge was Alexandria Pace.

Despite his views of Hollywood, television, and talk show stars, Nick had been as caught up as any housewife in the life of Alexandria Pace, former society beauty and film star, present Empress of Tokal.

Even more than her red-blond beauty, he had admired the cool Dashiell Hammett heroine air she had displayed in the half dozen movies she had made before the Emperor had proposed.

For two hours that past spring, along with millions of others, he had watched her TV special—a guided tour of her oriental palace—and been charmed by her portrayal of the new role she had assumed.

And despite himself, Nick was intrigued by the knowledge that she was an Empress, that she came from a socially prominent family, that she broke all the rules. She was so much the American dream, even in her escape from America.

". . . like you to meet Nick Meyer, the son of the founder of our hospital," Cecil was saying.

"I enjoyed your father," Alexandria Pace said, holding out her hand. "We used to talk about money."

Nick smiled and took her hand. "I don't know what to do with this. Am I supposed to genuflect, shake it, or touch it lightly with my lips?"

"Since you're the most attractive male I've seen in the last month, I think you'd best touch it lightly with your lips."

He did so, and thought it was probably the most expensive-smelling hand he had ever come into contact with.

"I've always like men named Nick. Major-domos and detectives are always called Nick. Such a sexy name. You could be in films."

She sat up and took his chin in her hand, examining his face. "Definitely. Especially in the films they're making today. You could play a street tough, the kind of person the people in power take advantage of until the last reel."

She was like a beautiful clock, he thought, one that had sat quietly on a shelf for a long time and then suddenly begun ticking. She wouldn't stop until she ran down.

"Do you ever get to Asia, Nick?" she asked, making room for him on the oversized chaise lounge. "Not your sort of place, I expect. You look too serious to join the hippies who smoke cannabis all day in the little squares, and you're obviously not a tourist. How different you are from Harry, and yet there is the same sort of strength, the same slow physicality that I for one find absolutely magnetic. Dear me, I am going on.

181

Cecil, what is the matter with me? Why are you allowing me to be so seductive?"

Cecil smiled and motioned Nick away from the chaise. He stood over her, examining her eyes, touching her neck under the fine red-blond hair.

The woman with the veil had come to stand silently behind him. "She'd better go downstairs immediately," he told her.

"Why? Why am I feeling so odd?" Alexandria Pace wanted to know.

"It's all positive, my dear Alex. The immunosuppressants are doing their job. You have a slight fever and you're understandably overwrought. I want to put you downstairs in an isolated germ-free room. It will be boring, but it's only for a day or two."

"The operation?"

"Two days, at the most. I promise, Alex."

She closed her eyes and stopped ticking.

Nick followed Cecil out of the room and waited while he gave Richard instructions to prepare Alexandria Pace for the IC Unit.

Richard stood at attention. "Yes, Dr. Paine. Immediately, sir."

Nick wondered what carrot Cecil dangled before Richard's coiffed head. A sex change?

Cecil guided him back to the elevators. "I'm going to have to beg off this morning's tour, Nick. I have to be scrubbed and in full surgical kit in ten minutes. Tomorrow, perhaps, we—"

"What kind of transplant is she getting?"

"Alex? A very tricky one. I've only performed it once before though Lord knows there have been enough tests. All positive, I might add. Oddly enough—and this is what troubles me—I don't know *why* they're positive. The immunosuppressants—"

"What is the transplant, Cecil?"

Cecil hesitated briefly. "A womb."

"A womb? Jesus, what does she want a new womb for?"

"This is extremely confidential, dear boy. As you might guess, she can't have a baby. And if she can't give her husband an heir, he'll have to divorce her. Not to worry, however; we have every reason to expect success, given the high level of histo-compatability between donor and recipient."

"Where's this histo-compatible womb coming from?" Nick asked, and then realized that he knew the answer. "The computer?"

"Of course." Cecil smiled as he used his card to summon an elevator.

"But what if—"

"Dr. Paine! Dr. Paine!" A concerned Richard was upon them. "You're wanted on twenty. Immediately."

"But I'm due—damnit, this *is* impossible!" It was the first time Nick had seen Cecil upset. "Pat is waiting for you downstairs, Nick, in her office. She'll take you to lunch. Perhaps you and I can meet tomorrow." He stepped into an elevator and the doors closed behind him.

Nick slid his new MatchCode card into the elevator call slot. "Who or what is on twenty?" he asked Richard as he stepped into the arriving car.

"I really couldn't say, sir," Richard said, smiling. "And don't forget, sir, the pool is available for your use at any time."

The elevator doors shut.

Nick placed his card in the slot by the "20" button. Nothing happened. I'm evidently not programmed for twenty, he thought. He put the card in the "9" slot and the elevator started down.

On the ninth floor, his card admitted him to the library where he had met Elliot Sarno, his father's lawyer. He had always felt eerie in libraries, and he felt especially so in this one as he checked to make sure he was alone. He went to the computer console he had remembered seeing in one corner of the big room and inserted the card into a slot at its side. A low hum came from the machine, and the screen turned a lighter gray, indicating it was operational.

He sat down at the console and punched on its keyboard what he guessed would be Alexandria Pace's MatchCode, trying to remember exactly how Arthur Fox had demonstrated the technique.

At first, nothing showed on the screen. Then, suddenly, words appeared.

-w-h-a-t/i-s/i-t/y-o-u/w-a-n-t/t-o/
k-n-o-w-

Nick thought for a moment and typed: "Source of donation."

-y-o-u/a-r-e/n-o-t/p-r-o-g-r-a-m-m-
e-d/f-o-r/r-e-q-u-e-s-t-e-d/i-n-f-
o-r-m-a-t-i-o-n-

184

"Is there anyway in which I can get the information without being programmed?"

```
-y-e-s/b-y/k-e-y/p-u-n-c-h-i-n-g/
c-o-r-r-e-c-t/c-o-d-e-
```

"What is the correct code?"
```
-y-o-u/a-r-e/n-o-t/p-r-o-g-r-a-m-m-
e-d/f-o-r/r-e-q-u-e-s-t-e-d/i-n-f-
o-r-m-a-t-i-o-n-
```

"Is there any way around this? Is there anyway to get at this information?"
```
-y-e-s-
```

"What is it?"
```
-y-o-u/a-r-e/n-o-t/p-r-o-g-r-a-m-m-
e-d/f-o-r/r-e-q-u-e-s-t-e-d/i-n-f-
o-r-m-a-t-i-o-n-
```

He wanted to hit it. He pulled his card out of the slot and the screen turned dark grey.

He put the cover back on the console and went to a corner shelf where he had seen telephone directories. He found the Manhattan Yellow Pages and thumbed through them, finding the address he wanted as the library door opened.

"I thought we were having lunch together," Pat Buckley said.

"We are. Let's go. Where do you want to have lunch?"

"The cafeteria?"

"Oh, no. Please. Let's get out of the complex

for a while. Look, I know a funny place on 57th Street that has just okay food but a terrific—"

"We don't have that sort of time, Nick," she said.

They left through a Madison Avenue exit, signing out in a ledger kept by the big doorman, who picked up his radio before they went out the door. Nick wondered who he was reporting to.

"We have to be back by two sharp," Pat said. "You're scheduled for a complete physical. Heart, lungs, all your organs. They'll take a blood sample, do a tissue evaluation—it's one of the benefits one receives working for the Harry Meyer. All medical care is free."

"I don't work for the Harry Meyer. Yet."

He looked at her solemn American face (with a tan and a real smile, he thought, she could be a California girl) and wondered what, if anything, they had on her. She was just convincing enough to be working for them for ten thousand a year and the good of mankind.

She took him to a coffee shop a block down on Madison Avenue.

Over tepid Manhattan chowder, he asked how she had known he was in the library.

"I looked in all the obvious places."

"That library doesn't seem to me to be such an obvious place."

"I just happened to think of it. ESP," she said, and he knew she was lying.

"What's on the twentieth floor?" he said, finishing his soup.

"Nothing," she answered too quickly. "A sort of display and an extra O.R."

He got a check from the peppy little waitress and told Pat to finish her coffee, that he would pay the cashier and come back with change for the tip.

He gave the cashier his money and asked her to tell the young woman he had been sitting with that he would meet her back at the office. "I'm sneaking out to buy her a wedding present," he said.

The cashier, a monumental woman who looked as if she were sucking on a large lemon, stared at him disapprovingly through the coffee shop's plate glass window as he went into the corner phone booth, made a call, and emerged to hail a taxi.

He told the driver to head downtown.

CHAPTER 19

The New York offices of the Basehart CVR Computer Manufacturing Company, the third largest supplier of computers in the United States, were located in an early Art Deco building on West 35th Street.

A guard with a drooping mustache connected to bushy sideburns let Nick in through an arched doorway. The guard's bodyshirt had a portrait of Sylvester Stallone on its front, a Rolls Royce Silver Cloud on its back, and half moons of perspiration stain under its arms. He took Nick up to the fourteenth floor in an antiquated but automatic elevator.

In a room created by plastic wall dividers, a woman with tightly curled hair told Nick to have a seat. "Fred Meiselman will be right with you."

Fred Meiselman appeared some twenty minutes later, wearing a white shirt with rolled-up sleeves that revealed unnaturally hairy forearms. He looked like the owner of an independent gas station in a town the new turnpike had passed by.

Nick told his story. He was the administrative director of the Presbyterian Hospital in Narbeth, Pennsylvania, and had been visiting a friend who held a similar position at the Harry Meyer Hospital. The friend had shown him the Harry Meyer computer and now he, Nick, was wondering if he couldn't convince his own Board of Directors to invest in one.

Meiselman offered him a tour of the plant, but Nick asked for just a demonstration of how a relatively small Basehart would operate. "The Board," he said, "will be a lot more interested in how our doctors can utilize the computer than in the actual machinery."

Meiselman led him through a large, antiseptic room filled with women sitting at computer consoles, key-punching data into the machines, filing printouts, chewing gum. Nick was reminded of old illustrations of immigrants laboring at sewing machines.

"We rent our services to companies who don't need their own computer," Meiselman said. "We keep magnetic tapes of their master files here and they send in an order when they want us to run something. Lot of time saved when you rent. Not to mention money."

"I think we'd want to own our own."

In a smaller room with unwashed, factory-like windows that let in a fair amount of thick grey light, Meiselman showed Nick the Basehart display console.

"This one's not operational, but it don't matter,"

he said. "Every computer we sell is programmed differently, according to the way the buyer instructs us. Think of it as if you're buying a car. It's a stripped down model—you can put in all the extras you want, providing you can afford it. Like it's a custom job."

Nick studied the keyboard. "What's this?" he asked, pointing to a bright red key next to the "z".

"That's your 'help' button. Say you got an untrained employee who needs to use the machine. He doesn't know how to ask for the information he wants so he presses this little button and the computer tells him how."

"I didn't see it on the Harry Meyer console."

"Sometimes it's not red. Sometimes it's hidden. But it's always there. We built our business on the 'help' button. Government was afraid some nut would devise a code so complex no one could get at the information. Now if you want a demo on an operating model, I'll take you up to . . ."

Nick told Mr. Meiselman that wasn't necessary, took his card, shook his hand and let the guard show him out.

He walked up Eighth Avenue. It was a humid day. His head needed a rest. He knew from experience that the best way for him to solve a problem was to get away from it for a while. There wasn't much he could do now anyway. He would have to wait for night before he could go back to the library, to the computer.

Maybe Shep was right. Maybe he was becoming obsessed, paranoid. "Obsessional paranoid." That would be the label they'd stick on his big toe when he was shipped down into the Harry Meyer basement to be ripped into a hundred or so reusable parts.

He needed a joint, but a glass of milk would do. He stood outside a corner luncheonette and drank it while people with unwholesome faces, wearing tan polyester pants suits, made for the Port Authority bus terminal and New Jersey. Others—blacks, Puerto Ricans, whores in hot pants, tough kids with tattoos and knives—stood in doorways, doing business.

It looked as if it might rain, and he hoped it would. It was too warm for September. The taxis, the busses, the trucks and the limousines emitted illegal fumes; short-order restaurants with open front windows and perspiring counter men gave off the sickly sweet smell of grilled chemicals.

He walked east on 42nd Street, passing the porn shops and porn movies. He pushed his way through crowds of hustlers in summer undershirts and pimps in powder blue jackets. The hostility was as thick as the rancid air.

An old man wearing a child's white-framed sun glasses sat on the pavement by a store front where junkies sold their blood. He was holding a cardboard sign that had been unevenly lettered with a black Magic Marker. The sign read: "The Nazis put me in jail and tortured me. Medical bills are very high."

Nick put a dollar in the cap in the man's lap, got into a taxi, and gave the driver the Harry Meyer address. Medical bills are very high, he thought.

He closed his eyes on New York, put his head back against the torn upholstery and wished Carla was back.

She was.

"You have a visitor, sir," Lawrence told him in a conspiratorial voice. "The young lady who was here with you on your first day. I let her in. I hope that was all right, Mr. Meyer?"

"Very good, Lawrence." Nick wondered why he disliked the man so much. If Lawrence kept his mouth closed, he thought, he could have a career as a state trooper.

"Oh! Mr. Meyer, sir! There's a communication from Miss Buckley."

Nick read it.

"Dear Nick: I suppose you had some reason for leaving me like that in the coffee shop, but I can't say it made me feel particularly positive about either myself or you. As I was supposed to be showing you the complex, I have not mentioned your unexplained defection to Doctor Paine. Tomorrow afternoon, we are scheduled to visit Genetics. Your physical exam is scheduled for the morning at eight A.M. sharp in Dr. Carlson's office (1242). Best, Patricia Buckley."

He tore up the note, started to hand the pieces to Lawrence, then stuffed them in his trouser pocket and went into the apartment.

All of the rotten odors of the day—the fetid animal aroma of the Marshal, the expensive perfume of Alexandria Pace, the cheap sex smells of 42nd Street—evaporated as soon as he saw her in the living room, standing by the one-way window.

"They called off the Gallo demonstration so I decided I'd better get my ass back where it belongs." She pressed the button that controlled the vertical blinds, making the room almost night dark. "You remember to water Baby Love?"

He put his arms around her and held her tight. "I've missed you so much," he said.

She kissed his neck. "Only four days."

"More like four years."

"I know. I've never been so lonesome in my life, Nicky."

She was wearing one of Harry's silk robes. He undid the sash and got her out of it, kissing her breasts, the space between her legs.

She pushed him away and lay down on the bed as he took off his clothes. He spread her legs and propped them against his chest, sinking himself into her. She put her arms around his neck and kissed him as he went in and out of her as slowly as he could, trying to make it last as long as he could.

"How many orgasms did you *have*?" he asked later, after they had made love again with less urgency.

"Orgasms! You're the only person under fifty and outside a classroom who uses that word. Besides, what do you think I have up there, an electronic calculator?"

He kissed her, putting his hand under the robe she had put on again. "I missed you so much, Carla."

"I got news for you, baby: I missed you, too."

He held her close to him for a while, and then he told her about Tony.

She already knew. She had called the office to report that she was back, and they had told her.

"I try not to think about him," she said. "But I can't help it." She began to cry, and he comforted her, stroking her hair.

Later she said, "I get so frightened when I think of Tony. He was too young."

"He had a little help with that accident."

She pushed him away. "What's that supposed to mean?"

"Forget it. I'm sorry I said anything."

"Listen, you bastard, you can't lay something like that on me and then hold out. You think Tony was snuffed?"

He didn't answer.

"By who?"

"I don't know."

"So why do you think it?"

He was silent, and she said, "You don't want to tell me, don't tell me. We got better things to do."

She took a bottle of baby lotion and poured some on the head of his penis. She started to rub her hand up and down on him.

"Jesus, Carla."

She got on top of him, opened her robe, and slid down on his penis.

"Jesus!"

"Relax, huh?"

It was midnight before he asked about the Chavez photographs.

"They're at the developer's now. I dropped them off on my way in from Kennedy. I think, I really think, they're dynamite, man. Too good for "OFF!" I know a photographer's rep who'll peddle them for me. *If* they're as good as I think they are. Cross your fingers."

"Ever the business woman."

"Don't do it to me, Nicky. I feel bad about Tony. But I'm not wearing black for the next ten years. I got Carlita to think about, man."

He got out of the bed to look for a joint.

"Why don't you put a fucken robe on?" she asked. "There's about three dozen in that closet. Your old man must have had a thing for robes."

"I don't get it," he said. "You were the one who thought I was uptight about being nude. You were the one who liked to run around with the shades up at high noon, the neighbors looking in."

"It's different in New York. Here."

"How?"

"I don't know, Nick. Different. This apartment and everything."

"Are you all right? Is something the matter?" He put his arms around her.

She began to cry—loud, child's sobs. "Nothing's the matter, man. I mean, like I started out at four A.M. trying to get on the plane and the stewardess gives me a lot of shit about my ticket and the fucken pilot thinks he's captain of the roller coaster, and then Tony's dead and you weren't here... Give me a chance to get it together, huh?"

He kissed the top of her head.

"I mean, Tony meant something to me too, Nicky. Like he gave me my first real job."

She pulled away. "Go put something on, huh?"

He wrapped a bathroom towel around himself. "You want to eat something?"

"No, man." Changing moods, she kissed him. "I'm going to pop a tranq and go to sleep. I'm cranky. Jet lag. Forgive me?"

"I forgive you."

She swallowed a Valium and switched off the lights. A hum cut off.

"You hear that sound that just stopped?" he asked.

"Nope." She arranged herself in her favorite sleeping position, on her side with her knees up, a pillow in her arms. Nick lay behind her, his arms around her.

He kissed her neck. She was asleep. He wasn't. Not even close. But he decided to put off the trip to the library; it seemed less urgent now that Carla was here.

He was hungry. He put on a pair of trousers and went down to the kitchen. He switched on the kitchen light and the noise began. It's making me crazy, he thought, as he ate a chicken leg he found in the refrigerator.

He went into the little downstairs bathroom and switched on the light, determined not to let the noise bother him. He switched the light on and off.

Suddenly, while he was urinating, it all came together. He knew why the sound was always there during the day and why it only came at night when the lights were on.

He looked in the mirror over the basin, half expecting to find it cracked. It was the way he felt inside. Staring at himself in the small cabinet mirror, he wondered, for the first time seriously, if he was crazy. Whether everything, in fact, had been delusion.

He shut off the light—and the sound—went into the kitchen, and switched off the overhead light there. Two small windows let in some light from the street, but not too much. He stood still for a few moments, waiting for his eyes to become accustomed to the dark.

In the butler's pantry, he found a screw driver and a step ladder. He placed the step ladder under the kitchen light fixture, climbed up, and unscrewed it.

He held the fixture in one hand and balanced himself on the ladder by keeping the other hand against the ceiling.

A coil of metal sprang out of the part of the fixture still fastened to the ceiling. In the dim light, it looked like an expensive, silver snake, something one would give a rich woman for her desk. It frightened him.

He forced himself to examine it. Thin wires ran through the coil, attached at the upper ends to the ceiling socket. The lower ends were affixed to a tiny TV camera, mounted on the coil with a swivel head.

It was all very clear. During daylight hours, the

cameras throughout the complex worked all of the time. At night, when there was less activity, the light switches activated the cameras. And probably alerted whoever was doing the monitoring.

Who? Cecil?

He replaced the fixture and put the ladder back in the pantry, where he found a pencil-sized flashlight on the shelf with the tools. He put the screwdriver and the flashlight in his trouser pocket.

He walked up the stairs, still surprised that he was able to function so calmly. In the bedroom, Carla turned over and peered up at him.

"Where you been, man?" she asked drowsily.

"Getting something to eat."

"How about a goodnight kiss?"

He kissed her.

"What about a goodnight fuck?"

"Too tired," he said.

"Say it for me once, Nicky. Say 'fuck,' please."

"Never and *nunca* and *jamais*."

She turned away, hugging her pillow. "Then goodnight, man."

He stood there, trying to analyze his feelings. And suddenly he had a thought. His stomach turned. Why did she suddenly want to cover up all of the time? Why wouldn't she make love with the lights on? The lights *and* the cameras.

He wanted to wake her, to ask her, to get some reasonable, reassuring answer. But his logical self, the self that had been operating so efficiently, stopped him. If she knew about the cameras, she knew about other things. She would tell whoever was behind all this that now he knew. They would stop him. And he didn't want to be stopped.

He put on a shirt and a pair of shoes.

It was time to go to the library.

CHAPTER 20

He let himself out of the triplex with his MatchCode card and went down the windowless third floor corridor of the hospital, cupping his hand over the pencil flashlight so that the cameras in the overhead light fixtures wouldn't be activated.

Walking as softly as he could, he climbed the steel steps of the emergency staircase. On the ninth floor, he used his card to open the door that led to Executive Services and used it again to get into the library.

He knew the computer screen would light up the moment he inserted his card, and guessed that its glow might be strong enough to activate the cameras. He considered covering the screen with his shirt and working under it like an old-fashioned photographer, and then decided that it would be easier to decommission the trigger device at its source.

He removed the dust cover from the console's

typewriter and lined it with his shirt to give it double protection against the light. Then, standing on a wooden desk-chair, he unscrewed the overhead fixture.

He decided not to unhook the neon bulb, in case simply touching it might set off some alarm. Instead, he wrapped the reinforced dust cover around the camera coil and the bulb, fit the glass fixture over them, and screwed it partially back into its base.

He slipped getting off the chair, but righted himself by clutching one of the bookcases. He could hear his heart beating in the soundless room. Despite the air-conditioning, he had begun to sweat. He thought he might become ill, shirtless and sweating in the cool room. Sickness seemed to be hovering about him. He told himself it was a matter of attitude; he wouldn't get sick if he was determined not to.

With a steady hand, he slid his card into the slot on the computer console. The console screen came to life, the light much stronger than he had expected. For a second he held his breath, thinking he had heard the hum of the camera. But it was only the hum of the computer.

The screen gave off enough light for him to see the keyboard clearly. It was as he remembered: there was no "Help" key next to the "z." He went down on his knees and examined the underside of the console. Several rows of screws ran along the front and side ridges. It took him half an hour to undo them all. Standing, he wiped the sweat from his eyes, wiped the palms of his hands against his trousers, and carefully lifted the hood.

The "help" button, a bright red, was where Fred Meiselman had promised it would be.

He sat down on the small swivel chair and typed Alexandria Pace's MatchCode as he supposed it should read.

```
MatchCode:   TOKAL-PACEal-28-RYLTY-
             F=RCPNT(A+)

             (CROSS REF:  NOT AVAIL-
             ABLE)
```

"Who is the donor?" Nick typed.
-y-o-u/a-r-e/n-o-t/p-r-o-g-r-a-m-m-
e-d/f-o-r/s-u-c-h/i-n-f-o-r-m-a-t-
i-o-n-

He pressed the "help" button and typed: "What is the code I need to receive donor information?"
The screen was blank for several moments. He was about to press the "help" button again when letters began to appear on the screen.
-k-e-y/p-u-n-c-h/a-l-t-e-r-n-a-t-
e/n-u-m-e-r-a-l-s/t-o-p/r-o-w/d-i-
g-i-t-s/f-o-l-l-o-w/b-y/d-o-u-b-l-e/
p-l-u-s/s-i-g-n/r-e-p-e-a-t/q-u-e-
s-t-i-o-n-

Nick typed 13579++, retyped Alexandria Pace's MatchCode and the question. The answer appeared immediately.

MatchCode: ZIP11963-PACEel-18-STU-
              F-POT.DON(A=)WOMB(PRI-
              MARY) - Heart (1) -
              Liver (1) PROJECT STATUS:
              IMMINENT

              (CROSS REF: TOKAL-
              PACEal-28-RYLTY-F-RCPNT-
              (A+))

He wrote down the zip code and the name and erased the readout on the screen.

He found telephone directories on a shelf behind a desk in a corner of the library. After a few moments with the Zip Code and Suffolk County directories, he learned that Zip Code 11963 was in Sag Harbor, Long Island, and that an Elizabeth Pace lived on Hampton Street in Sag Harbor.

He felt an almost overwhelming temptation to go to the telephone and call Elizabeth Pace, tell her to get out, to run, to protect herself. But the library phone was probably bugged. And Elizabeth Pace could only think that such a call in the middle of the night was from some nut case.

He replaced the hood on the console and took his card from the slot, turning off the computer. In the dark, he got back on the chair, unscrewed the light fixture, and removed the dust cover and his shirt.

The glass fixture was slippery in his wet hands, and as he began to screw it back onto its base, searching for the screw holes with his fingers, it began to slip. Grasping at it, he fell off the chair, one hand automatically going out to break the fall, the other holding the fixture in the air as if it were a victory trophy.

He sat still for a moment on the carpeted floor, then found his shirt and put it on. He felt less vulnerable. He climbed back onto the chair and carefully screwed the fixture into place.

Keeping his hand cupped over the beam of the flashlight, he made certain that everything was as he had found it in the library. Then he left. It took what seemed a monumental amount of time to get down the stairs to Harry's apartment. He felt as if he were a very old man who had been called upon, unfairly, to perform some strenuous act.

In the triplex, he rested for a moment on a silk-upholstered bench just outside the bedroom door, then stood and took off his sweat-soaked clothes. He carried them into the bathroom and dropped them into a hamper built into the wall. He toweled himself off in the dark and went back into the bedroom.

He got into the bed. And listened. The only sound in the room was Carla's steady breathing.

The hum. It was the first thing he was aware of in the morning. He opened his eyes trying not to look directly up into the light fixture. If they were watching on the other end, they would see the fear on his face.

He had to get out of the room, the hospital, as soon as he could. He had to get to Sag Harbor and Elizabeth Pace.

The door opened and Carla came in. She carried a tray on which sat a glass of orange juice, a glass of milk, a plate of buttered toast.

Holding the tray away from her so that nothing would soil her new and, for Carla, restrained outfit, she set it carefully over his knees. She kissed his forehead, then looked down at him.

"You feeling all right, Nicky?"

"Not bad."

Her green trousers were tailored; the sweater was a safe, pale green. The only things from her wardrobe that he recognized were the American Indian turquoise earrings.

"Where you going?" he asked.

"The developer's. I don't want anyone laying their fingers on those negatives without me being there.'

It made sense. But the words sounded rehearsed.

"Thanks for breakfast," he said.

"Don't mention it."

He fought back the questions he wanted to ask. She strapped her cameras around her and kissed him, this time on the lips.

"Maybe tonight," she said. "we can go out to some ritzy restaurant and celebrate."

"Celebrate what?"

"Your money. My photographs."

"Fine."

"What're you going to do today?" She didn't know how to leave the room.

"Relax. Maybe see Shep." He forced himself to sip orange juice, to eat some of the toast.

She went to the door. "You sure you're feeling all right? You look like shit."

"I'm fine."

"Maybe you should see a doctor?"

That made him laugh. "I don't have to."

"Okay. Then I'll see you later, huh?"

He wanted her to go. *"Vaya con Dios."*

"You too, baby." She pantomimed a kiss and left.

He got out of the bed, trying not to look as if he were hurrying, trying not to think about Carla. He was too aware of the camera's hum. He imagined it rotating on its swivel head, following him around the room.

What he wanted to do was put on his clothes and race out. But he didn't. He showered because he showered every morning. And he dental flossed his teeth and brushed them, then shaved and patted his cheeks with Harry's expensive after shave lotion.

It was eight thirty by the time he left the complex, and Lawrence was on duty. "What time do you think you might be home, sir?"

"I don't know, Lawrence."

"I only asked, sir, in the event that Miss Buckley or Dr. Paine..."

"Tell them I withheld the information, Lawrence."

"Very good, Mister Meyer, sir."

He walked down Madison a few blocks and looked back. He didn't think he was being followed. There was no one; the shops didn't open until ten. He found a phone booth and dialed the Sag Harbor number.

The line was busy.

He walked east and then farther downtown, stopping at phone booths, continuing to get a busy signal.

He told himself that there had to be enough time to get to Elizabeth Pace and somehow convince her she was about to be murdered by people she didn't know, for a reason that would be very hard to believe. There was a phone in front of Cakemaster's on Third Avenue. Still busy.

In a booth on Second Avenue, he asked the operator to break in on the line—this was an emergency call. After a moment, the operator told him that the number he was trying to reach was out of order.

He tried Shep at his office, but a secretary assured him that Mr. Gordon had taken the day off "to be somewhere private with his family. He very deliberately didn't leave a phone number. Why, I couldn't get him if the President of the United States wanted him!" She sounded excited by the prospect.

At a Hertz office in the east 60s, he rented a car, a green Ford Fairlane, for more money than he had thought possible. He charged it on the American Express card Tony had given him for "OFF!" expenses. He drove over the 59th Street Bridge to Queens Boulevard, then got onto the Long Island Expressway.

It looked as though it was going to rain.

He liked driving, but not what he had to drive

207

through. Coram. Medford. The towns that lined the Expressway sounded as if they were named after DuPont fibers. The houses looked as if they had all been modeled on the same mean little shoe box. Signs invited him to "Inspect Our Swiss Chalet, $21,500." Even the church on the Brook Haven cutoff looked like a poor man's ranchhouse; the cedar shingles on the facade had not aged fast enough.

He knew these houses and these roads; he had spent a fair amount of time on Eastern Long Island in the past few years. "Fucking in the Hamptons," Tony used to call those weekends when they'd drive in Tony's Porsche to Easthampton, where Tony's mother's friends would them to radical-chic parties attended by a great many accessible celebrities. Nick had often wondered why the celebrities all became so terrible the minute they were packed into a room or a garden together. They were so much more decent when met privately, face-to-face.

Of all the Hampton villages, he had enjoyed Sag Harbor most. It was less desperate than the others, more like a real place. Though it too had its pretensions, too many New Yorkers peeling asbestos off the cottages they had bought from families who had moved into split levels on the edges of the town. He had thought he wouldn't mind owning a house in Sag Harbor, a ginger-breaded house from which he, too, would peel the asbestos. He had talked to Carla once about spending a long summer weekend there, and she had said, "They let Ricans into a place like that?"

He shivered inside the over-air-conditioned Ford.

At a macadam rest area, he stopped and tried Elizabeth Pace's number again. This time it rang. It rang seven, eight, nine times.

He tried the number again, thinking that perhaps he had dialed incorrectly, but he hadn't. After another half dozen rings, he gave up. He leaned against the car. The air was hot and heavy with moisture. He wished it would rain.

He watched a field rat attempt to get into a plastic bag of garbage someone had dumped by the corroded drum that served as the area trashcan. He was wasting time, he thought. Elizabeth Pace's phone would never answer. He should turn around, go back to New York.

The hoped-for rain forced him back into the car and onto the Expressway. The rain stopped after a few minutes, but it had cleaned the air; he was able to shut off the air-conditioner and open a window. He decided to drive on. He would find Elizabeth Pace.

As he turned onto Route 27, he switched on the radio and picked up WLNG from Sag Harbor, a determinedly local station that had made him feel, on those weekends with Tony, as if he were actually in mid-America, not in another outpost of Manhattan.

"Swapshop" was on. Listeners were calling in, offering used washing machines and cotton slipcovers and badminton sets for sale or trade.

The announcer interrupted every few minutes to allow shopkeepers to advertise themselves, or to give local events some publicity.

He turned off the radio when he reached the Bridge-Sag Turnpike and was soon in Sag Harbor. The sun had come out, brightening up the day. He cut across Jermain Street, passed Otter Pond, drove down narrow streets bordered by small, shingled cottages that had once housed working men and their families.

Hampton Street was where he remembered it. The houses were larger here, and handsome. He stopped at one. A good-looking man in his sixties, wearing Bermuda shorts, was mowing the lawn.

"Can you tell me where the Pace house is?" Nick asked.

"Sure can," the man said, coming forward. "See that funeral parlor over there? Go four houses past it, on the right. Pace is that wood-shingled one set back from the street, the one with the blue trim."

"Thanks."

"Don't mention it."

Nick drove on to the Pace house, a modest, attractive one, smaller than its neighbors, surrounded by dogwood and mimosa trees.

He walked up the front path and climbed the wooden stairs to a porch with a glider on it, and a furled American flag resting against one of the columns. Through a window, he could see a wallpapered living room filled with mahogany furniture too big for it. The telephone, on a little table against a wall, was a pink Princess model, incongruously modern in the old-fashioned room.

He knocked on the door, and a voice off to his right said, "Ain't nobody home."

A woman in her late fifties, her head covered with white curls, stood on the porch of the house next door. She wore round glasses, a faded sun dress, stout white Minnie Mouse shoes.

"I've been trying to telephone..."

"Phone was out of order," the woman said in a precise, dry voice. "Receiver off the hook. Drat cat, as an aunt of mine liked to say." She stared at Nick. "I put the receiver back when I went over to borrow milk for the doughnuts I was making for the bake sale. You have any problems with that?"

He hesitated.

"You want to tell me what you want? Maybe I can help you. Of course, maybe I can't."

"I wanted to speak with Elizabeth Pace."

"Lord, you'd have a heap of trouble doing that. Elizabeth's been dead near on ten years."

"Are you positive?" He felt like a fool the minute he said it.

"I'm her sister-in-law, Mister. So I should know. What'd you want to talk to her for, anyway?"

"I'm from the telephone company. We had a report the phone was out of order. It's listed in her name."

"Poor Morty never had the heart to change it. Well, thanks for checking. The phone company's

211

usually not so up on things. Your people used to be neater, though. You know you got a button missing from that shirt, young feller?"

Nick said he did, his wife would attend to it that evening.

He got back into the Ford, drove on a few blocks into the village, and pulled into a supermarket parking lot. He tried to think.

The computer had made a mistake, he told himself, or the information had been deliberately scrambled. If it had been scrambled, that would mean they knew what he was up to.

He pulled out of the parking lot, switched on the radio, and headed back toward New York.

Big Mama must have made a mistake, he decided. Computers did, he knew from controversies over department store charge accounts. Or there was something he didn't know. Or he was imagining everything. He turned up the radio to drown out the sound of his thinking, and a part of his brain, the part concerned with trivia, recognized the last bars of a song he had always liked. "... you are my last love ... until tomorrow." The announcer came on. "That was the Du-Ops, and their hit, 'Last Love.' And now, folks, from the front porch of our own National Hotel, the results of the Pierson High School senior class cookie bake—and it's good news! A sell-out, not a cookie or a crumb left! The sale was sponsored by Mrs. Helen Brown, manager of the National, and all proceeds will go to the Animal Relief Fund. In case you're wondering, that huge upside-down cake—fifteen pounds, six ounces!—was bought by the Sag Harbor Volunteer Fire Company. Let's hear it for the volunteer firemen, ladies and gentlemen! And let's hear it for the two Pierson senior class members who baked that monster, Norma Epstein and Betty Pace. . . . Now for a song that's one of my very own personal oldies-but-goodies. . . ."

Nick switched off the radio. Fighting off panic, he turned the car around and headed for the National Hotel.

On the porch of the hotel, a large, red-brick building dating from the last years of the whaling industry in Sag Harbor, two young girls, sisters with taffy-colored hair, dressed in shorts and sweaters and eye shadow, were folding bridge tables. A formidable young woman in gray pants and a black sweater was directing them.

"Clear the tables before you fold them, Heather," she was saying as Nick climbed the porch steps. "And Sharon Lee, do please stop eating the crumbs! It can't possibly be healthy." She turned to Nick. "Hello. . . ."

"Too late for the cake sale?" he asked.

"I'm afraid so. We're just cleaning up." She folded a bridge chair.

"I was looking for Betty Pace."

She looked at him inquiringly.

"She's my cousin."

"I didn't know Betty had any cousins."

"We're not very close."

"You just missed her," the young woman said, losing interest. "She hung around until it was time

213

to clean up, and then she evaporated like the others."

"Do you know where she went?"

"I'm afraid not."

"I do," said one of the taffy-haired girls. "She and Mrs. Brown went to the P.T.A. picnic at Sagaponac Beach. It's the last picnic of the year, and we're supposed to be there too, you know, but—"

"You're not supposed to be there, Heather," the young woman said as Nick turned to go. "It's only for the senior class. Now you and Sharon Lee get cracking with those chairs."

*   *   *   *

"Why did you want to stop at the drugstore?" Mrs. Brown asked. Her safety belt was securely in place, her hair was tied securely back.

"Tampax," Betty said, trying to concentrate on Mrs. Brown's big old Buick. She didn't feel comfortable behind the wheel, but she never said no to an opportunity to drive.

"Dear me," Mrs. Brown said. "You don't mean to say you're having your period?"

"I do," Betty said. "I am."

"Well then, dear, you'd better pull over and let me drive."

Betty did so, but not happily. She had just begun to get the feel of it, and now, as soon as they left the village, Mrs. Brown insisted on taking over.

214

"You're not intending to go swimming?" Mrs. Brown said, her big hands—gloved, though it was still virtually summer—grasping the leather-covered steering wheel.

"Sure. It's warm enough."

"In my day, no girl would dream of going swimming when it was her time of the month."

She was such a queer duck, Mrs. Brown. No one really knew her very well. And now she wasn't saying a word, her lips pressed together in tight disapproval. Betty looked at Mrs. Brown's capable hands in their driving gloves, then looked away at the deserted, not very pretty road that connected Sag Harbor with Sagaponac Beach. Now she was determined to go swimming. She wished she had gone with Norma and the others. But Mrs. Brown had asked her to help count the money, and then it was too late. Well, they'd soon be there.

They were coming to the top of the narrow wooden bridge, the one that spanned the railroad tracks. For some reason, Mrs. Brown had picked up speed. Her foot, in its heavy brown leather shoe, was pressed down on the accelerator, even though everyone knew this was a dangerous spot.

Betty grasped the door handle as Mrs. Brown deliberately—or so it almost seemed—crashed through the fence on the left side of the ramp leading off the bridge and, without losing speed, drove straight across Irene Lagarta's potato field. Betty closed her eyes, letting out a half scream of disbelief as the car drove right into the old Moody pond.

215

She could hear the ducks shrieking as they flapped away, as the old car began to sink. She pulled at the handle of her door, but it wouldn't come open. Turning, she saw Mrs. Brown opening the driver's door, getting out. Thanking God Mrs. Brown was so agile for such a large woman, Betty slid across the seat to Mrs. Brown's arms—arms outstretched, ready to help her.

The pond wasn't that deep. There was still plenty of time.

Betty moved into Mrs. Brown's hands, proud that she was not panicking. But the hands weren't helping her out of the car. One of them was reaching for her face; she could feel the other circling her neck. Betty began to scream as Mrs. Brown's big, capable, gloved hands grasped her head firmly and held her until the water was all around her.

*   *   *   *

By the time Nick got directions and followed Madison Street out of the village, past the new, look-alike houses, until Madison became a lonesome rural road, it was too late.

He could hear the sirens before he crossed the wooden bridge. He pulled over when he saw the police cars—there were three of them—parked at the edge of a potato field beside a large pond. A dozen people stood looking down into the pond, where the top of a submerged car floated like a piece of ice in a tepid bowl.

Close to Nick, a man was observing the scene from a beat-up International Harvester truck, wiping the back of his sun-wrinkled neck with a handkerchief.

"What happened?" Nick asked.

"Young kid driving too darned fast. Kid from Sag Harbor. Morty Pace's girl."

"She okay?"

"Not much chance, from what I could tell. They got her over in that whirly-bird over there. Rushing her into New York."

For the first time, Nick saw the helicopter at the edge of the field. As he looked, its blades began to whirl.

"Woman who was with her, she seemed all right," the man in the truck volunteered. "Kept saying she should never have let the girl drive. Too late for that kind of talk now, you ask me."

The helicopter rose slowly into the air and circled cautiously, attempting to find the right wind pattern.

"Some of us have to work," the man in the truck said, starting his motor and backing up.

Nick looked up at the plastic-paneled sides of the helicopter hovering over him. It hung there for a long moment, as if it were having trouble deciding where to go. Finally it gathered the strength it needed to fight the wind, and flew off with Betty Pace's body in the back.

Nick got into his car. But not before he had seen Pat Buckley's worried face pressed against a window of the helicopter.

217

CHAPTER 21

The clouds came again as he drove onto the Expressway and the rain broke a few moments later—a light, steady drizzle. Funeral rain, he thought.

He was caught in the late afternoon traffic. Factories, more thoughtfully designed than the housing projects that separated them, disgorged an infinite number of cars. He felt that it had been deliberately arranged to frustrate him. He was anxious to get back to Manhattan, to get started.

As he passed the idling cars headed the opposite way in the far lanes, he stared through the Ford's rain-splattered window at the patient, defeated men trapped in their air-conditioned cells, seemingly hypnotized by the rhythmic beat of their windshield wipers.

A helicopter flew above him, headed for New York. He wondered for a moment if it was the one carrying Betty Pace, and knew, of course, that it wasn't. She was already at her destination.

His nervousness diminished as he decided what he had to do, deliberately planning each move. He understood himself well enough to know that he had to keep his emotions under wraps.

The rain had begun to come down more heavily by the time he had maneuvered through Manhattan's cross-town traffic and arrived at the Harry Meyer. He left the car on the Central Park side of Fifth Avenue in front of a half-assembled reviewing stand. A pink sign attached to a lamppost read: "No Parking. Parade Tomorrow. NYPD."

Lawrence's evening replacement stood at attention at the street entrance to the triplex. Opening the door for Nick, he said that it was a wet afternoon.

Nick went into the kitchen, where he poured himself a glass of milk and, mindful of the camera, drank it as slowly as he could. I have to do what I always do, he told himself. I have to act as I always act.

He went up to the bedroom. She was there, standing at the one-way window, looking at the Park.

"Hello, Carla," he said.

She turned. "Hi, Nicky."

He crossed the room and kissed her. He felt as if some theater director had told him to cross the stage and embrace the leading lady. I must be natural, he told himself. But he was too aware of the light, the faint hum of the camera.

"You're all wet," Carla said.

"That's what they all say."

"It might help if you put on dry clothes." She went to his closet and brought out one of the rugby shirts she had given him. "What're you saving this for?"

"I was planning to put it out on the terrace and let it age gracefully."

"Just put it on before you catch cold."

He changed his shirt and found a dry pair of trousers. "How were the proofs?" he asked.

"I'll know more on Monday. Too soon to tell. But I've got my fingers crossed." She tried to smile at him.

"Let's go out for a drink." It sounded about as natural as Tiny Tim's voice. But he had to get her out, away from the camera.

Her smile was still forced. "Sure, Nicky. I don't know why I'm feeling so down and dirty today. The weather, maybe."

"That's it," he said. "The weather."

They found a big black umbrella in the downstairs hall closet and ran, under its protection, to the Ford.

"Where'd you get the tank?" she asked as they got in.

He didn't answer. He drove down Fifth and across Central Park at 66th and turned up Central Park West.

"Nicky," she said to him once, putting her cool hand on his arm.

He still didn't answer, but concentrated on finding a parking space. He found one finally, opposite the Museum of Natural History, under a pair of low hanging trees.

220

He looked out at the large sign over the Museum entrance that said it was open late on Wednesday nights. The rain came down harder, but the only person in sight, a man strolling down Central Park West, didn't seem to mind getting soaked. Nick couldn't make himself look at Carla.

She said, "What the fuck is the matter with you, huh?"

He looked at her then. Her face was angry and hard, but her fingers, with their black painted nails, were touching her lips, as if they were sore and she was kissing them, making them better. It was a gesture he knew. It meant she was at her most vulnerable, not far from tears.

But still he couldn't speak.

"Would you mind telling me why you've been treating me as if I were a two-dollar whore, and you were the madam's brother?" There were tears in her eyes, but they didn't spill out. She hated anyone to see her cry; she had told him once that if the tears didn't run down her cheeks, it couldn't be counted as crying.

"Nicky," she said in a softer voice, "what's the matter?"

"How come you don't want to make love with the lights on?"

"What? What're you talking about?"

"How come you've been walking around in Harry's silk robes and getting me to wrap towels around myself?"

"What're you, nuts? What does that have to do with the price of eggs, for Christ's sake?"

"You used to say you were happiest in your

birthday suit, and now suddenly you're Miss Modesty. Something's funny about that, Carla."

"You're not laughing."

She was playing for time, he could tell. "No, I'm not laughing," he said.

She laughed, startling him. It was genuine, the last thing he had expected to hear.

"Okay," she said. "But, I mean, this is hard for me to say, man. I been thinking about what you kept asking and I kept refusing. I mean—don't laugh now—suddenly Mrs. Nicholas Miller doesn't sound so bad to me. I mean, like I feel I'm really in love for the first time. Not 'True Romance' love. Or even the kind of love where you're both good in the sack. But—Jesus, I'm saying this badly—for the first time I feel I can trust a man. I can trust you, Nicky. And so I'm getting into the idea of being a married chick, of having a kid, living a life. You know? But then I say to myself—how are his fancy friends going to react to Carlita Carmen Hilda Ponce Vasquez? I mean, man, we're living in a Fifth Avenue triplex. Not even a duplex. A triplex! So I was starting to clean up my act. Mrs. Nicholas Miller ain't running around bare assed, fucking with the lights on, is she?"

She did not wait for him to answer. "For Christ's sake, man, you haven't noticed anything! Have you? Have you seen what I been wearing? Carla wants to be a lady, man! I'm throwing out all my bangle beads and I'm shopping for fucken little pearl earrings. I'm trying to talk like you

222

talk, like that Pat Buckley bitch with her teeth frozen together. Fuck it! I'm even trying to walk different, with my ass all pulled in. Man, I love you! I want to be your wife. I dig it now. Okay? So now you know!"

She turned her head away because now the tears were spilling over.

"Why'd you ask?" she said.

He couldn't speak.

She turned to face him, the tears running down her cheeks. "Man, why'd you ask?"

He told her, his voice flat, about the hidden cameras. He told her how they recorded everything. He told her about Alexandria and Betty Pace, and he told her about Tony and his father, and he told her what business the Harry Meyer Hospital was really in.

And he told her he had thought she had known. That she knew about the cameras. And if she knew about the cameras, she knew about everything.

She slammed him across the face so hard he thought he had been punched. But her hand had been open.

"You fucker! You cocksucking, shit-eating scumbag! You creep! There I was trying to act like a woman good enough for you, and you—"

"I'm sorry, Carla. I was under a lot of—"

"—a lot of pressure. Yeah, I know that line! Let me out of this car!" She reached for the door handle, but he pulled her to him, holding her arms down. He kissed her.

"I love you, Carla. I love you."

After a while he let go of her arms, and she put them around him. "I love you too, man."

"You still want to be Mrs. Nicholas Miller?"

"I still may consider it, yeah."

He kissed her again.

Suddenly she pulled away. "Jesus!" she said. "I got goose bumps all over me. You mean they snuffed Tony and your father, just like that? You mean they just went out and hit somebody because she happened to be related to some rich bitch who needs a new womb?"

"That's one way of putting it."

"Jesus!"

He held her for a long time. Then he started the car, U-turned, and drove down Central Park West and back across the Park.

"Jesus," she said again. "Jesus."

"Please stop saying that."

"Why do you think those cameras are up there, Nicky? Why do you think they're keeping tabs on you?"

"Maybe they were watching Harry and are just keeping the process going," he said. "Or maybe they think I know something I shouldn't."

"We're going to be all right, aren't we, Nick?"

"Sure."

"Keep driving. Right over the bridge to California. Let's blow this town."

He stopped the car by a telephone booth on Third and 65th, one of the booths from which he had tried earlier that day to call Elizabeth Pace.

He felt as if he had made that call on a different planet during another lifetime.

The phone rang half a dozen times before Brendi Gordon answered.

"Oh, Nicky," she said. "I only answered because I thought it was the baby sitter. I—"

"I have to talk to Shep right away," he said.

"No social chit-chat with me?"

"No social chit-chat."

There was always an odd note of regret in their voices when they spoke to each other. He thought about that and about her while she went to get Shep.

"This better be good, Ace," Shep said, and Nick pictured him looking very earnest, his pipe in his mouth, his blue eyes quizzical. "This is the first day we've had to ourselves in a year. We're getting ready to go out to a party, and I promised Brendi no phone calls, no sudden—"

"Shep, I'll be there in five minutes," Nick said.

In the car, Carla tried to do something to her hair while looking in the sun-visor mirror. "I feel like I'm wearing a used Brillo pad on my head," she said.

When they parked in front of the Gordons' house, she said, "Is the wife going to be there?"

"Of course. Come on."

"I'll wait here."

"You're coming with me," he said.

CHAPTER 22

Brendi opened the door of the brownstone and stood there for a moment, framed by the doorway, looking concerned, beautiful, and very rich. She wore a strapless black evening dress that made her shoulders look like white marble. There was a diamond on the thin chain around her neck. She looked like the Queen of England, Nick thought. Carla, in her new dark clothes—Carla, who should always wear color—and her flying hair, looked like a girl who had been roughed up by her pimp.

Nick introduced them.

Another woman might understandably have taken pleasure from the situation, might have enjoyed her own contrast with her visitor. Brendi didn't seem to. "Shep wants to see you alone, Nick, in the den," she said. "You know where it is." She turned to Carla. "May I fix you a drink, Miss Vasquez?"

"Sure," Carla said, undaunted. "A great big

one. And do call me Carla."

She'll be all right, Nick thought, heading for the den.

Shep was wearing a black tuxedo, a frilled shirt, and a silk handkerchief in his breast pocket. He looked as if he had been waiting for a servant, and not patiently.

"Talk," he said to Nick, not getting out of his leather reclining chair. His black patent leather pumps caught the reflection of the light from a lamp across the room. "We're going to a party, Ace, a very important party. We were supposed to be there ten minutes ago—and that would have made us twenty minutes late. So talk. And talk fast."

Nick sat down in a straight-backed chair and talked for forty-five minutes. He left nothing out.

When he had finished, Shep stared at him, banged his fist on the arm of his chair, then stood up and left the room. Nick could hear him talking to Brendi. "Call the Duanes. Tell them we're going to be late. Very late."

Shep came back into the study and poured two glasses of Scotch. He gave one to Nick and got back into his recliner.

"You're telling me," he said, knocking down the Scotch as if it were water, "that the most prestigious hospital in the world engages in a little murder on the side? You know that if you're even a tiny bit right, this could make Watergate look like Jersey City. Ace, tell me this is one of your elaborate jerk-off jokes. Please!"

"You know damn well what I'm saying makes

sense," Nick said. "You know that African murderer isn't in there because he's got a bad case of tonsillitis."

"The Marshal! For Christ's sake, Nick, he never *ever* leaves Africa! He never even leaves his own country—his own *palace*! And if he were here, don't you think I would know?"

"Why would the second in command of The United States Economic Recovery Program know a thing like that?" Nick said, smiling.

"Ha," said Shep.

"Isn't there someone you could call who could tell you where the Marshal is now?"

"Yeah, there's someone I can call," Shep said, reaching for the telephone. "There's always someone I can call, Ace."

He dialed a number that seemed to have more digits than a social security card. It took three or four minutes before it was answered, and while he waited, Shep refilled his pipe. He was a man whose hands and mouth were always occupied.

"Luke?" he said, putting down the pipe. "Shep Gordon. No, this is something else. No, no need for that. All I want is a yes or a no. Listen, is your man, by some weird chance, here, in New York, in a hospital at this moment?"

He listened. As he did, his blue eyes narrowed in the kind of dramatic gesture an old-fashioned actor might make. Playing the role, Nick thought.

"I can't tell you that now, Luke," Shep said. "Some other time. Let's just say I owe you one."

He hung up the phone and looked at Nick, his eyes still narrowed. He took another long pull at his drink, finished it, and reached for Nick's glass.

"Okay. Maybe you shouldn't be put in a straightjacket. Say I believe you. Say I go along with the whole thing on the strength of that one fact. What the hell do you want me to do, Nick?"

"Stop it. Stop them."

"I can't call out the palace guards, Ace. Not just on the basis of what you say."

"I'm Harry Meyer's son. I'm worth a little money. Somebody should listen."

"They'll say you're a loony tune, a nut. You'll make page three of the *News*, and then they'll lock you up for twenty years. Nobody will listen, Nick."

"Then tell me what to do. There must be something I can do."

"Get some proof."

"Like?"

"Like Rosalynn Carter's eyewitness account of Cecil Paine murdering Johnny Carson with a scalpel on prime time TV. Barring that, something concrete. Something I can put into The Man's hand before he raps me in the mouth." He put Nick's glass down, empty, and picked up his pipe. The Scotch didn't seem to have affected him. "Or forget the whole thing. Chalk it up to Acute Shock During Bereavement Over Father's Death. Go back to Philadelphia and play sedition with Tony Lyle."

"There is no Tony Lyle," Nick said.

There was silence for a moment while they looked at each other.

"I'm sorry, Nick. I forgot."

229

"I'm not forgetting, Shep."

"Get me something concrete. Some proof."

"All right."

"When?"

"Tonight."

"It has to be good, Ace."

"It'll be good. Keep Carla here, all right?"

"I'll see if we have any chains in the playroom."

Nick followed him through the dining room and into the kitchen. "Tell her what I'm doing," he said.

"Tell her yourself."

"She'd want to come with me."

"All right," Shep said. "But listen, Nick, don't come back here. I don't want Brendi or the kids involved if this thing blows. Come to my office—downtown, on Centre Street—tomorrow morning. The building's supposed to be closed—the Jewish New Year—but there's always a man in the lobby. If you're not there by noon, I'll forget we ever had this conversation." He scribbled the address and handed it over.

"Take care of Carla," Nick said, as he went out the kitchen door into the narrow back alley.

"Take care of yourself, Ace," Shep said.

Shep closed the kitchen door and locked it. He stood still for a moment, and then he went into the pantry. Maggie, the cook, was sitting on a high stool, studying what appeared to be a recipe book.

"I think you have to go shopping, Maggie. Cookies."

"But it's Rosh Hashanah eve, Mister Gordon. All the bakeries will be closed."

"Still."

"Emergency cookies, Mister Gordon?"

"About a pound. With a lot of those little nuts on top."

CHAPTER 23

He left the car on Madison and 68th by a meter.
It was almost seven P.M. and the Avenue was
deserted; it was a tradition for New York to shut
down on the eve of a major Jewish holiday. In
Philadelphia, Nick thought, you'd never know it
was the night before the Jewish New Year.

There were no people on the street, and few
cars. A couple of passengerless taxicabs, their off-
duty signs lit, were making their way uptown to
garages in the Bronx. The avocado Ford, the only
car parked on the block, looked as if it had no
business being there.

Which was the way he felt as he went into the
Madison Avenue entrance of the complex,
nodded at the doorman, a Nazi-youth-poster
model he had seen before, and walked directly to
the elevator bank.

He entered one of the elevators, counted ten,
and walked back to the doorman.

"Excuse me," Nick said, "but I left my card in

the triplex, and I was supposed to be upstairs a half hour ago for a meeting with Dr. Paine. You want to punch twelve for me?"

"Yes, sir." The doorman walked with him to the elevator taking his MatchCode card from his breast pocket. Nick took the card from his hand, stepped into the elevator, blocking the doorman with his body, and slipped the card into the slot by the "20" button. He withdrew the card quickly and returned it to the doorman.

"Thanks," Nick said, as the elevator doors shut.

He held his breath until the car slowed at the twentieth floor. It was a long shot, he knew, starting at twenty. But something told him that this was the place to begin.

The elevator doors opened, and he stepped out into a narrow, vault-like landing. There were no windows, only bare walls and arched doorways.

He opened a swinging door and saw an operating room, a replica of the one on the fifteenth floor. Another door led into what looked like a well-equipped laboratory, but everything in it seemed out of scale, small, as if it had been designed for children.

He crossed the landing to an archway that framed a gray steel door. The door had no handle or knob.

Suddenly, startlingly close, he heard the familiar hum of a camera. Looking up, he saw it, fully exposed, swiveling on its coil above the archway. It looked like a snake about to strike, and for a moment he was hypnotized, unable to move.

233

Then a movement before him took his attention from the camera. The grey steel door was sliding up and back, like a garage door. When it was fully up, Nick stepped through the doorway.

He found himself in a large, windowless room, perhaps forty by twenty feet, with walls of the same grey steel as the door. The ceiling was very low; it cleared his head by no more than inches, and he resisted the impulse to stoop. Rows of glass-enclosed display cases divided the room into a series of corridors. The cases glowed softly, the objects in them lit from below.

At the far end of the room was another low, arched doorway, another grey steel door.

The door began to slide slowly up, and Nick forced himself to walk toward it.

Ssssst ... Sssst ...
He turns away from the young woman, moves across the room toward the monitor screens, his round eyes half open, peering.
Hsst ... Hsssst ...
He stops before the central screen, studying the figure it reveals.
Wsshh ...
He spins himself around, nods quickly at the woman. Twice.
Ssst ... Wsssh ...
He turns back to the screen as the woman starts for the door.
Fsst ... Fssst ... Ssst ...
He glides closer to the screen, so close that he is

234

almost touching it, as if he wished to feel as well as see the expression on the face he is observing.

Whssshh . . .

He spins around again.

Sssssst . . . Sssst . . .

He moves quickly away from the arched doorway as the door begins to rise.

Hsst . . .

He stops. His eyes are half closed again. He listens.

At the arched doorway, Nick halted. Someone was coming toward him from the other side; he heard the tap of heels on the floor.

"Nick, what are you doing here?" Pat Buckley asked in her calm, hostess voice. But her smile was as insufficient as ever and her eyes, behind the trendy glasses, were wide with some suppressed emotion.

"Twenty is the only floor I've missed," Nick said.

"That's not true." Pat put her hand on his arm, attempting to move him away from the open door. "You haven't been to ten or to—"

He didn't move. "Well, it's the only important floor I've missed. I pressured the doorman into getting me up here. You look as if you're about to scold me for being a naughty child."

"And so you are. Only authorized personnel are allowed up here." Pat stood before the archway with her arms folded across her chest like a safety guard in a school corridor. "Where's your friend?"

It took him a second to realize who she meant.

"Carla's spending the night with her sister," he said. "Why?"

"No reason. I just thought you spent all your free time with her. I had every intention of showing you the twentieth floor. As a matter of fact, this was where we were scheduled to come when you didn't keep your appointment with me."

He knew she was lying.

There was a medicinal odor in the room, and now it became stronger and more unpleasant, mixed with the aroma of a household deodorant spray, the pine scented variety.

"Well, I'm here now," he said.

Pat glanced back through the arch she was guarding. "Of course." She assumed her cicerone's voice. "We are now in the prosthesis room. Dr. Paine has collected prosthetic devices from ancient to modern times, and they are displayed here for the edification of the staff and visitors."

"What's in there?" Nick pointed toward the room behind the arched doorway.

"Various ultra-sensitive temperature controls and equipment for the maintenance of the hospital plant."

"I'd like to see all that. I like machines."

"Only authorized staff is allowed back there."

"But certainly I—"

"Even you, Nick, will have to get clearance from Doctor Paine."

It took him a minute to decide not to force his

236

way in. If what she had said was true, if there was only equipment in there, he would needlessly have put them on their guard.

"Now this wooden leg," Pat said, leading him away from the arched doorway toward one of the glass display cases, "is believed to be fourteenth-century Italian. The wooden hinges are still attached, though the leather straps that were used to hold the piece onto the thigh no longer exist."

He sensed that she was as aware of the other room, of another presence, as he was, that she was forcing herself to go on.

"If you'll look closely," she said, "you can see the indentation where the silk was placed to soften the pain. There is a great deal of pressure, as you can imagine, when an adult torso is supported by a two-pound wooden prosthesis."

He looked into another case. "What's that? It looks like—"

"Just what it is— a penis and scrotum. Early eighteenth century. One of the more notorious sultans, Mahmud, had it constructed for a eunuch who saved his life. It's very clever. The penis is wood. The scrotum, probably made of goat skin, was filled with liquid, and when the tiny pin valve in the penis was pulled open, the liquid could be ejaculated from that little hole in its tip. We don't know anything about the jade eyeball in the corner of the case except that it was designed for a noblewoman in China around the beginning of the eighth century."

Taking his arm, Pat led him along the row of display cases. "Here are the most modern prostheses. This limb was developed for a thalidomide victim. It's extremely versatile, with six variations of movement. Yet it's easy enough for the child to use instinctively. He can eat with it, dress, write, go to the bathroom, and so on. Now, the devices in this case here are powered by the small electrical signals generated by muscle fiber when it contracts. By twitching a muscle, the wearer can control a number of movements of a prosthesis. This one here is called 'the hook.' It gives a firm three-point grip of up to ten pounds. It can be unplugged and exchanged for a more human-looking hand—like this one, the Dorrance. The thumb and first two fingers can be moved towards one another in a caliper motion to give the wearer a fingertip force of six pounds. Power is taken from a lightweight battery strapped to the—"

"What's that?" Nick interrupted, moving into another corridor of display cases, one that led back to the arched doorway at the far end of the room. He pointed to a machine that resembled an enormous spider.

"A perambulating machine, very much like the one used on the moon by the astronauts. Though smaller, of course. This one can walk up and down stairs."

"And what's this?"

"An electric typewriter that can be operated by the mouth."

"And this hand?" They were back in the antiquities section, about six feet from the archway door.

"Designed by Ambroise Paré, a sixteenth-century French military surgeon."

Nick stared into the half dark beyond the archway. He thought he could see something move.

Pat, still talking, took his arm, pulling him back. "The hand was for soldiers. Primarily cosmetic, but still enormously sophisticated for the time. The joints work and it is fitted with . . ."

He pushed her arm away and started forward, but as she did, the door at the far end of the room behind him slid open. He turned. Cecil stood there, rubbing his big hands together.

"Nick, old boy. Patricia." Cecil strode across the room to the arched door and pulled it closed. "Who in blazes left that open? Patricia? You know that machinery is far too delicate to be exposed to all this light and dust." He turned to Nick. "Enjoying your tour? Fascinating up here, isn't it?"

Cecil was still wearing his surgical coat and conductive boots. A thin line of red ran along the front of his coat, as if a child had shot him with a water pistol filled with blood. He must have come directly from the operating room, Nick thought—from Betty Pace.

"The entire complex is fascinating, Cecil," he said.

"Then you are planning to take your father's place?"

"After what I've seen, I don't think I have any choice."

"That's wonderful news, Nick. Tomorrow will

be a slow day. Shall we lunch together and discuss it? I'll have Patricia call you in the morning and set something up."

Nick forced himself not to recoil when Cecil put his hand on his shoulder and guided him to the outer door.

"Now if you're through up here, I have a little work I'd like to do in the laboratory," Cecil said.

He shut the steel door behind him and walked with Nick and Pat to the elevator. He took off his gold-rimmed glasses and began to polish them with a handkerchief. "I'll see you tomorrow then, Nick. Goodnight, Patricia." The elevator doors closed.

Pat escorted Nick to the triplex, and he invited her to come in. He had a couple of hours to kill, and the thought of being alone with the television cameras was not a comforting one.

In the living room, he switched on the lights—let the cameras roll, he thought—and sat her down with a glass of club soda. He got himself a glass of milk from the kitchen, returned to the living room, and sat next to her on the white-pillowed sofa, wondering if she had arranged Betty Pace's accident or had been sent along only for the pick up.

"You've cut your hair," he said. "And you've stopped smoking? Or you've cut down."

"No, I've stopped. At least I think I have."

"Do you feel any different?"

"Freer. That's why I had my hair cut. Do you like it?"

"Very much. You look much younger."

240

"Thanks." She sipped at her soda, searching for something to say. "You don't like alcohol? Like your father?"

"I have a drink once in a while." He put down the milk and looked at her. "How'd you get involved with the Harry Meyer, Pat?"

"It was years ago." She moved across the room to the oriental chest that served as a bar and poured more soda into her glass. "I was a patient."

"What were you suffering from?"

"Suffering is the right word. I was blind in both eyes."

Pat stared at the painting above the chest, a huge portrait by Chuck Close of a woman called Phyllis.

"Doctor Paine gave me sight," she said. She said it as if Cecil was God.

"Were you blind from birth?" Nick asked, and then caught himself. "Listen, if it's too painful, let's not talk about it."

"No." Pat turned to face him. "Dr. Paine says I should talk about it." She paused for breath, a swimmer about to plunge into cold water.

"My father," she said, "was a psychiatrist here in New York. When I was eight years old, a psychotic patient stabbed him to death with a bayonet he—my father—had kept as a souvenir from the war. His office was at the end of a long hall in the house we lived in. I had just gotten home from school and put my books down on the table in the foyer when I heard him call out. I ran down the hall and opened the door to his office, something I was never to do, under any circumstances. But I did, and I saw the patient—a very young man, very small—standing there with the bayonet in his hands. My father was still conscious, and he kept saying, 'Sit down, Allen. Just sit down.' But Allen didn't listen. He grabbed me and began beating me around my head, punching at my eyes until my mother and a colleague of my father's came in. He said he hadn't wanted to hurt me, but he didn't want any witnesses."

She had told the story as if she were giving him the synopsis of a television play.

He went over and put his arm around her. She felt soft and firm. "I'm sorry, Pat," he said.

Her body relaxed and she lay back, her head against his arm. "The worst wasn't the actual attack. I was too hysterical to know what was going on and I supposed I blocked it. It only came out much later that I thought I was being punished for opening the door when I had been clearly told not to. I mean, Nicky, for years I thought—unconsciously—that I had deserved it. And I was one of those children who are terrified of the dark. And suddenly it was dark all of the time."

She took off the aviator glasses, and he held her more closely in his arms.

She pulled away and dabbed at her eyes with a handkerchief. "I mustn't feel sorry for myself," she said. "Because I have my sight now."

"And you can see perfectly?"

"Twenty-twenty."

242

"But the glasses..."

"I'm self-conscious." She finished her club soda and set the glass down on a lacquered tray. "There's scar tissue that never quite healed."

He studied her. Her eyes were more silver than grey, perfectly shaped, and framed by thick blond lashes. "I can't see any scar tissue," he said and then, surprising both of them, he kissed her. Like her body, her lips were both soft and firm.

At first she responded, and then she pushed him away. "You don't have to feel sorry for me, Nick..."

"I usually pat women I feel sorry for on the shoulder." He reached for her hand. "I kissed you because I felt close to you."

"Perhaps," she said, taking back her hand. "But I don't think that explanation would go down very well with your friend." She walked to the door. "I'd better be going. We have an important operation tonight."

"Tonight?"

"Yes," she said, putting on her glasses. "We often perform experimental operations at night. Especially when they may be controversial. The night crew comes on at eleven and nonessential staff are sent home."

He followed her up the spiral staircase to the connecting door on the third floor. Before she went out, she gave him a long look through the unnecessary glasses. "Are you in love with her? I know it's none of my business, but I would like to know, Nick."

"Yes," he said. "I'm pretty sure I am."

"Goodnight, Nick. And thank you," she said, and was gone.

He thought about her, about her touch, her smell, all so different from Carla's, and he realized that he wanted to make love to her.

Then he heard the sound of the overhead camera and was again aware that he was being watched, that they had both been watched.

He went back down to the kitchen and looked into the freezer compartment of the refrigerator, hoping for ice cream. He shut the freezer door quickly and made do with an American cheese sandwich and more milk. There had been a leg of lamb in the freezer, and he tried not to think of the associations it brought to mind, of what he still had in front of him that evening.

Painfully aware of the cameras, he went up to the bedroom, took off his clothes, turned on the television set, and pretended he was watching.

He decided he would wait until ten, when Cecil would presumably begin preparing for the experimental operation and concentration would be off Harry Meyer's apartment.

When the ten o'clock news came on—"Do you know where your children are?"—he turned off the set and the light above the bed, and had the small satisfaction of hearing the camera above him switch off. He lay in the exact center of the circular bed, thinking about Carla and Pat, aware that his heart was beating too fast, that his mouth was too dry.

Then he took a half dose of one of Carla's

tranquilizers, got dressed, and went into Harry's study. He found the screwdriver and the pencil flashlight in the desk drawer where he had left them and transferred them to his trouser pockets. On impulse, he took the picture of his father as a young man and put that in his pocket too, understanding now why otherwise sane men wore St. Christopher medals, crosses, Stars of David.

He was going into action and he needed all the help he could get.

CHAPTER 24

The corridor seemed especially dark. He felt his way along it, attempting to keep his use of the flashlight to a minimum. He felt more anticipatory than anxious, like a kid playing night games. Unlike Pat, he had been a child who was comfortable in the dark, not needing or even wanting the hallway lights Harry had insisted be left on for him.

Touching the wall as he walked, he arrived at the stairwell emergency door, slid his MatchCode card into the slot and went through, still feeling adventurous. Maybe it's the tranquilizer, he told himself.

At the bottom of the stairwell, he inserted his card into another slot and walked confidently through the steel doorway, expecting to find himself in the entrance room to Storage. Instead, he almost walked into the arms of a garage attendant. Fortunately, those arms were engaged in opening the door of a dark green Porsche Targa with M.D. plates.

Nick dropped down behind one of the parked limousines and edged his way along the wall of the garage away from the attendant's booth. Somehow he had miscalculated; he had thought the stairs would lead him below street level into the Storage department, not into the garage.

The confident feeling was gone. Fright and disorientation had taken its place.

Taking a chance—he could always say he was in the garage on legitimate business; he was Harry Meyer's son—he stood up. The attendant was talking to a bald doctor in the Porsche, one hand on the radio-beeper attached to his belt, the other behind his back in the military pose all Harry Meyer service men seemed to find comfortable.

The big garage was fairly well filled, the cars parked in spaces defined by cement columns. There was an elevator on the far side, but he would not be able to reach it unobserved. And even if he could, he had no assurance that his card was programmed to operate it.

He scanned the ceiling for the fixture cameras. There were only two of them, one over the elevator, one over the garage door that led to 70th Street. The rest of the illumination, round circles of severe light, came from bulbs set in ordinary garage fixtures.

As the Porsche drove out the exit door, he saw another exit, a pair of swinging doors, between a Lincoln Continental and a BMW sedan. They were halfway around the garage, and he guessed that they would lead into one of the lobbies in the complex. Once in the lobby, he might be able to bluff his way into the elevator he and Pat had taken to the parts bank.

He began to make his way around the outer edge of the garage. Whoever had parked the cars had backed them into their spaces with great precision—in each case there were only six inches for Nick to slide through.

The garage was unexpectedly clean—the grey cement floor had recently been scrubbed down. No oil pools or tire marks defaced it. Each car had a yellow plastic pyramid on its roof, bearing a number for the owner to call when retrieving his car.

A pyramid had been placed too far to the left on a sloping Imperial roof, and as Nick squeezed by, his body brushed the car. The pyramid fell to the floor, creating a sound like a cymbal clash.

"What the Sam Hill..." The garage man put down the clipboard he was studying and came toward the Imperial.

The space next to it was empty; there was no place to hide, no way to turn and go back the way he had come. Then the elevator opened, a voice with a Middle European accent called out, "Number Fourteen, please. The black Bentley," and the garage attendant about-faced and trotted away.

It's like a ballet, Nick thought. Sweat stung his eyes.

By the time the attendant had delivered the

Bentley and was able to think about the Imperial again, Nick was at the swinging doors between the Continental and the BMW, searching for the MatchCode card slot. There wasn't any.

He pushed against one of the doors, but it didn't give. He knelt for a moment, wondering how he would be able to retrace his steps, hoping neither the Continental nor the BMW owner would have a sudden inclination to take a drive. Then the doors began to open, and he had just enough time to duck behind the BMW.

Two women in their mid-thirties with loose, low-cut dresses and the kind of simple haircuts that cost fifty dollars on 57th Street came through the doors and stopped a few feet from where Nick was crouching. They stood in the doorway arguing in polite East Coast voices about a subject that seemed to be important to both of them.

After a moment he had a feeling he was going to sneeze or cough, and he knew he couldn't stay crouched much longer. He tried to ease his position.

The women shifted their envelope purses from their hands to under their arms, and went on arguing.

"I was hoping for a different answer. From a person like you—"

"You haven't a clue as to what kind of a person I am, Eve, and I resent—"

"You resent everything. I wonder who you see me as? Probably your mother."

"Don't put me through your famous Freud trip, please. Spare me just this once, I beg you."

"Ladies," said the attendant from the other side of the BMW, startling Nick. "You're letting the air conditioning out."

The women came forward, allowing the swinging doors to close. Nick caught one door with his foot, almost toppling over with the effort, and when the women and the attendant were at the front of the garage he crept out into the September night air.

He was in a triangular courtyard. At the apex of the triangle was a door which led to the indoor pool. Another set of doors led into the section of the complex set aside for the nurses. The women who had entered the garage must have come from there.

At the far end of the base of the triangle was a narrow driveway leading to 71st Street. In the center of the base, under the overhang of the upper floors, was an opening of some sort. The windowless lower walls of the complex gave an eerie, other worldly feeling to the courtyard; its brick-paved floor made it seem almost medieval.

The only illumination came from the high-powered headlights of an old-fashioned white ambulance. Nick pressed himself against a wall, thanking the architect for the shadows made by the overhang. The back doors of the ambulance were open. In the reflected light, it looked like a bakery truck.

Two men in white shirts and trousers were removing what might have been sacks of flour, loading them onto shiny steel gurney carts, and wheeling the carts to the opening Nick had noticed. Here the sacks were unloaded and placed on a conveyor belt which fed into the opening. It took him a moment to realize that the sacks contained the cadavers Mr. Rios had spoken of as "night deposits."

He watched the two men working silently, sweating in the Indian summer night. A canvas sack ripped as it was being put on the conveyor belt, and something fell out. It was a hand, long and white. One of the men fitted it back and sent the sack down into the basement of the Harry Meyer.

When the ambulance was empty, the men closed the back doors, got into the front seat, and drove off down the driveway that would take them to 71st Street. The ambulance's headlights showed Nick the outline of a Harry Meyer doorman waiting to let them out.

With the ambulance gone and the small triangle of sky blocked by clouds, it was almost totally dark in the courtyard.

Nick waited until he heard the doorman shut the gates of the driveway before he approached the opening. He pushed aside a vinyl flap and shone his pencil flashlight through the square hole into which the cadavers had gone. He saw a canvas gondola, about six feet long and three feet wide, at the top of the conveyor belt. When he grabbed the edge of the gondola, the belt began to move; it was self-activating. The gondola, he reasoned, must be programmed to deliver its contents down into the Storage area—Mr. Rios would check his consignment in the morning—

and return automatically to the top of the conveyor belt.

He knew if he let himself think about it, he wouldn't be able to do it. Holding the gondola with one hand, steadying himself against the brick wall of the complex with the other, he stepped in and crouched.

He had prepared himself for the total absence of light, for the roll of the conveyor, for the claustrophobic feeling of hurtling down a narrow chute. He had not thought about the smell of formaldehyde, the curiously wet canvas that enclosed him, the shallow pool of some unidentifiable liquid on the bottom of the gondola. The liquid was seeping into his trousers, touching his skin, and he realized that it had drained off the cadavers. It was not blood; it wasn't thick enough. He tried not to think.

The gondola stopped abruptly and its front end opened. Nick found himself sliding down the conveyor belt into an aluminum chute neatly lined with cadavers in canvas sacks. The sack in front of him was torn; when he pointed the pencil flashlight at it, he could see part of a face, the eyes disconcertingly open.

He heard the front of the gondola snap shut as it began its return to the top of the conveyor. He climbed over the side of the aluminum chute and shone the flashlight about him. He saw a series of steel tables, instruments enclosed neatly in Lucite boxes, and several stainless steel trolleys, each one holding a canvas sack.

He stood against a wall of refrigerator

compartments, listening to the sound of the refrigerator motors, trying to get it together. He wasn't sure he could. The light from his flashlight hit a steel pan filled with entrails, and he put his hand to his mouth. After a few seconds he realized that his hand was wet with the liquid from the bottom of the gondola. Some of it was in his mouth. He vomited into a steel sink. Each time he thought it was over, the taste of the liquid came back to him, and he vomited again. It took almost ten minutes before he stopped for good, before he felt he could move again.

He would have to be methodical, he told himself; he must leave no trace of his visit. He found a green sheet, cleaned up the mess he had made at the sink, and stowed the sheet in the back of a compartment that seemed to be a repository for odd cleaning equipment. When the sheet was found, it would be attributed to a queasy first-year medical student.

He checked the ceiling of the dissecting room. The light fixtures were of thick plastic; they were unlikely to be hiding motorized cameras, so he could probably turn on the lights with little risk. In the end he decided not to, fearing that cameras might be hidden in other places.

He stepped out into the central corridor, rubbing his hands against his trousers. He had washed them at the sink, but there was still a residue of sticky liquid on them.

He had become confused when Doctor Pollette had taken him through the maze of rooms in full light. Now, with only the illumination of his pencil flashlight, he was afraid to wander too far off the main corridor. He looked for familiar machinery as he walked, and was reassured. The Van de Graaff accelerator was a landmark, as was the hyperbaric perfusion unit, a white plastic chest-high object that Dr. Pollette had pointed out just before she had taken him into the storage areas.

The first storage room he entered contained the freezer chests he remembered. When he opened one of the chests, his flashlight revealed neatly labeled vacuum flasks arranged in metal racks, each containing a freeze-dried human heart valve. Directions for soaking the valves in solutions of penicillin so that they would regain their former texture had been taped to the inside of the freezer door. Each flask was labeled with a coded strip of plastic, giving the MatchCode of the donor, the date of deposit.

He left the freezer door open as a sign post and went into the adjoining room which was lined with similar chests. Opening several of them, he found that he was becoming used to the kidneys and the hearts and the unidentifiable organs stored in the transparent plastic flasks, each with its own MatchCode label. None bore the MatchCode he was searching for.

The next door he opened led into a narrow hallway Doctor Pollette had not shown him. At the end of the hall was a steel-walled room that contained a six-by-six-foot walk-in freezer locker. He opened the heavy door and went in. The locker was several degrees colder than any other part of

254

the storage area; his breath formed little clouds of steam in the light from his flashlight. He rubbed his hands together, trying to keep circulation going.

The door closed itself behind him as his flashlight played on the narrow stainless steel drawers that filled the locker. Each drawer had a label next to its handle. Only two bore current dates.

He pulled out one of the drawers, trying to prepare himself for what might be in it. No amount of preparation could have protected him. A mutilated male body lay in the drawer. It had been slashed open from the neck to the penis. A piece of rubbery pink cord trailed out of the incision, curling on the bottom of the drawer. It was, he realized, part of the cadaver's lower intestine. He wanted to stuff it back in, to somehow close the obscene wound. The body's face was a young one. Its eyes were closed, a thin yellow mustache giving it a rakish air.

Nick slammed the drawer closed, and the freezer reverberated with the noise. He told himself that he had to be clinical, objective. One part of him was. The other was screaming.

He shone his flashlight on the face of the cadaver in the next drawer he opened. A girl. Snow White after she ate the witch's apple and fell into a deep sleep. Her long black hair had been arranged to frame her white oval face. Her eyes were closed, her lips looked as if they had been recently made up. Lying there, she seemed to be waiting. For the Prince?

Nick moved the flashlight down past the young breasts, and then he shouted as if he had been stabbed. The body had been cut literally in half. Everything below the rim of the pelvis was gone.

He dropped the flashlight, but it didn't break. He picked it up carefully and aimed it at the cadaver's arm. He read the plastic tag around its wrist:

ZIP11963-PACEel-18-STU(=)

On the hand was a mock gold ring, indicating that this was a member of the senior class of Pierson High School. The ring was a fraudulent piece of jewelry with a red-glass center. It made her seem not only violated, but pathetic. He touched the hand. It was frozen solid. He tried to remove the ring, but the finger was bent as if it had been frozen in the act of grasping something. He pulled down hard on the finger, knowing what would happen, assuring himself that this wasn't bothering Betty Pace.

He heard a snap and looked down disbelievingly at the thing in his hand. He removed the ring, and placed the finger on the bottom of the drawer and shut it slowly, as if afraid to wake her. He pointed the flashlight inside the ring and read Betty Pace's name and the date of the anticipated graduation.

She already has graduated, he thought, putting the ring in his pocket. He went to the freezer door. It didn't give on the first try. Or the second or the third. Or the tenth. He began to shout out, to beat the door with his fists. The sound of his shouts boomeranged around the freezer and came back to him. He stopped shouting and stood back. Steadying his hand, willing himself to be calm, he played the flashlight methodically around the frame of the door. The lever was high up, to the right. He pressed down on it and let himself out.

His hands immediately began to burn fiercely. A good sign, he told himself; it meant he wouldn't have frostbite. The sharp pain in his hands eased as he searched for the freezer compartment door he had left open as a sign post to get him back to the main corridor. But it wasn't where he thought it should be. After five minutes of wandering around, he knew he was lost. The compartment doors, he realized, were like the freezer door; they had been designed to close themselves.

It took him what seemed like hours to get back to the dissecting room. It didn't matter; he was almost finished, almost home free. He found Dr. Pollette's office and used his MatchCode card to get in. The room was large, warm, painted a surprising peach color. A poster designed to look like a window had been pasted on the wall; through the fake window, sitting on a country fence, plump bluebirds sunned themselves. Two modern chairs, wood slatted affairs, faced a dark red Formica Parson's table that served Dr. Pollette as a desk. There were white-painted metal file cabinets against the wall. A strong odor of perfume hung about the room, a reminder of her considerable presence.

The computer terminal sat on the right side of the desk, a final touch to the modern woman's office. It was, in its way, as frightening as the rest of the Storage area.

He stood on the desk and undid the light fixture, careful not to step on the plastic cubes that contained pictures of fat children and thin, vulnerable parents.

He slid his MatchCode card into the terminal and typed out Betty Pace's MatchCode. After a moment, white letters appeared on the gray screen.

```
Revised
MatchCode:   ZIP11963-PACE-el-18-F-
             STU-(=)WOMB (=) Status:
             PRJCT XCTD

             (CROSS REF:  TOKAL-PACEal
             -28-F-RYLTY-(+))
```

He pressed the "Printout" key on the console, and a thin sheet of yellow computer paper slid out of the machine with the revised MatchCode on it. He put it in the pocket of his jacket where he had stored the ring.

Then he obeyed an impulse that had been in the back of his mind for some time: he typed his own data on the console keyboard. The white letters appeared on the screen, heightening the arid taste of fear and vomit in his mouth.

MatchCode: ZIP19106-MILLER*-28-
            RPRTR-POT.DON(A==) ALL
            ORGANS - ALL LIMBS -
            (PRIMARY) Status: HOLD-
            PRJCT PENDING name at
            Birth: MEYERn

            (CROSS REF: NOT AVAIL-
            ABLE)

CHAPTER 25

He used his MatchCode card to unlock the outer door, attempting to keep the significance of his own readout under wraps, under a rock, under something, anything. He was afraid to take it out, examine it, accept what it meant.

But it kept popping up, that significance, so fast and so hard it left him breathless.

They weren't keeping him around, making TV movies of his life, because he was Harry Meyer's son or even because he was one of two men who had control of one hundred million dollars.

They were keeping him around because they wanted *his* parts.

He thought of Betty Pace's half body in the steel drawer. Despite the refrigerated air, he began to sweat again.

Why they wanted his parts—*All organs ...limbs primary...status: Prjct Imminent* —was something he didn't really want to know. He did know that he didn't want to end up in the back freezer with his intestines creeping out of his stomach, his heart beating in somebody else's body.

His heart was going to stop beating entirely if the elevator didn't come. He jiggled the card in the slot. The possibility that the elevator had shut down for the night became more certain when he reinserted the card and heard no sound of responding equipment.

And there was no other way out. *All organs . . . limbs primary*. What did that mean? The conveyor belt was activated by the gondola, and that was at the top of the belt awaiting new arrivals. *Prjct imminent . . .* How imminent? Tonight? Tomorrow morning? He realized he was no longer the boy sleuth, looking for clues. He was a man on the run, and he had trapped himself very successfully. It would be convenient for them; they could kill him and dissect him in one easy location.

There was one possibility.

He forced himself to go back inside Storage, to walk past the dissecting rooms and the hyperbaric perfusion unit to the dumbwaiter Dr. Pollette had demonstrated, the one that could rush parts to the operating room.

The dumbwaiter's door was open. He stood on a chair and maneuvered himself into it. On his knees, his chin against his neck, he was just able to reach out and touch the button that shut the door and set the dumbwaiter in operation. It rose smoothly and silently for several minutes and then it stopped, and he climbed out.

261

He was in a small, dark, tiled room about four feet wide and five feet long. There was a light fixture, but since there was no direct light, the camera would be inoperative. There was a door at one end, a window cut into a long wall. He went to the window and found that he was looking out onto the stage of the fifteenth floor's main operating theater. The experimental operation Pat had mentioned was about to be performed.

The stage was crowded. Robed figures moved back and forth across it in choreographed movements.

The stage was set up very much as it had been when he and Pat had witnessed the monkey-to-man heart transplantation. The huge kettledrum of operating lights was again ablaze, illuminating the two operating tables, each with its own complement of surgical teams, scrub nurses, draped Mayo stands. The two anesthesiologists sat behind their Lucite screens, fiddling with equipment, checking the computer screens at the rear of the stage which reported on their patients' life functions.

TV cameras suspended from cables over the operating tables relayed what was happening to the theater's monitor screens. There was also a monitor in the room from which Nick was observing, next to the window, and he switched his attention to it. The screen showed the two operating tables. On each was a draped, anesthetized patient. Only small strips of skin were exposed, just below and above their shoulder and hip joints.

He had to get out of that little tiled room. The door led him into a narrow hall that extended to the left wing of the operating stage. Some ten feet away, halfway between him and the stage, was a door that he hoped would lead to the central corridor of the fifteenth floor.

Two doctors in gowns and masks emerged suddenly from that door and stood looking through the big picture window across the corridor at the activity on the operating stage. There was no way he could get past them; he would have to wait until they moved. He stepped back into the tiled room and returned to the window and the monitor screen.

Pfft ... Pfft ...
His left arm reaches out.
Pft ... pft ...
The largest of the screens set into the computer wall glows with light.
Pfffffft ...
He brings the left arm back to its original position, folds it along his side, the elbow joint facing outward.
Mssssh ...
He elevates himself so that his eyes are level with the TV screen.
Whft ...
The volume level rises. Now he can hear as well as see what is taking place on the fifteenth floor operating stage.

Cecil, in surgeon's coat and mask, stood at the

center of the stage between the two operating tables, his tall body dwarfing the surgical teams about him. A thin cord ran from under his mask, connecting a miniature microphone to a battery unit in the pocket of his coat. Both his voice and image were being recorded by a tape camera set in an overhead track.

Nick turned up the volume control of his monitor. Listening, he thought how theatrical Cecil was.

"...will provide the doctors of the world," Cecil was saying, his gold-framed glasses glinting in the reflected lights above and around him, "with a visual blueprint of a revolutionary transplantation, one that has never before been successfully completed."

He stepped away from the operating tables as other doctors began to attach tubes to the patients on them.

"In transplantation research," Cecil went on, "there has been a tendency for certain achievements to be greeted by the medical community as the last word, so to speak. We have now succeeded, say these self-appointed guardians of public funds; there is no more to be done, no higher plateau to be reached. Yet for thirty years I have been attempting to climb ever higher, to scale a peak my colleagues, to a man, have said does not exist. It is perhaps immodest of me, but I am happy to announce that today I shall conquer that supposedly nonexistent peak."

Removing the gold glasses, he pinched his nose as if he were weary from long hours in the laboratory. Then he replaced the glasses, looked directly into the camera with a wide, engaging smile, and began to speak again as the camera moved over the bodies of the men on the operating tables.

The man on the right was identified as Buddy Gerber, twenty-four years old, Caucasian, a man with a history of incapacitating illness. He didn't look like a sick man, Nick thought. Even under the surgical draping, strong muscles were apparent. He looked like a man in his prime. The patient on the left was Morris Gerber; he was fifty-eight, the father of Buddy. Morris Gerber was so short as to be abnormal. The draping seemed to end halfway to where his body should have extended.

"The details," Cecil was saying, "of how we conducted experiments on thousands of creatures we designated X/Gf mice, of the long years we spent working with those remarkable and admirable animals, will be recounted elsewhere in a work now in progress. Suffice it to say that the X/Gf mice are an albino strain developed here at the Harry Meyer. They are exceptionally free of spontaneous cancers, viruses, and other foreign infiltrations. We needed a reliable test subject for the immunosuppressant we conceived—an immunosuppressant that acts very much the way cancer does in hoodwinking the body into accepting an alien. In the written text I've alluded to, you will find details of the various steps and procedures we took to ensure that the immunosuppressant—named, appropriately, X/Gf—

did indeed do what we hoped it would: short-circuit the immune response to major limb transplantation. Today, you will see..."

Nick went to the door and opened it. The two doctors were still in the corridor, watching through the picture window. *All organs...All limbs (Primary)...* He went back to the monitor.

The screen showed the men on the operating tables. Metal frames extended over each table from just below the patients' faces. Scrub nurses were draping the frames with blue towels, creating tents that would keep the patients' breaths from infecting the wounds the surgeons would make.

Nick studied Morris Gerber's face. His deep set eyes were surrounded by wrinkles and lines; the skin hung loosely from his face. His son Buddy, on the other hand, had good facial skin, strong and taut.

"This filmed procedure will serve as an historic record of the first successful transplantation of human limbs from one individual to another—from a son with a critical heart malfunction to a father whose circulatory problems have caused him to live for years in a state of near paralysis. We can be sure that..."

Nick was surprised that it was the young, healthy-looking Buddy who was ill, that the father was to be the recipient. He was conscious suddenly of his own arms and legs.

"...the father's limbs were removed exactly forty-two days ago. Mister Gerber has made a remarkable recovery, both physiologically and psychologically. One week after the multiple

266

amputation, he began receiving hourly injections of X/Gf-1, which will effectively suspend the immune response to the transplanted limbs, while leaving enough of the response intact to ward off common bacteria and viruses. Even so, for precaution's sake, he was kept in germ-free isolation. Mr. Gerber experienced remarkably few side effects due to the injections—fever, fairly low-grade; a few aches and pains. All expected. All softened by his knowledge of the pivotal role he is playing in the furtherance of medical science. And, of course, by the knowledge that he would soon walk again, would soon be able to use his hands and arms.

"We began our search for the perfect patients several years ago, when development of X/Gf-1 was still in its infancy. We had hoped for twins, because similarity of tissue is the key to this operation, but in some ways a father-son pair offers a more valid test . . ."

Nick turned down the volume and looked out into the corridor again. The two doctors hadn't moved. He wondered if he could bluff his way out, but without a surgical coat and mask he wouldn't have much of a chance. And now it wasn't merely a question of being reprimanded. *All organs . . . All limbs (Primary) . . .* He would have to wait until the operation was over. He turned the volume up again.

". . . to begin, we will perform a dual interscapulothoracic on Buddy and immediately transplant his upper extremities onto the torso of Morris. While that transplant is taking place, a second team of surgeons will be performing a dual hemipelvectomy on Buddy, after which his lower limbs will be transplanted onto his father."

Nick hoped that the two doctors blocking his exit would be part of the second team. Looking at the monitor, he wondered if Buddy really had a bad heart.

"The interscapulothoracic amputation," Cecil was saying, "is a radical amputation of the shoulder and upper extremity. The operation entails *en bloc* resection of the entire clavicle, scapula, shoulder and upper extremity. In addition, the entire axillary contents are removed." Cecil wiped his glasses with his handkerchief and looked toward the table on which Buddy Gerber lay. The camera switched its focus to the table.

A surgeon held out his gloved right hand. A nurse slapped a scalpel into it. The surgeon looked at the anesthesiologist, received a go-ahead, and inserted the scalpel deep into Buddy's left shoulder, peeling the skin away as if it were the outer layer of an onion.

"The incision," Cecil's voice went on, "has been made directly over the clavicle from the sterno-clavicular joint to within three centimeters of the acromioclavicular joint. The clavicle is being transected with a Gigli saw to provide a five centimeter segment."

Nick watched the surgeon's hand insert what looked like a wire with saw teeth into the bloody mass of exposed muscle, while an assistant angled Buddy so the surgeon could maneuver inside the incision. The surgeon gave the saw to the nurse and held out his hand for the scalpel.

"The incision is being carried inferiorly and the pectoralis major muscle is being divided on the chest wall. The subclavius muscle and fascia are now divided into the area of the segmental clavicular resection. The underlying subclavian artery is dissected cleanly for a distance of two centimeters. All superficial adventitia will be removed before an attempt is made to ligate the vessels."

Nick moved away from the monitor, unable to watch them systematically take Buddy Gerber's arm from him. He could not move away from Cecil's relentlessly informative voice.

"...finally, the levator scapulae and the rhomboidcus major and minor are divided along the medial border of the scapulae, and with this the entire upper extremity, with its axillary contents, is removed from the chest wall."

A soft, sucking sound, as if a plumber had finally unclogged a blocked-up drain, came from the monitor's speaker. Nick looked back at the screen. Two surgeons were carrying Buddy's blood-dripping left arm and shoulder to the table upon which his father lay, holding it as if it were the specialty of the house.

Morris Gerber, his limbless torso exposed now, lay quietly in sedated sleep. Using forceps, a surgeon carefully lifted the folds of the skin where Morris Gerber's shoulder should have been and began to fit the new shoulder, his son's shoulder, onto his body.

Nick turned from the monitor and stared through the window at the stage. Another surgeon had just inserted a scalpel into Buddy Gerber's right shoulder.

Nick went to the door. He was breathing much too fast, and his body was again soaked with sweat. He felt sick and weak. But the two surgeons were gone from the corridor, presumably to take their place on the stage, to help quarter Buddy Gerber.

Nick shut the door quietly behind him and ran down the corridor to the exit door. Before he opened it, he looked back through the picture window at the stage and was immediately sorry that he had.

Buddy Gerber's right shoulder and arm were being wrenched away.

CHAPTER 26

The corridor ended in a flight of carpeted stairs that led down to the fourteenth floor and a door that required the use of his MatchCode card.

The room behind the door smelled like the common room of his old fraternity house—an aroma of sweat, cigarettes, beer and marijuana. He knew immediately where he was: the foreign students' dormitory.

The designer had not been as lavish here as with the rest of the complex; the room was unappealing in its shoddy modernity. The floor was red linoleum tile; the walls were plasterboard white; and the windows, fronting Madison Avenue, were covered with bamboo blinds. The furniture—vinyl sofas, plastic game tables—might have been ordered from a catalogue. Twin sets of swing-doors faced each other from opposite ends of the room.

The sight of Buddy Gerber's arm and shoulder being taken from him returned suddenly, and

Nick closed his eyes for a minute. When the nauseous feeling passed, he crossed the room to the nearest set of doors, looked through a round glass set in one of them, and saw an elevator bank. He was about to push the door open when he heard footsteps, and then a uniformed guard came into sight, patrolling the floor.

He moved back into the room and sat down at a desk on which someone had left an empty eyeglass case and a copy of *Rolling Stone*. Opening the newspaper, his attention was caught by the framed "Student Regulations" on the wall before him.

Thick red letters gave a long, numbered list of rules for all interns living in the foreign-student wing of the Harry Meyer complex. Most of them were predictable prohibitions—no alcoholic beverages were permitted in the students' rooms, etc.—but Number Nine was especially interesting. "All students not on duty are encouraged to spend weekend and holiday time away from the complex. Permission must be granted by the individual's section chief. The student must sign out upon leaving, and in upon returning, in the register kept in the student common room."

A final paragraph noted that there was a twenty-four hour manned elevator, and that students were not to discuss hospital affairs with outsiders.

Nick reached over to the little stand on which the register lay. Two students with the word "Israel" after their names had signed out to spend the Jewish holiday at an address in Scarsdale with a family called Shapiro. The register indicated that they shared dormitory room number 11.

"You new here?"

Nick closed the register and turned. They put the second team up here, he thought; this guard was noticeably older than the others. "Yes," he said, trying for a British accent. "Only arrived today."

"No one told me about a new arrival," the man said, aggrieved. "What's your name?"

"Anthony Lyle. Doctor Paine told me I needn't go through the formalities until tomorrow morning. Of course if there's something I should be doing...?"

"No. That's okay. As long as Doctor Paine said..."

"He and my father are great chums. They went to school together."

For a minute Nick thought he had overdone it. But the guard said, "Well, that's all right then. But be sure and see Miss Youngman in the morning."

"I'll do that. Goodnight."

"'Night."

When the guard had left, he walked through the doors at the other end of the room into a corridor lined with closed doors. Behind them, he heard rock music and people talking. He sniffed. Someone was smoking marijuana. He wished he could share it.

Number 11 wasn't locked or even, he discovered when he got inside, lockable. He did not switch on the overhead light, but crossed the room and raised the bamboo blind, letting the Madison Avenue street light in.

The room was small and grey, with industrial carpeting on the floor. There were two beds, two chests of drawers, a Klee print over one of them, and two metal lamps on a shared night stand. The shallow closet held a few jackets and trousers of Israeli design; a dozen stiff white intern's uniforms were piled on the top shelf. The chests of drawers held underpants and khaki shirts. There was an Israeli flag and a half eaten chocolate bar in one top drawer. Suddenly hungry, Nick ate the chocolate.

He lay down on one of the beds, on top of a bedspread made of a material the consistency of cardboard. He got up almost immediately and let down the blind. Back on the bed, his hands behind his head, he listened to a muted conversation, in what seemed to be French, coming through the thin walls. He attempted to make out occasional words, his mind refusing to acknowledge what he had seen, what he had to do next.

In the morning, when the sun came up, the overhead cameras in the triplex would tell them he wasn't in Harry's circular bed. They would search the whole complex. Eventually they would get to this room. They would find him. And they would know that he knew. *All organs . . . All limbs (Primary) . . . Prjct imminent . . .*

The only plan he could come up with was to wait until morning and then, pretending to be an intern, simply leave via the elevator. It probably wouldn't work, but it was the best he could do. He closed his eyes, just for a moment.

They didn't open again until nine o'clock the next morning.

It took a few seconds before he knew where he was. When he did know, he got up from the bed and opened a door across the room, expecting that it would lead to a bathroom, which it did. What he hadn't expected was a bathroom that could also be entered from another bedroom. A small, hairy man stood at the basin in white intern's trousers, shaving.

"Who are you?" the man asked, not surprised.

Nick stepped back. He could hear the camera in the bathroom. "Tony Lyle," he said, holding out his hand. "Newly arrived."

"And they put you in David and Moishe's room?" The man spoke with a distinctly French accent. "It would have been amusing had they been there."

"Doctor Paine said it wouldn't matter for the one night."

"Doctor Paine?"

"Yes. He and my father are great chums."

The lie impressed the little Frenchman as it had the guard. He finished shaving with one swipe of his lethal looking razor, wiped his hand on a towel, and extended it. "My name is Jacques Barmont. I welcome you to the Harry Meyer. They work us too hard, but it is a very interesting, exciting place."

Nick shook the hand, but hung back in the doorway to David and Moishe's room.

"Please," Jacques said. "I am finished. It is all yours." About to leave through the opposite door, he turned. "Would you care to have breakfast? A few of us are going out in about ten minutes to a horrible place with terrible food and extravagant prices. But it is better than the cafeteria." He looked down at his white trousers. "I am, unfortunately, on duty at noon."

Nick said yes, he would like to join them, and Jacques left, closing the door behind him. Nick switched off the light and stepped into the bathroom.

When he had finished, he went through the Israelis' effects and found a pair of drugstore sunglasses and a tweed cap. He tried on one of the intern uniforms. The trousers were short, but would do. He borrowed a pair of Moishe's—or David's?—white socks, put on his own loafers, transferred everything from his pockets into the uniform, and hung his own clothes in the back of the closet. He hoped the boys wouldn't fight over them.

With the cap in his pocket, but wearing the sunglasses, he went into the common room.

"You look like a medical James Bond," Jacques said, introducing Nick to the two Indians, Dal and Kumar, and the Italian Paolo, who were waiting with him. Nick shook their hands, said the appropriate things. His hope now lay in the possibility that they still hadn't discovered he was missing.

In the corridor with the other men, he waited anxiously for the elevator. An ordinary push button called it; a Harry Meyer uniformed guard ran it. The guard stared at them, not shutting the doors. "You guys sign out?"

"Certainly," said Jacques, winking at Nick. "Not once, but twice."

"Wise guys." The guard took them down.

They came out into a lobby that faced Madison Avenue. Nick started for the exit, but Jacques took his arm. "No, *mon ami*. Closed. It's a holiday. The Jews' holiday. We have to walk through to Fifth Avenue."

Feeling as if each camera they passed under was focused on him, Nick tried to walk naturally, to respond to Jacques's conversation. They were going to be great friends, it seemed. Jacques chatted amiably. "...most of them are from countries you have never heard of. Uncivilized..."

The two doormen at the Fifth Avenue entrance stood with their backs turned. Their attention was on the crowds, the parade. They barely noticed as Nick and the four interns came out into the September morning.

"What is this celebration?" asked Dal, a dark-skinned man with a skimpy beard.

"You don't know?" Jacques laughed. "It's the pederasts."

Fifth Avenue was a sea of marchers and floats. Musicians and protesters, frustrated vaudevillians, and vociferous supporters of gay rights filled the Avenue for as far as the eye could see, a solid body of good-natured movement, everyone swimming with the tide. Policemen lined the curbs behind sawhorse barricades, attempting to contain the crowds on the sidewalk.

Nick felt as if he had stepped out of the twentieth century and back into the Middle Ages, into a riotous fair. Even the costumes of the marchers—gold lamé jump suits, sturdy patterned ponchos—had a timeless quality about them. The men with their finely-shaped beards and the women with their long, free-flying hair could have come out of an illustration from a book of Arthurian legends. He put on his borrowed tweed cap and followed Jacques and the others up to the barricades, only dimly realizing that he was free.

Jacques was explaining how the parade had become a political issue, and how the mayor had attempted to sidestep it by issuing a permit for the day of the Jewish New Year, thinking no one would march. "He is a little wrong, do you not think?" Jacques said, waving his hand at the crowds, enjoying both the event and the mayor's chagrin.

A group of women marched by bearing placards reading "Out Of The Closet And Into The Streets," "Gays Do Not Rape," "Save Our Children From Anita Bryant." Behind them a group of young men wearing skull caps and tight shorts carried a banner reading, "Start The New Year Right! Fight For Gay Rights!"

"It is Gay Freedom Day," Jacques explained unnecessarily. "Oh, *Mon Dieu*, look at that!"

Five men in pink trousers and T-shirts were

passing. They carried a pink banner that read, "Anita Sucks Oranges"; over and over again they chanted, "Human rights are absolute." More men and women, grouped according to sex, came after them carrying red, white, blue, green placards with slogans favoring equal rights for homosexuals.

Nick glanced back at the complex. At the Fifth Avenue entrance, the two doormen were still enjoying the parade, but Lawrence was there now too, talking earnestly into his radio.

He looked for a way to escape across Fifth Avenue. Too tough. The policemen were in riot gear.

"We are Proud Gay Parents," proclaimed a sign held aloft by a middle-aged couple. He was dressed in a business suit; she wore a hat. They looked as if they were going to church.

Lawrence was scanning the crowd. The doormen were back at their posts now, talking into their radios.

A squad of men on motorcycles, dressed in black leather jackets, trousers and boots, drove by. The Greek letter, Lambda, symbol of the homosexual movement, was painted in silver on the backs of their jackets.

The elevator man who had taken Nick and the interns down was with Lawrence now, talking, his face red.

A flat-bed trailer carrying Lesbian mothers and their children went past. Nick tried to move back, but the crowd behind him pushed him up against the barricade.

Lawrence was holding a pair of binoculars. They were aimed directly at Nick.

A float carrying college kids in blue jeans and T-shirts passed by. "Straights For Gay Rights" was painted on its side in orange and pink day-glo letters. A stocky boy in his early twenties was talking into a microphone. "I'm as straight as they come," he said. A group of male marchers in white gym shorts shouted, "Sure!" "But I believe," he went on, "in the struggle for rights. We have got to support our gay brothers and sisters..."

Why weren't they making any attempt to get him? Then Nick saw two men standing at the outer edge of the crowd behind him. They were not in uniform, but they were burly enough to be Harry Meyer guards.

The policeman in front of him was as nervous as he was. Nick could see the sweat spreading under the man's arms, darkening the sides of his blue shirt. What was he afraid of? A riot? The people on the sidewalk were pushing towards the street, trying for a better view. Nick was afraid to turn around. He looked at his watch. It was ten forty-five. He had little more than an hour to get to Shep at his office.

A huge float, designed to look like a battleship, distracted everyone as it sailed up Fifth Avenue. The long banner at the ship's masthead declared, in blue and gold glitter letters, "The Gay Liberation Front." On the side of the ship was painted, "USS Freedom." A group of young men stood on the deck dressed in chorus-line versions of World War II sailor suits. They were posturing, trading insults with the crowds, their hands on their hips, their lips pursed, caricaturing stereotypical homosexuals.

As the crowd laughed at the most outrageous sailor, Nick risked a turn. One of the men who might have been a Harry Meyer guard was a few feet behind him. The other was advancing to the left. At the hospital entrance, Lawrence still held the binoculars to his eyes.

Nick edged past the barricade, pushed the sweating policeman aside, and moved out into the street. "Hey, sailor," he called up to the crowd's favorite. "Want to have a little fun?"

The cop made an ineffectual grab for Nick as he walked up to the side of the float. The crowd cheered.

"Climb aboard, baby," the boy said. He threw a rope ladder over the side. Nick grabbed it and climbed up. The crowd was applauding. The boy shouted, "One more for our side!"

Once on top of the float, Nick looked back. The two men he had thought were after him were standing where he had left them, their eyes on the next float. Lawrence and the doormen were still at their posts, their radios back in their belts.

"This ain't no free ride," the boy was saying, imitating Mae West. "You're going to have to work off your passage, honey."

"Oh, yeah?" Nick said, moving across to the other side of the ship. He was relieved to see another rope ladder hanging there.

"Oh, yeah. First I want a little kiss. For rescuing you. Then..."

The boy looked older up close. Under the makeup, his spoiled angel's face was sour and angry.

Nick kissed him on the cheek, put his tweed cap on the boy's head and went over the side, climbing down the rope ladder. He could hear the sailors wise-cracking as he descended: "Don't worry Steven, there are other fish in the sea . . ." "But he was the only man I ever loved!"

The crowd was thinner on the Central Park side. He pushed through it into the park, wondering why they had made no effort to get him. Had Lawrence received orders on his radio not to pursue him?

He looked at his watch again. It was almost eleven. He began to run, passing joggers and the slower bikers. It was a beautiful September day, still pleasantly warm. The sky was comic-book blue and the trees looked as if they had been lifted from a Disney cartoon. He felt as if he were running in a tricky animated short; he was real, but everything else had been drawn.

He came out of the park at 59th Street, but the parade was still blocking Fifth Avenue. It took him a valuable ten minutes to get to 57th Street, past the hot dog, falafel and knish stands, the pretzel ladies, the barefoot kids with their tape decks, the tourists—men with sideburns, women with Farah Fawcett hair-dos—all open-mouthed at what was moving up Fifth Avenue. At 57th Street, where the cops were letting the cross-town traffic through, he got across. On Madison Avenue, he stuffed the eyeglasses and the intern's jacket into a garbage can, turned uptown and kept walking. The green Ford was where he had left it, at Madison and 68th.

It was eleven thirty-five; there was still time to get to Shep before noon.

Driving up Madison, before he swung right on 70th Street, he saw the Harry Meyer Hospital ahead of him, looking as solid as if it had stood for centuries—safe, serene, secure. He wondered why he didn't just pick up Carla and head for the hills. But deep in his gut he knew that no matter how far he went, they would be waiting for him.

CHAPTER 27

At five minutes to twelve, he parked the Ford in a near-empty lot across from Shep's office building on Centre Street, deserted now except for early lunch takers.

Like the other melancholy government buildings on Centre Street, Shep's building had gone up in the 1930s. It was tall, narrow, its once white concrete façade a dirty grey, the black Art Deco frieze at its top chipped and fading. Nick walked up the few steps that led to the glass front doors and knocked. Inside, an old, fat man wearing a faded khaki shirt and trousers got up from his desk with what seemed enormous effort. He walked slowly to the doors, opened one of them slightly, and glared at Nick.

"Building's closed today. Jews' New Year."

Nick grabbed the door before he could close it. "I have an appointment with Shepard Gordon."

The old man relaxed his hold on the door.

"Nick Miller," Nick said.

"Miller?"

"Or Meyer?"

"People getting so they don't know their own name." The old man admitted him and waddled back to his seat. "Elevators back there. Last car's working. Push seven."

"Mister Gordon up there?"

"I only open doors in this building. Information gal comes on tomorrow morning at nine." He bent over the puzzle he was working on in an old copy of *Presbyterian Life*.

Guy has a lot of charm, Nick thought. Walking across the black marble lobby, he wondered where all the money had come from to build this kind of building in 1936, and if it was entirely occupied by government organizations. There was no directory in the lobby, only an empty lacquered-wood information booth at the head of a stairway. Above the stairway hung a sign that said: "Subway—Uptown-Downtown IRT." Below that another sign informed the public that the nearest operating station was two blocks north.

Nick got out of the elevator on the seventh floor. His stomach had begun to churn, and he longed for a glass of milk, a tranquilizer, a joint, a motherly woman to kiss his forehead and tell him he was a good boy.

"Shep!" he shouted into the empty, unlit reception area. It was Standard Government Waiting Room in design, honey-colored chairs lined up in even rows, waiting for people to sit down and wait. "Shep!"

"Nick? In here."

He went through a low wooden gate and past several incredibly neat desks, each phone in its proper place, each blotter a virgin. He opened a thick, paneled door that had been left slightly ajar.

It was a large office with four windows with vertical blinds, two sofas, covered in what might have been green leather, one upholstered wing chair, and another impossibly neat desk with Shep behind it. On the wall behind him was a signed photograph of the President. The other walls bore studio photographs of Brendi and the girls wearing expensive dresses. A computer console sat on a corner table, next to a plastic coffee making machine.

"So you're a four-window man." Nick said.

"I told you I was a big shot, didn't I? You want coffee? You look like death."

"Death warmed over," Nick said, sitting in the wing chair.

"What?" Shep was busy at the coffee maker.

"The cliché is: You looked like death warmed over."

"You'll accept my apologies, Ace." He handed Nick a ceramic mug of coffee and a packet of non-dairy creamer.

"Where you been, Nick? Your lady friend was climbing the walls all morning, doing irreparable damage to our decorating scheme. 'Where the fuck is that cocksucker?' Brendi reported she said over breakfast. The girls are getting an education."

"I've been locked up in the Harry Meyer Hospital, playing with cadavers and computers, watching an old man get his son's arms and legs glued onto him. Can I have some sugar for this coffee?"

"Wait a minute." Shep reached under his desk.

"Don't tell me you're putting me on tape?"

"I want The Man to hear it in your words. Now start talking. Tell me everything you can that's pertinent. Start with your name."

"And serial number?"

"Cut the shit, Nick."

He talked for half an hour, trying to get in every detail, every name he could remember. It came out, he thought, surprisingly well organized, as if he had worked on it, edited it, toned it up. When he was finished, Shep switched the recorder to rewind and gave him a second cup of coffee. "Let's see the ring and the printout, Ace."

Nick pushed Betty Pace's class ring and her "PRJCT XCTD" printout across the desk.

"We've got enough evidence to start," Shep said. He put the printout and the ring into a small manila envelope. "I have an appointment with The Man this afternoon. He moves quickly when he moves." He took a cassette from the machine under his desk and put it into the envelope. Then leaned back and rested his hundred-dollar rust-colored suede shoes on the desk.

"Here's what I want you to do, Ace," he said. "Go back to the hospital."

"You're out of your mind!" Nick came out of the wing chair. "They want to take me apart and deposit me in their bank. I'm not going anywhere near there. They're not only hip to me, Shep—they want me."

"They can't touch you, don't you understand? You're Harry Meyer's son. Listen, Nick, if you don't go back, they'll clean up everything. They're not dumb."

"Shep, I'm not going anywhere near that place. You get your boss to raid it right away, tonight."

"Carla's there."

"What?"

"Carla's there, in your father's apartment. She went back about an hour ago. At my suggestion."

"How could you do that?"

How could Shep have sent her back? How could he, knowing what he knew?

"Nick, you came to me with this. I didn't ask for it. Okay, now I've got it, and I have to work it the way it should be worked. You go back to the hospital and take it easy. You'll both be safer there than hiding out somewhere. Leave the rest to us, the pros."

Nick went to the paneled door. "If anything happens . . ."

"Believe me, nothing's going to happen, Ace. Now get your ass out of here. I have to talk to my boss." Shep took the receiver off the cradle, laid it on the desk, and reached for his Rolodex.

Nick closed the door behind him and went straight to the phone on the nearest desk. He depressed the lit button and picked up the receiver hoping that Shep's receiver was still on the desk, that Shep was still dialing.

He listened to the sound of Shep's breathing, to the telephone ringing on the other end of the line.

You don't send your friend's woman into the lion's den just so you can get him there too, he thought. And you don't look up your boss's telephone number.

Sssss . . . Sssss . . .

The phone had been answered but with an odd, sibilant sound.

"This is Shepard Gordon," Shep said, as if he were reporting to a telephone answering device. "He was here, sir, and just this moment left. I got him to go back to the hospital."

The sound came again—*sssss . . . Sssss*—and then whoever or whatever was at the other end hung up.

Nick waited for Shep to hang up and replaced his own receiver so that the signal light wouldn't give him away. Fighting back the urge to go into Shep's office and hit him, he walked quietly out a door marked "Stairs" and ran down the seven flights. Anger flooded him with energy. That was why they hadn't tried to capture him during the parade—they had Carla. They knew he'd come back for her.

He emerged on the main floor behind the information booth. The watchman sat at his desk, concentrating on his puzzle. Nick was about to cross the lobby when he saw the familiar two-way radio on the watchman's desk—and then, through the glass front doors, a flash of what might have been Harry Meyer green. He ducked back behind the booth.

They were waiting for him.

But why here? Why weren't they waiting to pick him up back at the hospital? Whatever the answer, he had to stay out of their hands if he was going to get Carla away from them.

Keeping the information booth between himself and the front doors, Nick raced down the stairs leading to the out-of-service subway station.

A train roared by as he reached the bottom, lighting up the shuttered token booth, the locked turnstiles, and the exit stairs at the far end of the platform. There was a wire gate at the foot of these stairs, with a sturdy lock on it. He saw a metal garbage can cover, picked it up and smashed it against the lock, praying that another train would come by to cover the tremendous noise he was making. Any second now they would realize that he must have found another way out of Shep's building.

The lock gave, but as it did he heard footsteps racing down the other staircase. He pulled open the wire gate and ran up into the brilliant sunshine of the street. Recovering his sight, he discovered that he had surfaced around the corner from the building's entrance. Standing at the corner, his back to Nick, was a man in a green Harry Meyer shirt.

Nick ran east, away from the government buildings and the empty, threatening streets.

CHAPTER 28

At the southern end of the seedy park on Bayard Street is a concrete play area filled with rusty swings. A number of elderly Chinese women, wearing purple trousers and long turquoise jackets, sat on the benches facing the swings, minding their children's children. They seemed content, Nick thought as he ran by, if not downright happy.

He looked behind him. Two men in green shirts were just entering the park. He crossed the street to a Burmese restaurant that bore a "Closed" sign across its beaded doors, and knocked. A very small, very beautiful woman came from the back.

"Sorry. Closed, sir."

"I'm ill. Sick. Can I use your bathroom?"

"Yes. Yes. Right there."

She let him in and pointed to a door. He hadn't been exactly lying. He felt sick. He waited in the bathroom as long as he dared, knowing that if they found him, he had given them a perfect place to take him. A tiny room without a window.

But they hadn't found him. He came out of the bathroom and smiled at the Burmese woman, who looked at him as if she were genuinely concerned. "You okay now?" she asked.

"Yes. Much better."

He left the restaurant and started walking fast, into Chinatown. He turned right on Mulberry Street because there were people there—conga lines of tourists following unhappy guides in and out of restaurants, bakeries, novelty shops; permanent-pressed Chinese businessmen bustling to late lunches; uptown couples shopping for woks and mushrooms. The people spilled over into the narrow streets, blocking traffic. Cars sat still, their exhausts smoking.

He turned up Pell Street and forced his way through the crowd coming toward him. The odors from the endless rows of restaurants made him alternately hungry and nauseous. He turned right at an alley called Doyers Street and emerged on the Bowery. Tourist buses were double parked. Yellow faces stared expectantly out of restaurant windows. It was probably bad luck to say it to himself, but he might have shaken them.

An ambulance drove north, lights flashing, sirens going. There was no hospital name written on its side. It tried to turn into Doyers Street, but the alley was one-way, the other way. A cop put his hand purposefully on the driver's door.

Nick jay-walked across the Bowery, ducking cars, and went up Division Street, past a butcher shop with candied, headless ducks hanging in the window.

The driver of the ambulance had had blond hair and wore a green shirt.

As he ran, Nick put his hand to his stomach to see if he could ease the pain. He tried to think of other things, to forget how afraid he was. I have nothing to fear but fear itself, he told himself, but he couldn't smile and he couldn't stop being afraid.

There were fewer people on this side of Chinatown and he needed people. The mass of a huge new red-brick building loomed oppressively over him. He went under the access ramp to the Manhattan Bridge and up Forsyth Street, and then he stopped. The two men at the far end of the street made him uneasy. He thought of turning back, but the ambulance was somewhere in that direction. They could be any two men, he told himself as he walked on. The Forsyth Street shops, all closed for the holiday, featured gold and silver charms behind their barred windows. He wondered if anyone wore charm bracelets anymore. He wondered why all he could think of was how scared he was. The street was deserted; he felt as if he were walking to his execution.

It was a very warm day, even for September. The heat was trapped in the baking street by the tall, ancient buildings, the overhead mass of polluted air. His shirt was plastered to his skin.

All they had to do, he told himself, was take him. As he got closer, he saw that they were very big men and occupied only with waiting. One of them took a step forward. Nick turned back. Nobody. Nobody to see if they dragged him into the car parked at the curb where they were standing.

And then, as they began to walk towards him, the doors of the boarded-up synagogue with swastikas painted over its few remaining stained-glass windows were thrown open, and about thirty young people emerged—boys, from one door, girls from another—engulfing him in their high spirits. The boys wore skull caps and looked thin and myopic. The girls looked fatter, but not healthier.

"Happy New Year," said one of the girls, giggling. She might have been fifteen.

"Happy New Year," said Nick. "You don't mind if I walk with you to the corner, do you?"

She giggled again, and he walked beside her in the middle of the crowd of orthodox Jewish kids, past the two big men, who retreated to their car. He stayed with the kids across Delancy Street, leaving them at Orchard.

There were people on Orchard, but not as many as he had hoped for. A few stores, Hispanic-owned, were open. The others, the shirt and pocketbook and underwear stores were "Closed for the Holiday."

"You look awful hot, sonny," said an incredibly fat woman, who was selling soda and pretzels from a wooden booth.

Above Canal Street, there were more people. His neck began to ache from turning around, though he hadn't seen the two men since he left Forsyth Street. Signs in the open shop windows said "Se Habla Espanol." Spanish women, leading families in brightly colored T-shirts, pushed their way along the sidewalk, making for their favorite shops, the best bargains, the cheapest shoes, the least expensive blue jeans.

He saw a flash of green behind him and turned at the first cross street, reasoning that if he was foolish enough to continue on to Houston Street he would be in a vast, lonely wasteland, everyone minding their own business. They could kidnap Elizabeth Taylor and all her husbands on Houston Street and no one would blink an eye.

Though the crowds thinned out on Rivington, more shops were open. He crossed Essex, where an enormous retail market attracted flies with its open displays of meat and fruits. By the time he had passed Norfolk and Suffolk Streets, the shop signs were offering *Comidas Criollas* and Religious Articles. He was in a new neighborhood, one no one ever came to because they wanted to.

He pretended to ignore the hostile teenage kids in their undershirts, clutching portable tape decks and smoking dope on the tenement stoops. Women, most of them fat, their breasts weighing down cotton halters, sat by themselves, drinking beer. Occasionally one would look up to yell at the little kids playing with the sticks of furniture abandoned in the burned out, looted lower floors of ancient buildings. There were smells now of backed up sewers, of rotting garbage, of urine.

Defeated people sat on the sidewalks on old chairs, their conversations ending as he approached, the men looking down, the women's angry eyes on him, full of hate and despair. He was frightened by the intensity of their impersonal dislike; there was no one here who would interfere with an attempt to get him into the ambulance.

A sanitation truck was backing up Attorney Street. The crew worked slowly, one man driving, one man picking up the trash cans, turning them over into the machine, tossing the cans down on the pavement. Up ahead, at the corner of Ridge and Rivington, was a *bodega*, a classic of its kind, breaking every conceivable sanitation law. Red meat hung in the window; flies crawled up the streaked glass and darted at the meat. A man in Bermuda shorts stood against the counter, his back to the window.

Across the street from the *bodega* was a small brick park, the back end of a new school. Six sad-faced old Puerto Rican men in undershirts and pleated trousers were sitting around one of the concrete tables, drinking beer. Another man, a little drunk, stood off to the side, singing, *"Quizas, Quizas, Quizas."* He sang it in Spanish, then in English. His audience was quiet, appreciative.

At another table, two men sat with their eyes on the street.

"The lovely señorita says no . . . but her eyes, how they glow . . ."

One of the two men, for some reason Nick

couldn't quite put his finger on, looked oddly out of place.

"Quizas, quizas, quizas..."

It was his shirt. The man was wearing a Chemise Lacoste, a green cotton shirt with an alligator on the front.

"We should go in and dance..."

The man in the alligator shirt stood up and Nick whirled. The ambulance was coming down Rivington Street toward him, lights flashing, its siren quiet. As he started to run, he saw the man in the Bermuda shorts come out of the *bodega*, his earnest Ivy League face set in a determined grimace.

"Quizas, quizas, quizas..."

Nick turned up Attorney Street as the ambulance reached the corner, and saw the sanitation truck backing slowly toward him. It would block the ambulance.

"What's the hurry, man?" the sanitation man asked as Nick ran by.

"Cops," gasped Nick.

The sanitation man stepped to the middle of the cracked sidewalk, blocked the man in the alligator shirt with his hip, and rolled an empty trash can into the man in the Bermuda shorts, who stumbled and fell.

"Sorry," the sanitation man said.

Nick turned left at Canal Street and right at Pitt. The thin soles of his loafers slapped the hot pavement. He ran under the Williamsburgh Bridge, past the live chicken market and the new red-brick police station. The pain in his stomach eased as he went past the Henry Street Settlement, and he risked a look back. They weren't there. They were going to use the ambulance. They weren't built for running. They were big and thick, but they were slow. They were built for beating up people.

He turned left under the FDR Drive and ran along the sidewalk up into the park that separates the East River from the Drive. He wondered what was taking them so long.

He looked behind him, to his right, and was reassured to see a woman and a dog. Then he looked to his left. The ambulance was next to him, Lawrence in the passenger seat. All Lawrence had to do was stick out his hand. But there was a high steel fence between them. For once, Lawrence's face wasn't cool. He was staring, as if his power of concentration could stop Nick, make him give himself up.

The ambulance was trying to keep pace with Nick, but drivers in the cars behind it were blowing their horns and shouting out of their windows for it to speed up. Nick slowed to a walk, trying to smile at Lawrence as he and the ambulance disappeared.

He went up onto the concrete by-pass that led to the west side of the Drive. From the top of the by-pass, he could see that the ambulance had picked up speed. It seemed to be making for the Houston Street exit.

The by-pass ended in a small park. A group of black and Puerto Rican girls, teenagers, were sitting on the ground at the far side, drinking beer, passing a joint around. He decided to try and get into one of the red-brick housing project buildings that surrounded the little park. He went down the ramp still scared, but exhilarated. He was going to win. He was going to beat them.

They had been crouching under the overpass, hidden from him—the green alligator shirt, the man in the Bermuda shorts. Each had a radio attached to his belt. He had been under surveillance all the time, he realized; they had manipulated him into running where they could spring the trap quietly, where there would be no people. He felt like one of the rats in the research wing of the Harry Meyer, beautifully programmed.

The alligator shirt had a hypodermic needle in his hand. "This will only take a moment, Mister Meyer," he said in an oddly boyish baritone. "No one wants to hurt you."

Bermuda Shorts had circled behind him and grabbed his arms. He tried to kick Alligator Shirt in the head, but succeeded in only keeping the needle away. He twisted an arm free and almost managed to break the other man's grasp, but this was their kind of action, the sport they had been trained for, and in a second the man had him again. Alligator Shirt closed on him, slicking back his lemon-blond hair with one hand, shaking the hypodermic with the other. Nick decided not to fight anymore.

Suddenly Alligator Shirt was down on the ground, blood pouring from his head; suddenly there were arms and legs everywhere. In a moment Nick was standing off to the side, free, watching. The beer drinking, pot smoking, teenaged girls from the little park were attacking his attackers with thick nickel-plated bike chains. The girl who seemed to be the leader couldn't have been more than seventeen. She had lovely thin arms, doe eyes. He thought of Carla.

"Fuck you, cop!" she said, slamming her chain into the crotch of the man in the alligator shirt. "Cocksucking bastard."

"Hey, baby, you better get your sweet ass out of here," another girl said to Nick. "They got reinforcements." The ambulance was coming over the by-pass, followed by patrol cars. All their sirens were going.

The girls ran into one of the housing project buildings to the north. Nick chose one on the west side of the park. He went up to the roof and lay down and waited, his eyes closed. He came down forty-five minutes later, walked over to Henry Street, and found an off-duty cab driver who, for ten dollars, went back on duty.

He got out of the cab a block from the parking lot where he had left the green Ford, across from Shep's building. He could see, as he approached the lot, that the Ford was still there, that there was still no attendant. A piece of luck, he thought—they didn't know about the car. All he wanted to do was get into it and drive someplace—a motel in New Jersey, maybe—where he could rest and think.

He did not see Carla until he entered the lot. She had been leaning against the far side of the car; when she saw him, she got into it.

"Where the fuck you been?" she whispered as soon as he was in the driver's seat. She put her arms around him and began to cry. "I thought they must have killed you! Jesus knows what I thought!"

He kissed her, thinking that she smelled so good. "How'd you get here?" he asked, not letting her go.

She kept her arms around him, her cheek against his cheek. "I didn't want to go back to the triplex, and I knew you were supposed to meet Shep at his office, so I came down." She kissed him again. "And when I saw the car, I decided to wait. You're not the kind of guy who runs out on a rental."

She pulled back and looked at him. "I been here nearly two freaking hours. Where you been?"

He turned the key in the ignition and put the car into drive. Out of the corner of his eye, he saw her take something from her purse. At first he thought it was lipstick. Then he thought it was a pistol. Then he saw what it was. But it was too late. She was already pressing the hypodermic gun against his shoulder; the pain he felt came from a needle, not a bullet.

He guessed he had about thirty seconds. He looked at her again because he wanted to see what was in her face. She looked frightened. She looked even more frightened when, with a final surge of energy, he pressed his right foot against the gas pedal, pushing it down to the floor, holding it there. He didn't try to steer.

The Ford broke through the lot's chain link fence and crashed into the back of a large blue truck that had stopped for a traffic light.

He stopped seeing Carla's face and saw flames.

CHAPTER 29

He woke once and began to scream. Someone dabbed his upper arm with alcohol; his skin felt as if it had been seared with a torch. By contrast, the needle entering his arm barely hurt. The smell of the macadam on which he was lying, mixed with the sour odor of burnt gasoline, made him throw up.

"Jesus," a man said. "That's all we need."

His face was wiped; strong hands under his shoulders, around his ankles, moved him a few feet to the right. Around him were legs in dark blue trousers.

A siren cut through the conversation above him. It was an ambulance siren, growing louder as it came closer. It frightened him.

He pushed the pain away and concentrated on forming words. "Where are you sending me?" he asked finally. His voice sounded like someone else's.

"What'd you say?" A big round, white face,

crowned by a policeman's cap came into his view.

"Where are you sending me?"

"Bellevue. You'll be all right, kid. Just rest."

He stopped thinking and let the pain take over.

He was dreaming all the time. Sometimes he knew he was caught up in a dream. Most of the time he thought he was trapped in reality. He knew, or thought he knew, that days, even weeks, were going by.

Once he heard someone say, "He is the noisiest critter on the whole damn floor and I don't mean maybe." The voice had a soft Southern accent, and the speaker seemed to be talking to herself. He was aware that that scrap of conversation had come from the real world. Other phrases, sentences, words, began to break through. They dealt with dosages, tracheal infections, uremia, splinter forceps, antimicrobial therapy.

After a while he found that he was no longer lying down all of the time, that he was occasionally sitting up, that he was doing what he was told to do.

But most of the time he dreamed.

The first full conversation he allowed himself to comprehend was about a nasal intubation. He found it interesting. He liked the way the Southern voice was explaining it, the air of recently assumed authority.

"Now this here patient can't swallow. I mean, maybe he can, but the doctor don't want to take a chance on his choking himself to death on account of the fact he's only half-conscious. So we're using a nasal feeding tube on him. See here?

This is a standard seventeen French rubber catheter passed through his nose into his upper esophagus. That pin and tape on the proximal end is so it don't slip down beyond reach. We began feeding him with a 100ml. every hour. Then we increased the amount and decreased the frequency until now he's getting about 500ml. four times a day."

"What's the matter with him?"

"That man is in shock. Due to a bad accident. Now come on, Rosemary, I still have to show you..."

He heard a door shut. He opened his eyes, but the light was too bright. He put his hand to his nose and touched the safety pin and the tape attached to the tube. They felt like bizarre extensions of himself, as if they had grown there.

He knew who he was, and where he was, and why he was there. But he didn't want to admit to all that knowledge. There didn't seem to be any reason to. He went back to sleep, to the dream he had been having.

The voices became more intrusive. As much as he wanted to, as hard as he tried, he could no longer shut them out.

"...can't even make an educated guess. It may be tomorrow or it may be never. This sort of shock is the kind we know least about. His body is functioning beautifully, if that's any consolation. There's no question of brain damage."

The other voice said something about a psychiatrist.

"He could do nothing with a patient who can't

talk. I'm not being much help, am I? As executor, you have a difficult decision..."

Nick opened his eyes just wide enough to see. The two men were standing by the door. One was obviously the doctor—tall, authoritative. The other man he recognized. He was thin; his skin was the color of tobacco, and his lined face was sour. Sarno. Elliot Sarno. His father's lawyer.

"...keep it in trust," Sarno was saying, "for at least another year, at which time..."

Nick wanted to say something to Elliot Sarno. He didn't know what he wanted to say, but it was important, very important. He made a sound, and the two men turned toward him.

"Dreams," the doctor said. "You could quite accurately say that he's living in a dream world. The real world was too much for him."

"His father's death, and then that friend of his."

"Exactly. Well, if you've seen enough..."

Nick tried again. He knew the word he wanted to say. It was only that he hadn't spoken for so long, he couldn't articulate it.

The door opened. Elliot Sarno looked at him and shook his head.

It was like getting a car to start after it had stood out in the cold for a couple of weeks. But if he tried hard enough, he would succeed.

He did. "Help," he said. "Help."

But the door had already closed.

"You kept calling for help," she said, rolling him onto his side to put new sheets on the bed. She wasn't fat, but she was big. Enormous breasts pushed out the starched fabric of her uniform so that she looked as of she were wearing round popcorn barrels, the dollar size, under it.

"Tell you the God's honest truth, I wished I could have helped. Oh, I know—nurses aren't supposed to get emotionally involved. And you were a pain in the you–know–where, but there was something very sweet and sad about seeing you lying there with your eyes all screwed up like someone was going to pry them open, holding on to the blanket and calling for help like a baby. Doggone it, I just wanted to shake you! And I thought maybe if I did, you might come round. But then I thought if I did it, and you had a stroke or something, there'd be hell to pay. And I got enough trouble paying the rent. That was a joke. Get it? Hell to pay, paying the rent?"

He smiled.

"That's better," she said as she finished making the bed. "You comfortable?"

"Yes," he said, though he wasn't. There were too many pillows behind his back.

"Today we are going to take one giant step for Nick Meyer, one small step for Bonnie Mae Phillips. You are going to try feeding yourself, my man."

She handed him the metal spoon from the tray she had brought in with her. He took it awkwardly, dipped it into the bowl she held for him, and slowly brought it up to his mouth. Some of the custard spilled back into the bowl.

"You got most of it. Bellevue's proud of you. Try again."

307

"You're a very patient woman, Bonnie Mae."

"Forget the sweet talk and make with the spoon."

He raised the spoon again and it fell, bouncing off the bed onto the floor. For a moment he thought he was going to cry.

"I'm feeling weak," he said.

"You been lying in that bed with a tube up your nose for almost ten weeks. If you didn't feel weak, there'd be something awful funny going on. Listen, this place makes me feel weak sometimes." She sighed. "I can think of a hell of a lot of other places I'd rather be."

"When I get out of here," he said, offering her a joke, "I'll take you to Miami."

"Not me, honey. I hear you're a rich man. You take me to Palm Beach or we're not going nowhere."

He smiled. "All right with me, but your husband might not be too happy."

"Him? Why, that little sneaky bastard would pay half the fare."

He laughed aloud.

"See?" she said, picking up his meal tray. "I knew you could laugh if you tried. Now go to sleep. There's been a million people asking after you, and I got to tell them you're better. 'The little prince laughed,' I'm going to say."

"Who? Who's been asking for me?"

"I wasn't supposed to say anything, so don't start bothering me with questions I have no intention of answering."

"Don't let anyone in, will you, Bonnie?"

"Honey, this door stays closed tighter than my mother-in-law's purse. No one gets past without three say-sos—yours, mine, and Doctor Beck's."

The intubation tube had been removed as soon as he worked up the strength to eat all of his meals by himself, and he was now sitting up most of the time, still without any desire to read, but beginning to be bored.

The ordinariness of his room offered little distraction. The window, opposite his bed, looked out on a red-brick wall, featureless except for a yellow-shaded window so far to the right that it was almost beyond his view. He had all sorts of fantasies, most of them sexual, about what lay behind that window. He supposed he was getting better.

His doctor, the tall authoritative man named Beck, inspired confidence. He answered Nick's questions simply, without evasion.

They had gotten Nick out of the Ford just before it and the truck he had slammed into exploded. "They" were the police and the driver of the truck.

Yes, Dr. Beck said, Nick was suffering from shock more than from any real physical damage inflicted by the accident. Aside from his weakness, there was nothing wrong with him physically.

There had, of course, been requests, once his identity was known, that he be transferred from Bellevue to the Harry Meyer Hospital. Dr. Beck had denied these requests, after consulting with several colleagues on the Bellevue staff and with Nick's lawyer, Mr. Sarno. Why had he?

"To put it bluntly, you seemed to have some sort of persecution mania about the Harry Meyer and Doctor Paine. You talk in your sleep, and to your nurse. I decided it would be a mistake to send you to a place you so obviously fear. That it might exacerbate your condition. Mister Sarno backed me up."

And Carla?

Dr. Beck said that the young woman who had been in the car with him had been taken, at her own request, to the Harry Meyer. Her condition had not been serious.

Having asked Nick's permission, Dr. Beck lighted a small cigar, and said that Mr. Sarno was now abroad with his wife, but had been notifed of Nick's improved condition and would pay him a visit when he returned next week.

"All that remains is for you to regain your physical—and mental—strength," Dr. Beck said, putting the cigar out in the visitor's ashtray.

"How long will that take?" Nick asked.

"That, of course, depends on you."

With Bonnie Mae's help, he began to walk around the room. He had expected to find himself weak, but he was surprised at how little strength he actually had, at how thin and pale he looked in the mirror on the bathroom door.

The first time he tried to walk by himself, he barely managed to get to the bathroom. He had to sit on the side of the tub, holding on to the safety bars, until his legs stopped quivering. He felt very old.

But on his second effort he made what he considered a wonderful discovery. The bathroom window directly faced the window in the brick wall. And its yellow shade was up. After he had rested for a moment on the side of the tub, he walked the few feet to his own window and pressed his face to the glass. Would any of his fantasies come true? I'll probably see, he told himself, an empty broom closet.

And then his eyes focused. The room behind the yellow shade was a shower room, and there were three naked women in it, showering. He saw their hair, wet and plastered to their faces. He saw their breasts, young and round and firm. He saw the black patch of pubic hair on the woman showering in the far corner.

He had to go and sit back down on the edge of the tub. He wondered if he were crazy. After a minute he went back to the window. One of the women had left; the remaining two—one plump, one lean—were letting the shower water massage their backs. He realized suddenly that he was looking into the Bellevue nurses' shower room. He started to laugh, but stopped as one of the women began to soap down the other. He loosened the knot of his pajama bottoms. Then, as if she were one of those people who could see through the backs of their heads, the plump nurse turned, walked to the window, and pulled down the shade.

Nick got himself back to his bed, closed his eyes

and reached down for his erection. He was definitely getting better.

He took to spending a great deal of time in the bathroom. "Honey, you are the cleanest patient I ever had," Bonnie Mae told him a few days later.

He had discovered that the nurses showered on regular shifts—one group in the early morning, another in mid-afternoon, a third late at night. The last group was the most interesting because they rarely troubled to pull down the shade and they kept the light on in the shower room.

He tried to remember what Peeping Tom's punishment was. Still, he rationalized, it was better than television, both aesthetically and intellectually. The window became his theater. He began to know the women, to give them names, to identify personalities. On the several occasions when they remembered to draw the shade, he found himself disappointed, like a child whose dessert has been withheld for no given reason.

On the fifth day after his discovery, at five P.M., a time when no nurses were scheduled to bathe, he was in the bathroom, drying himself after his own shower, when he happened to glance across at the nurses' window.

It was a dark, rainy afternoon, and the light was on in the nurses' shower. He went to his window and looked across as a naked woman came to the opposite window. For a moment he thought she had seen him, and then he realized that her smile was only for herself. She reached for the shade and pulled it down.

He pulled his own shade down, went into the bedroom, and sat on the edge of the bed. He had seen that smile before. It wasn't a sexual smile. It was beatific, holy, and it was the smile and the face of the nurse who had helped him on with his conductive booties before he witnessed his first operation at the Harry Meyer Hospital. He remembered the saint's face clearly because it had been so incongruous above the Jane Mansfield body. Her naked breasts had been just as large as he had supposed them to be.

He tried to convince himself that she might have switched jobs, come to work at Bellevue.

But he knew she was still a nurse at the Harry Meyer, and that she had been taking a shower in the Harry Meyer nurses' shower room, and that he was sitting on a bed not in Bellevue, but in the patients' wing of the Harry Meyer Hospital.

When Bonnie Mae came in and switched on the light, she saw that the bed was empty. She thought he was in the bathroom again.

He wasn't. He was standing behind the door, and when she was well into the room he slipped out into the hallway. From the far end of the familiar corridor two men dressed in white uniforms started towards him. The last time he had seen them, one had been wearing a green alligator shirt, the other Bermuda shorts.

He immediately knew where he was—the back end of sixteen, the patients' floor. He turned a corner and ran along the green-and-white wallpapered corridor. They were chasing him now—the male nurses, Bonnie Mae. He made as much noise as he could, banging on doors as he ran. Patients were looking out of their rooms, asking their servants to find out what the commotion was all about.

He was in a cul-de-sac with only one door. He crashed into the door, knocking it open, and fell exhausted onto the carpeted floor.

The male nurses came in and picked him up while Bonnie Mae chastised him. "Now what you want to go and do something like that for, Nick? I'm going to get in a whole mess of trouble..."

He wasn't listening to Bonnie Mae. With the nurses gripping his arms, he stood staring at the old man sitting on the edge of the bed.

Rolls of butter-colored flesh spilled over the top of the old man's undershorts, the kind that had three snaps at the waistband. He had breasts as large as a plump girl's, divided by a clump of sparse grey hair that matched the toothbrush mustache on his lined face. His faded, convex eyes were transparent, like tiny empty goldfish bowls.

Morris Gerber sat grasping the mattress with both hands, his legs crossed in an oddly nonchalant pose. His arms and legs were several shades darker than the rest of his body. They were a young man's arms and legs, the muscles beautifully defined, the skin covered with thin dark hairs.

Morris Gerber lifted his strong right hand to his face, and Nick saw that it was a vibrant, alive hand with long, thick fingers. It was much too large for him.

"Sorry about this, Mister Gerber," said one of the nurses, Alligator Shirt.

"About what?" Morris Gerber smiled and looked at Nick. He stood up, an old man with an old man's quivering yellow torso, dark young limbs attached to it.

"Disturbing you, Mister Gerber. This guy's gone berserk..."

"Forget about it, sonny," Morris Gerber said. "I'm feeling fine. Never better. Don't mind me." He walked awkwardly on his thick strong legs to the bathroom, and the door closed behind him.

Nick felt the prick of a needle as Bonnie Mae injected his arm, and then the two male nurses were escorting him back to his room.

CHAPTER 30

Bonnie Mae was shaving his body, starting at the top of his chest and working down to his legs. Nick wished he could fight her off, or at least try, but the shot she had given him made him helpless. It was not like the other drugs they had given him—no fantasies or little trips. It had simply immobilized him. His mind was perfectly lucid. He wished it weren't.

Cecil came into the room and watched as Bonnie Mae slid the razor expertly over his skin.

"How many milligrams did you give him?" he asked, lifting the gold-framed glasses from his nose and rubbing the bridge with his thumb and forefinger. Nick wondered if the familiar gesture was a deliberate one, designed to suggest that though he might look and act like Jehovah, he was in fact a mere mortal with weak sight.

"Two hundred plus the Demerol, Doctor Paine."

Cecil put his glasses back on. "How are you,

Nicholas?" he asked, smiling kindly.

"You know what you can do with your benevolent God act, Cecil," Nick said. "You're not God. You're a murderer, a pimp, a disgusting..."

"I suppose I am a murderer, Nick. But a pimp?" Cecil paused, as if to consider the charge. "I don't think so. If you're thinking of Carla, that little lady is in business all by herself."

Bonnie Mae folded the razor, placed it on a tray, and began to rub Nick down with alcohol.

"Get away from me, Cecil," he said. "Get out of here."

"You're so much like your father, Nicholas. I liked him too. He was so wonderfully naïve. He never understood why he shouldn't always get what he wanted, why everything wasn't exactly what it appeared to be. But you understand, don't you, Nick? You're so much more sophisticated. It might be easier for you if you weren't. I know it won't help, but I must tell you that I am sorry there wasn't some other way." He turned toward the door.

"I want to see Carla." His voice was a stranger's whisper.

"It will only make you feel worse, Nicholas." Cecil considered for a moment. "But why not? It all depends, of course, on whether she wants to see you."

Bonnie Mae finished swabbing his body and wrapped him in a sterile sheet. "What you want to see that good-for-nothing bitch for?" she whispered, her face close to his. "Huh?"

He turned away from her. In a moment she said, "Goodbye, Nick," and left the room, carrying her equipment on a white plastic tray.

Carla came in ten minutes later.

She didn't look like his Carla. She looked like *Vogue*'s Carla. Her hair was longer and seemed to be of a different texture—silkier, finer. She wore it pulled back so that her cheekbones and her charcoal black eyes were now the dominant features of her face. Her makeup was different; it was lighter, changing the color of her skin. She wore no jewlery. Her dark red lipstick matched the red of her dress, which fell gracefully away from her body, just touching her breasts.

She closed the door behind her, looked at him briefly, and walked around the room, touching things. Her nails were no longer painted black; they were dark red, like her lips and her dress, like congealed blood.

She sat down in the green visitors' chair and crossed her legs. "You wanted to see me, Nicky?"

It was not even Carla's voice anymore. There was nothing of Puerto Rico in it. She sounded as if she came from California via Park Avenue.

"Even your accent was fake..." he said.

She smiled and looked down at her hands. "What difference does it make, Nicky?"

"What about the plant? What about Baby Love? You faked that, too?"

She looked at him with sad, amused eyes. "Now that you've seen me, Nicky," she said in her soft new voice, "is there anything else?"

318

"You're not Carla."

"I never was."

She stood up and went to the window. She even moved differently.

"Help me. You could help me."

She didn't turn. "I don't want to help you, Nicky."

"I'd give you the money." He felt helpless, emasculated. The drug was making it difficult for him to speak. "It's a lot of money."

She came away from the window, looked down at him, and then at the blank wall behind his bed. She tried to laugh. "You bought it all, didn't you, Nicky? I'm not in it for the money."

"What *are* you in it for?"

"I like being in the center, Nick." She began to pace. The sleeves of her dress were slit so that he could catch glimpses of the soft skin of her arms. "And right now, this is the middle of the world. Anyone who's going anywhere—anyone who's already arrived—is going to have to pay a call on the Harry Meyer. Sooner or later. Everyone, Nick. Presidents, kings, oilmen, astronauts. We have what they all want. All they have to do is pay for it."

"And how are you paying for it, Carla?"

She closed her eyes for a moment "In my own inimitable way, Nicky."

She moved to the bed, bent down, and kissed him. The smell of her now, expensive and artificial, made him sick. He turned his head away.

She straightened up and smiled. "As Carla would say, 'Baby, you were a great fuck.'"

"Is that my epitaph?"

"It could be worse." She went to the door, but turned when he spoke again.

"And I have a few last words for you, too," he said.

"Yes?"

"Fuck you, Carla," he said. "Fuck you."

Cecil entered a moment after she was gone. The two male nurses were behind him, wheeling a trolley.

"Not exactly what you thought she was, old boy?" Cecil said, undoing the sheet Nick was wrapped in and injecting another needle into his arm.

"What's that?"

"Only a little more of what we gave you before. It's a marvelous drug. Affects only motor reactions. Your mind will stay clear, you can be assured."

"Give me something to fog it up."

Cecil smiled and signaled the nurses to move the trolley next to the bed. The nurses picked him up and placed him carefully on the trolley. He could smell their after-shave lotion.

"Cecil, what are you going to do to me?" he said.

"It's not what *I* want to do, Nicholas."

"Then who?"

"He wants to meet you. Now."

CHAPTER 31

Fear cut across him like a knife, despite the drug, and when the elevator stopped on the twentieth floor, he closed his eyes. The male nurses rolled him out, one on each side of the trolley, calm giants taking the disturbed prince for an airing. Cecil followed as they moved past the small operating theater and through the arched entry into the room where the prosthetic devices were displayed.

Pat Buckley stood by the archway at the other end of the room, her face pale, her arms folded across her chest. The two nurses remained with her. Cecil wheeled him into the room on the other side of the archway, and then went out and left him there alone.

Sssss... Sssss...

He stared up at the low, smooth ceiling. The sounds were like the ones he had heard over the telephone in Shep's office. He raised his head slightly from the trolley so that he could look around the room.

The wall closest to him was covered with television screens, each revealing a different location in the hospital complex. On one screen he saw the room from which he had just been taken. A woman with a kerchief around her head was mopping the floor.

Hssst... Hssst...

Nick turned his head slowly away from the wall of television screens.

A few feet away, a small man, not much bigger than a ventriloquist's dummy and with something of the same frozen expression, was watching him from a vehicle that resembled a wheelchair. It took Nick a few seconds before he realized that the man was not actually that small, that his torso was of normal size.

But that was all there was. A torso. No arms, no legs. Just a torso and a head.

It was a perfect doll's head. Round and smooth, with a thin coating of dark hair that looked as if it had been painted on. A dimple in the chin; two bright circles of red on the cheeks. The eyes, fringed with dark lashes, were the color and texture of old-style Coca Cola bottles, thick and green.

He looked like a discarded toy, a toy whose arms and legs had been torn away.

A thin plastic tube was secured to his neck by a wire frame that held the end of the tube close to the heart-shaped mouth. From there the tube ran down to the base of the chair-like vehicle; from the base, it snaked across the floor to the computer that covered the entire far wall.

"I am Brown."

The voice was flat and thin, as if it came from a machine.

"My body is an extension of the computer you see behind me. That computer is an extension of the one on the nineteenth floor, which weighs two hundred thousand pounds. It is programmed to record my various functions. I will demonstrate. Look at the monitor in the center."

I will tell myself that you are real, Nick thought, and therefore I am not insane. I will listen to what you are saying; I will do what you tell me to do; I will not let myself think.

He forced himself to turn his eyes away from the talking doll called Brown to the computer against the wall. There were three monitor screens. The first and third were blank. The one in the middle listed functions.

```
HEART - NORMAL

LUNGS - NORMAL

KIDNEYS - NORMAL

BLOOD - NORMAL

EXCRETORY - NORMAL
```

The last entry on the monitor changed from NORMAL to FUNCTIONING.

Shssss... Shssss...

Brown took his lips away from the plastic tube as his chair rolled silently closer to Nick.

"My bowels are moving now," Brown said. "A radio-physicologic stimulator is attached to my colon. Electrodes are implanted in my detrusor muscles. At the appropriate moment, an electrical signal contracts the muscles and evacuation commences. When it is complete, the computer alerts the plumbing system, which then removes the waste. A deodorant chemical is simultaneously discharged."

Nick heard a soft *hssss* from under Brown's chair and the sharp, familiar smell of a pine-scented aerosol spray was suddenly in the air. On the monitor screen, the EXCRETORY function changed back to NORMAL.

"My organs have been adapted by the computer," Brown said in his flat, metallic voice, "to a range of situations and stimuli. My metabolism is maintained at minimal levels and accelerated only when necessary. The computer, therefore, preserves my organs. It keeps them young. There are two control systems at my disposition. One is dependent upon a series of electrodes placed within my body; these put me 'on line' with the computer. When an action is required, I breathe the appropriate code into the tube you see here at my mouth, and these impulses are transformed into instructions for the computer. I will demonstrate."

Pffft . . . pfft . . . pfft. A metal arm rose smoothly from the side of Brown's chair. The hand at the end of the arm had four steel fingers, each with three joints. *Hssst...hssst...hssss....* The steel fingers writhed in the air only inches from Nick's neck. *Pfft...pfft.* The arm sank back to the side of the chair.

"The other control system," Brown said, "is a back-up system. I am able to contract certain muscles in my torso and neck, which then give off myoelectric signals. The computer takes these signals and reapplies them to activate the appropriate prosthesis. I will demonstrate."

Brown made a jerking movement of his head, and the metal arm rose from the chair again, swung over Nick's head, and returned to its place.

Nick closed his eyes for a moment. When he opened them he saw that Cecil had come into the room.

"I have demonstrated, Cecil," Brown said. "And now it is time for him to learn our history."

"Yes," Cecil said. "It is time." He removed his gold-rimmed glasses and rubbed the bridge of his nose. "Tell him. We have only a few more minutes."

Nick saw Brown's sleek, round head turn slowly toward him, saw the small pink tongue flicker over the parted lips.

"I am Cecil's brother," Brown said in his flat metallic voice. "Harry Meyer was my brother. You are my nephew. I need you."

Nick closed his eyes again.

CHAPTER 32

"Listen carefully, Nicholas," Cecil said. "It is important for you to understand." He turned to Brown. "There is very little time."

Brown's lips pursed, close to the plastic tube. *Whhft...Whhft...* The photograph of Harry Meyer as a cocky young man appeared on the central computer screen.

"The animal..." Brown said, and Nick sensed the hatred in his machine-like voice. It was the first time Brown had shown emotion of any sort.

The words came again. "The animal..."

"Your father was not kind to Brown, Nicholas," Cecil said. His tone was that of a teacher concerned that his prize student was missing a basic fact.

Ptth...Ptth... The photograph of Harry was replaced by the one that showed his family on the eve of their emigration to America.

"Harry and Ruthie were fifteen when that was taken." Cecil said. "Notice how your grandmother clings to Harry's arm. He was everything in the world to her."

Ptth... Ptth... The screen went blank.

Nick wanted to put his hands over his ears, to shut out Cecil and his sentimental concern, to shut out the sound of Brown and his commands into the plastic tube. He wanted it to be over. He wanted not to know what was coming, not to know what had been.

"You're repulsed?" Cecil asked. "My dear boy, there was a long period in Brown's life when he was offended by himself."

Nick forced himself to look at the doll-like head so close to his own. Its eyes closed for a moment, then opened to stare at Nick. The pupils were glassy bright.

"Your grandmother wanted to leave him in the snow when he was born," Cecil said. "But father and I, we saved him."

Brown breathed a command. *Ptth.* The monitor screen now showed a close-up of the left side of the photograph; the tall young man holding what appeared to be a large baby in a nest of wraps.

The young man was Cecil.

The baby was Brown.

"He was kept in the barn with the animals," Cecil said. "It was my job to care for him. Just as it was my job to care for the chickens and the horses. Brown was ten years old when that photograph was taken, and he had never once slept in a house. I was fourteen. They were leaving the next day for America. I begged them to take us with them."

327

As if he were quoting, Brown said, "'They wouldn't let you in. There are no monsters in America.'"

"That was what our mother told Brown," Cecil said. "She wouldn't even look at him. But Father gave me a wallet with some money in it, and that night Brown and I traveled to Warsaw. It was the first step in a long, difficult journey that brought us eventually to England. We chose England because I knew from my schoolbooks that England was the center of the modern medical world. In England, we began anew. The social agencies were kind to us; they gave me my new name, they found us a place to live.

"I can remember a kindly woman from one of the agencies looking at Brown in his swaddling clothes and asking me how I planned to care for 'the baby.' The truth of the matter is that Brown, in the end, took care of me. I took a job with a company that made artificial limbs, a rather successful company; there were a great many young men in England then, victims of the first World War, who needed artificial arms and legs. Brown improved on the designs I brought home to him, and we were able to market his improvements. We earned enough money to put me through medical school. I became a surgeon specializing in research. Much of our most important research was carried on in the laboratory we constructed in the cellar of our house in London. The world believed me to be a brilliant and innovative surgeon. But it was Brown who made the discoveries. It was Brown's mind, Brown's genius, that led us on. Do you understand that, Nicholas?"

Nick nodded, trying to focus his attention on Cecil, trying not to look at the monstrous doll next to him, trying not to believe this was his uncle.

"Brown's goal has always been to have real arms and legs," Cecil said, as if explaining to a child. "He has dedicated his entire life to making his body complete. And I am the instrument by which he will succeed. I was already a successful surgeon when we came to this country after the second World War, but the enormous funds we required were beyond us. But not, you see, beyond Harry. Harry had made his hundreds of millions; he was not, as you can imagine, thrilled to see us. But he had the money we needed, and fortunately we were able to help him. We gave him a new heart; he made it possible for this hospital to exist, for our research to continue, for Brown's plan to reach its final stage. And your father, Nicholas, gave . . ."

He was interrupted by three faint but urgent beeps from a speaker in the corner of the room.

"Harry gave us," Cecil said, speaking more quickly now, "the most important gift of all, the vital piece of equipment. He gave us you, Nicholas. In a few hours, Brown will be equipped with your young arms and legs. In time, he will leave this computerized prison, and begin to live the life of which he has always dreamed. He will be treated with all the respect and adulation he deserves as the greatest medical genius who ever

329

lived! Think of it! Think of what he has accomplished. He has provided mankind with the key to eternity."

There were two more beeps from the speaker, and then Nick heard his own voice. It seemed to be coming from a long way off.

"And me? What about me?"

"You will be kept alive, of course, Nicholas, in as much comfort as we can achieve for you."

"And when Brown's heart starts to go . . . ?"

"Exactly. You're his insurance. Your tissues and blood factors are as compatible as if you came from the same egg. But you can console yourself, Nicholas, with the thought that you are serving not only science, but all of mankind. And, of course, you will live a very long life; your organs will be preserved by the computer as Brown's have been. You will learn to make the most of your disabilities. You will learn to use your mind, to—"

A single, long, urgent beep came from the speaker.

"It is time," Brown said, and Nick thought he saw the little lips turn up, as if they were smiling.

The two male nurses came in, and he felt his trolley being turned, felt it begin to move toward the arched door.

Cecil's hand touched his shoulder as the trolley passed through the archway. "Good luck, Nicholas," Cecil said.

CHAPTER 33

A man without a face was standing over him, a hypodermic in his hand.

The sting of the alcohol diluted the dream. The alcohol was being sponged onto his skin, around his shoulders and thighs. It felt cool, pleasant. Then he was spun around, lifted onto another, higher surface.

He opened his eyes and realized that the faceless man of his dream was Doctor Beck wearing a surgical mask. The doctor raised a weal on his shoulder; rubber gloved hands inserted a twenty-two gauge needle through the weal. A second; then the needle plunged down through subcutaneous tissue—and again deeper.

He kept his eyes open, despite the overhead light, as the doctor began the same process at the top of his right thigh. He saw other masked, gowned doctors standing at their posts. He wanted to call out, to get their attention, their help. He couldn't.

He turned his eyes and saw Cecil, also gowned and masked, standing by another operating table only a few yards away. Brown's truncated body lay on the table. He lay perfectly still, his doll's head unmoving, his round eyes open, his lips still pursed in a little smile.

Nick felt as if he, himself, were truncated—the preliminary anesthesia had already begun to deaden his limbs. He prayed that it would quickly deaden his mind. He saw Cecil and Beck step back as the anesthetists came forward to the operating tables, saw the anesthetists nod to each other as they completed the ritual check of procedures. It was going to happen; the operation was about to begin. He tried to cry out, but already his speech function was paralyzed. He saw Cecil make a little motion with his right hand, indicating that the anesthetists were to proceed. A vision flashed in his mind of a scalpel being slapped into Cecil's hand, of the hand being raised to make the first incision, of the scalpel slicing through skin and flesh, carving him away. A scream rose in his throat, but there was no way for the scream to be released; it swelled inside him.

Cecil's eyes changed above his mask. They were wide now with some new emotion.

Fright. He's frightened, Nick thought.

A young doctor was standing next to Cecil, talking, alarmed.

It was impossible to make out what the young doctor was saying; he was drowned out by the electronic hum of the operating room equipment, by the murmur rising from the other doctors. On the operating table a few yards away, Brown's round head had turned; he was looking toward Cecil, his lips working uncertainly. Cecil turned away from the young doctor, took off his mask, and used it to wipe the perspiration from his face.

"Cecil," Brown said. "Cecil, what is—"

Across the room, the doors from the corridor swung open. It was Pat Buckley who had opened them. She was pushing a wheelchair. She rolled it directly to the table where Brown lay, with Cecil standing beside him now.

Morris Gerber sat slumped in the chair, covered by a sheet, a curious, dazed expression on his face. Pat Buckley brought the chair to a stop and pulled the sheet off the old man, as if she were unveiling an statue in the park.

Nick saw Brown's round head turn slightly so that his eyes could fix on Gerber. Cecil was already staring down at him.

The old man's torso was the same unhealthy butter-yellow color it had been when Nick burst into his room. Only the color of his new arms and legs had changed. They were no longer a vibrant tan.

They were blue.

And they were dead.

Morris Gerber raised his head slowly to look up at Cecil. He was smiling, a rueful half-smile, as if he were about to tell a risqué joke in mixed company.

"Didn't work after all," he said. "To tell the

God's honest truth, I never did think it would."
He sighed. "All his life, Buddy was useless to me.
Still is."

The room was silent now. Nick heard only the
faint, labored sound of his own breathing. And
then Brown spoke, his metallic voice flat, showing
no emotion.

"Find out what went wrong, that's the first
step," he said to Cecil. "Get those limbs off
Gerber. Report to me as soon as possible. Now I
want to go upstairs. Bring my chair."

Nick saw white-coated figures surround
Gerber and the table on which Brown lay. Then
they came for him, lifted him onto a trolley, and
rolled him out of the operating room.

CHAPTER 34

They kept him in the triplex bedroom.

There was a wire grill now over the light fixture. He had tried once to remove it, standing on a chair, and an electric shock had knocked him off the chair.

The door to Harry's den had been walled over; he could no longer remember exactly where it had been. He could not let himself out onto the third floor landing; there was a new MatchCode slot by the bedroom door.

At the end of the first week, he tried to throw the television set through the floor-to-ceiling one-way window. The window didn't break, but the set did and they didn't replace it for several days. He had to ask, and ask nicely. He had no illusions about how difficult it would be to live without it. Television filled his mornings with news shows and reruns of series he had seen when he was young. In the afternoons, he watched what was left of old films after the commercials and censors had gotten through with them.

He talked to no one except Lawrence, who brought him his meals and kept up the fiction that he was a servant and Nick was Mister Meyer, sir. Twice he had tried to attack Lawrence. All that had happened was that he found himself being flipped over onto the circular bed. It had been painless but humiliating. Lawrence had enjoyed it.

Evenings were the most difficult. Lawrence brought him dinner, exactly at six thirty. Forty-five minutes later he would come for the silver-plated tray. "Have a nice evening, Mister Meyer."

"Up yours, Lawrence."

He didn't watch much television at night. The fake kids in the fake high schools, the wholesome families that never existed, the serious, unreal, dramas on the public station, made him feel unreal, one-dimensional. He would read the *Times*, saved from the breakfast tray; he would try to read the books he had ordered and Lawrence had delivered, mostly mysteries. He still, he told himself, wanted to figure out who done it.

But there always came a moment when he couldn't read any longer, when he would get off the bed and pace, looking up at the camera-light fixture. Sometimes, after several weeks had gone by, he would start to scream. After two months had gone by, he began to throw things at the wire grill. Then Lawrence would come in and give him a shot of something that made him go to sleep and

336

kept him docile for the next day.

He was allowed only a small amount of wine, no marijuana. His meals were beautifully organized plates of well-balanced, complementary foods. They were keeping him healthy.

They began to allow him 10mg. of Valium each evening, in place of the occasional shot. "Don't want you getting a habit, Mister Meyer," Lawrence said. He would save the pill for the moment when he was in bed facing the fact that he wouldn't be able to sleep—the moment when he would want to start beating on the door; the moment when, against his will, he would begin to cry like an animal in pain. Then he would swallow the pill without water, as if it were candy, a reward he had worked all day to deserve.

The lights, controlled from outside the room, went off every night at eleven. He was usually asleep by midnight.

As more weeks passed, the Valium began to lose its effect, and he spent entire nights banging his fists against the door. Lawrence began to give him shots again, seeming to take a kind of sexual pleasure in looking for a vein, inserting the needle, letting the fluid escape slowly into Nick's arm. Despite the shots, there were nights when he tried to attack himself. Once he broke the mirror in the bathroom cabinet and almost succeeded in slashing his wrists before they got to him. They did not replace the cabinet mirror. The mirrored wall in the bathroom was indestructible.

He waited. He knew that they were getting

ready to perform the operation, that by now they must have solved whatever the problem was before.

He lay on the bed, looking up at the camera-light fixture, and screamed until he lost his voice.

The knock on the door didn't make any sense. Lawrence never knocked; he didn't need to.

The knock came again.

"Who is it?" he asked, his voice hoarse, unsure. Perhaps they were coming for him.

"Me. Pat Buckley. May I come in, Nick?"

"Just a minute."

He knew immediately why she was there. She was the only one they had who wouldn't make him crazier. Pat was to be a human tranquilizer; she would talk to him, soothe him, help him through his final nights.

He wondered what he looked like. He put on one of Harry's silk robes, a blue one with polka dots. They had taken away the belt; he had to hold it closed with his hand.

"Come in," he said.

Lawrence opened the door, let her in, and went out, closing the door.

"Hi, Nick," Pat said.

She had changed—or maybe he was seeing her differently. Her hair was blonder and softer; her eyes were older, kinder. She seemed more sure of herself.

"I like the beard, Nick," she said. "Makes you look all serious." Her voice was determinedly cheerful, and he realized that she was not going to acknowledge his melancholy state.

"I am serious." He tried to smile, but didn't. He couldn't decide whether to go on standing or to sit down. The months of isolation had stripped him of his social reflexes.

"What're you doing here?" he said. "Visiting Harry Meyer's very own private breeding farm?"

"I wanted to see you, Nick. They said you needed company, and I—"

"They ordered you."

"—and I volunteered. I've wanted to see you for a long time, Nick, but they wouldn't let me."

He sat down on the bed, and she took a chair facing him. He could smell her perfume. It went with her crisp, New England manner. Now, he thought, she's offering me help. Before, she was looking for it.

"I want to ask you something," he said. "Before we become dearest friends, sharing our darkest secrets."

"Go ahead."

"Have you always been hip to what goes on here? Have you always known about the computerized killings?"

She glanced up at the fixture, and then directly into his eyes. "I've only known for a short while. Since Betty Pace died. Before that, I thought all the donations were legitimate. It's not a subject I want to discuss, Nick." Her eyes flickered upward again.

He understood. Up there, on the twentieth floor, Brown was listening.

"Okay, let's talk of other things," he said.

"Eritrean rebels? I'm very up on the news. I read the *Times*, *Post*, and the *Village Voice* classifieds. I watch 'Eye-Witness News' six times a day, and I. . . ."

She let him talk. He hadn't for so long, it was a relief to babble, to say all sorts of inane things, to talk to someone who seemed to be listening.

She came to see him regularly after that night. She brought books and magazines. She told him about her youth, about how deserted she felt when her father was killed, about the nightmare of being blind, about the operation Cecil had performed that gave her back her sight.

Nick told her how he had been brought up, and how he had always wanted to write, and how satisfying it had been working for the magazine, working with Tony Lyle.

He spent his days waiting for her to come.

"I brought Scrabble," she said one night. She was like the old Pat that night, her eyes nervous and afraid. "Want to play?"

"A dollar a point."

"Piker," she said, setting up the board.

He wondered why she was nervous. Whatever the reason, it didn't interfere with her game. She was a good player. She knew the value of the blanks and the 's's; she knew how to wait and build for a seven-letter word.

At the end of the game, she announced the score. "Four hundred to three eighty-five."

"Who's favor?"

"You owe me, Mister Meyer, fifteen dollars."

"Let me see that scorepad."

She tore the top sheet off the pad and handed it to him, then began to pack up the game. In a moment she stood up awkwardly, spilling tiles onto the floor, giving him a chance to conceal from the camera the shock of what he had read. He got down on his knees and helped her to put the tiles back in the gray plastic bag.

"Tomorrow night?" she asked, as she always did.

"I'll be here."

Watching her use her MatchCode card to get out of the room, he wondered if the camera would pick up the fact that her hand was shaking.

He waited until the lights went off at eleven before he went into the bathroom, where he tore the scorepad page into tiny pieces and flushed them down the toilet.

Even with the Valium, he couldn't sleep. He could not stop thinking about the words Pat had carefully copied out on the scorepad:

COMPUTER READOUT - 6455-t-3/8

Revised
MatchCode: ZIP10021-MEYERn*-28-M-
              UN-POT.DON(A==)ALL ORGANS
              - LIMBS (PRIMARY) Status:
              IMMINENT/PENDING FINAL
              TESTS *aka: MILLER

              (CROSS REF: NOT AVAIL-
              ABLE PRJCT XCUTION DATE
              0-4 DAYS)

CHAPTER 35

Pat did not come the next two nights. The third night she did, the Scrabble set under her arm, the nervousness again on her face. "I heard you didn't eat your dinner," she said, looking at the tray with the glass of milk on it.

"Lawrence should publish a little newspaper," he said.

"You're too thin as it is."

She set up the Scrabble board, not bothering to ask him if he wanted to play, and they played two games. He won both. Then Pat packed up the Scrabble set, touched his hand, and left.

Nick wondered how either of them had gotten through the evening.

He glanced at the score pad. There were only the Scrabble scores on it, written in Pat's neat, girls'-school hand.

He drank the milk Lawrence had brought with his dinner and then began to pace. He didn't stop when he saw it, but kept moving back and forth across the room. The tip of the plastic pouch that held the Scrabble tiles was sticking out from under the edge of the bed.

It was half an hour before the lights were turned off and he could get to it; even then he reached for it with as inconspicuous a movement as possible. There were no tiles inside the pouch. It must have been an extra one she had held in her hand when she came in and later slipped under the bed.

Inside the pouch was a pencil flashlight like the one he had used to explore Storage, a MatchCode card, and a note. In the big closet, using the flashlight, he read the note. *Come now. As soon as you find this. I'll be waiting.*

He put on trousers and a shirt and shoes. He had not worn shoes for a long time and the loafers felt unnatural; he had grown used to the soft padding of Harry's slippers.

He did not realize how frightened he was until he tried to fit the MatchCode card into the slot at the side of the door. His hands shook; he had begun to sweat.

Could he trust Pat? His rational mind told him he had nothing to lose. His irrational mind told him to stay where he was, to get in the bed, to swallow the Valium.

When he managed to slip the MatchCode card into the slot, the click of the door opening sounded like a bomb exploding. He stood still for a minute, listening, his hand on the door knob. There was only silence.

He took a deep breath, pulled open the door,

and played the pencil flashlight quickly over the landing. The beam fell on Lawrence, standing only a few feet away, his servant's grin slightly broader than usual, his hands reaching out.

"Sorry, Mister Meyer, but you—"

A slender figure came swiftly and silently out of the dark behind him, and there was a soft, thudding sound. Lawrence stood very still, his hands outstretched before him. Then the right hand moved slowly upward and back, as if he wanted to pat the back of his head, and he began to sag. He fell to the floor and lay still.

It was as if he had been hit with a hammer, Nick thought, and in the same instant he realized that Lawrence *had* been hit with a hammer, from behind, by Pat. She stood there, holding a heavy surgical hammer, her eyes wide with fright.

"Did I kill him?" she whispered.

"No," he said, taking the hammer from her and laying it gently on the floor beside Lawrence.

They went to the door at the far side of the landing. Pat's MatchCode card let them into the complex, and they made their way silently down the third floor corridor to the emergency stairwell.

In the total blackness of the stairwell landing, he felt the pressure of Pat's body against him. He put his arms around her and kissed her.

"Thank you," he said.

She pulled away. "I love you, Nick," she said matter-of-factly.

"And I—"

"Not now," she said. "Just be quiet and follow me."

344

They went slowly up the metal stairs, being careful to make no sound. It was a quarter of an hour before they came out into the vaulted corridor of the twentieth floor. The memory of what had confronted him before, the thought of going back, made him sick with fear. "I can't," he said.

"You have to," she said. "You have to help me, Nick. I can't do it alone."

He pointed to the camera visible above the arched door, but Pat said simply, "He's otherwise engaged," and took his hand. He let himself be led through the room where the prosthetic devices were displayed, through the second arched doorway into the place where Brown lived.

Chsst!.. Chsst!.. Chsst!.. Chsst!.. Chsst!..

Brown's commands to the computer seemed to fill up the room, as if they came not from him but from deep within the building. The sounds were ugly, ancient, almost a chant. Nick wanted to run, to cry out.

It took a moment before he realized what he was seeing.

In the dim light at the far side of the room was an inflatable rubber mattress. Carla lay on it, face up. She was naked. She looked like Medusa—the long coils of black hair were snakes about to strike. Sweat streamed down her face; her dark eyes were wide open but unseeing. Her legs were extended above her, straight up and wide apart, held at the ankles by stirrups attached to a track in the ceiling.

Chssst!.. Chssst!.. Chssst!.. Chsst!..

Brown hovered in the air above her like a

grotesque, pink-white wasp, his naked, truncated torso grasped by the computer-controlled fingers of the metal arms that rose from the side panels of his wheeled chair. The plastic tube, still held in place by the mount about his neck, ran across the room, connecting him to the computer.

Chssst!.. Chssst!.. Chssst!.. Chssst!..

The metal arms, obeying his commands, raised him, pushed him down into Carla, pulled him back out, then down again.

Chssst!.. Chssst!..

Nick sensed that Pat had left his side, but he could not take his eyes from Brown. The doll's eyes were closed, the bow lips pursed in a smile. His unclothed torso seemed curiously complete, seamless; his erect penis was like a hypodermic needle as it plunged into Carla, withdrew, and plunged again.

CHSSSSTTTTT!

The steel arms held Brown down into Carla as he achieved orgasm. His head, held up and away from her body, shook slightly while he emptied himself. The smile did not leave his face. His expression was that of a child martyr undergoing some divine experience.

Brown opened his eyes slowly and saw Nick. His lips went instantly to the plastic tube.

Phffft . . . Phffft . . .

Nothing happened.

Phffft . . .

Still nothing.

Phffft . . . Phffft . . .

Brown tried once more, but still the steel arms held him down into Carla.

"The computer," he said. "Get me to the computer."

Carla pushed him up and out of her. She eased him into his chair, disengaging the steel hands.

There was total silence as Brown's head swung slowly from Nick to Carla and back to Nick again, searching for an answer. And then they all heard it. A reassuring, everyday sound. The sound of someone typing.

Brown's eyes turned to the far wall, to the computer. Pat Buckley stood at the console, key-punching a message into its brain. The other end of Brown's plastic tube was visible on the floor a few feet away. It was no longer connected to anything but him.

"Stop her," Brown said. "Stop her."

Carla moved toward Pat, but Nick stepped in her way. Her bare breasts glistened in the dim light, and he could smell the familiar musky odor of her body and her perfume. He was afraid of her.

Her right foot lashed out at his groin, but he caught it in his hand and jerked. She grabbed his leg as she fell, and he went down on top of her. He tried to pin her arms behind her, but she was slippery with sweat and amazingly strong; she broke away, then flung herself on top of him, driving into him with her knees, clawing at his face. He threw her and rolled so that he was now outstretched on top of her; they were like two people parodying the act of love. He twisted her arms under her. Holding her down, he seized her throat with his free hand. She lay still.

Pat Buckley's hands moved quickly over the

computer's console. The tapping stopped. She stepped back from the console.

Sssss.... Brown made a small, useless sound. His eyes widened as they fixed on the computer's central monitor screen. His round head began to shake violently.

```
HEART - NORMAL

LUNGS - NORMAL

KIDNEYS - DYSFUNCTION

BLOOD - DYSFUNCTION

EXCRETORY - DYSFUNCTION
```

Nick heard a rush of air, and then the smell of the pine-scented deodorant spray filled the room. A second later the pine smell was overwhelmed by the putrid odor of excrement.

Carla had gone limp under him, and he relaxed his grip on her throat. He kept his eyes on the monitor.

```
HEART - NORMAL

LUNGS - DYSFUNCTION

KIDNEYS - DYSFUNCTION

BLOOD - DYSFUNCTION

EXCRETORY - DYSFUNCTION
```

Brown's eyes had become mirrors, reflecting the monitor screen. He watched himself die as the monitor registered the last change.

```
HEART - DYSFUNCTION
```

"He's dead," Pat said. "I programmed him out."

Nick got up, letting Carla move away, as Pat came toward him. He put his arms around her. "Let's get out of here," he said, and turned her gently toward the arched entrance to the room.

"What about me?" Carla whispered.

She went to Brown's chair. The little pink body had slumped sideways. The eyes were closed now, but the lips still held the plastic tube.

"What about me?" she screamed. "What about me?"

Nick and Pat kept walking.

They were halfway down the corridor when the elevator doors opened and Cecil stepped out. He stood for a moment, staring at them, and then he began to run toward the room where Carla and Brown were waiting for him.

DAVID A. KAUFELT was born in Elizabeth, New Jersey, in 1939. After being graduated from the University of Pennsylvania's Wharton School of Finance and Commerce, he received his M.A. from New York University and subsequently spent two years in the Army in Georgia. Mr. Kaufelt pursued a career as an advertising copywriter until 1975, when he retired to work with the Henry Street Settlement in New York as Director of the Public Interest, and to write. Mr. Kaufelt is the author of two earlier novels, *Six Months With An Older Woman* and *The Bradley Beach Rumba*. He lives with his wife, Lynn, in Manhattan and Sag Harbor, Long Island, where *Spare Parts* was written.

THE BEST OF THE BESTSELLERS
FROM WARNER BOOKS!

DAUGHTERS OF THE WILD COUNTRY   (82-583, $2.25)
by Aola Vandergriff
THE DAUGHTERS OF THE SOUTHWIND travel northward to the
wild country of Russian Alaska, where nature is raw, men are
rough, and love, when it comes, shines like a gold nugget in the
cold Alaskan waters. A lusty sequel to a giant bestseller.

THE FRENCH ATLANTIC AFFAIR   (81-562, $2.50)
by Ernest Lehman
In mid-ocean, the S.S. Marseille is taken over! The conspirators
—174 of them—are unidentifiable among the other passengers.
Unless a ransom of 35 million dollars in gold is paid within 48
hours, the ship and everyone on it will be blown skyhigh!

DARE TO LOVE by Jennifer Wilde   (81-826, $2.50)
Who dared to love Elena Lopez? Who was willing to risk reputation and wealth to win the Spanish dancer who was the scandal
of Europe? Kings, princes, great composers and writers . . . the
famous and wealthy men of the 19th century vied for her affection,
fought duels for her.

THE OTHER SIDE OF THE MOUNTAIN 2   (82-463, $2.25)
by E.G. Valens
Part 2 of the inspirational story of a young Olympic contender's
courageous climb from paralysis and total helplessness to a use-
ful life and meaningful marriage. An NBC-TV movie and serialized
in **Family Circle** magazine.

Ⓦ A Warner Communications Company

- -

Please send me the books I have checked.

Enclose check or money order only, no cash please. Plus 50¢ per
copy to cover postage and handling. N.Y. State residents add
applicable sales tax.

Please allow 2 weeks for delivery.

WARNER BOOKS
P.O. Box 690
New York, N.Y. 10019

Name ....

Address ....

City .... State .... Zip ....

_____ Please send me your free mail order catalog

THE BEST OF THE BESTSELLERS
FROM WARNER BOOKS!

THE KINGDOM by Ronald Joseph (81-467, $2.50)
The saga of a passionate and powerful family who carves out
of the wilderness the largest cattle ranch in the world. Filled with
both adventure and romance, hard-bitten empire building and
tender moments of intimate love, **The Kingdom** is a book for all
readers.

THE GREEK TYCOON by Eileen Lottman (82-712, $2.25)
The story of a romance that fascinated the world—between the
mightiest magnate on earth and the woman he loved . . . the
woman who would become the widow of the President of the
United States.

**FISHBAIT: MEMOIRS OF THE CONGRESSIONAL
DOORKEEPER** by William "Fishbait" Miller (81-637, $2.50)
Fishbait rattles every skeleton in Washington's closets. Non-stop
stories, scandal, and gossip from Capitol Hill, with 32 pages of
photographs.

THE WINTER HEART by Frances Casey Kerns (81-431, $2.50)
Like "The Thorn Birds," THE WINTER HEART is centered upon a
forbidden love. It is the saga of two Colorado families—of the men
who must answer the conflicting claims of ambition and love and
of the women who must show them the way.

 A Warner Communications Company

- -

Please send me the books I have checked.

Enclose check or money order only, no cash please. Plus 50¢ per
copy to cover postage and handling. N.Y. State residents add
applicable sales tax.

Please allow 2 weeks for delivery.

WARNER BOOKS
P.O. Box 690
New York, N.Y. 10019

Name ....

Address ....

City .... State .... Zip ....

_____ Please send me your free mail order catalog